Also by Chris Curran

Mindsight

Her Turn to Cry

Her Deadly Secret

All the Little Lies

WHEN THE LIGHTS GO OUT

CHRIS CURRAN

ONE MORE CHAPTER

One More Chapter
a division of HarperCollins*Publishers*
1 London Bridge Street
London SE1 9GF
www.harpercollins.co.uk

HarperCollins*Publishers*
1st Floor, Watermarque Building, Ringsend Road
Dublin 4, Ireland

This paperback edition 2022
1
First published in Great Britain in ebook format
by HarperCollins*Publishers* 2022

A catalogue record of this book is available from the British Library

ISBN: 978-0-00-853450-9

Printed and bound in the UK using 100% Renewable Electricity
by CPI Group (UK) Ltd

To Paul – always. Thank you for making the lockdowns almost pleasurable!

Chapter One

A jolt and, 'Oh, god. Oh shit,' from the driver's seat.

Ava gripped her own seat. Hard.

The car swerved across the country lane. Swerved back, then back again. The sky whirled overhead. There were trees closely packed on both sides of the road. Too close.

Screeching brakes. A sickening lurch. And they were juddering onto the grass verge. Plunging amongst the trees.

A shudder, a crunch. Something huge and black rushing at them.

Then. Nothing.

The taste of dust or talc, a strange smell, and pain in her chest and legs. She couldn't see. A spike of terror, her hands scrabbling at her face, pushing bits of something that felt like fabric or rubber away from her eyes and nose. Spitting out the dust.

Memory coming back. An airbag. It must be the airbag. They had crashed. And, thank god, she could see. A tree trunk, wide and dark, blocking the shattered windscreen.

They had crashed into a tree.

A screech of metal. And she flinched, expecting something to fall on her, or for the car to burst into flames. But it was her door being wrenched open. A woman, brown face smeared with black, shouting in at her, 'You need to get out, Ava. Come on, get out.'

Ava struggled for a name. They'd only met for the first time this afternoon when the woman picked her up from the station. As she kicked and fought to free her legs, the name came to her. Lally, the woman was called Lally.

A fierce shaft of pain shot through her knee as Lally dragged at her arm. But then she was free, tipping slowly out onto the bare prickly earth under the tree. Together they hobbled to the grass verge and lay back. The grass was beautifully soft and, although she ached all over and her legs were throbbing, she knew she was all right.

How long she lay there she couldn't tell. It could have been a minute or an hour. Just glad to be still, and still breathing. Eventually she became aware of a series of choking coughs on the grass beside her. She forced her eyes open and herself up onto her elbow. 'Lally?' her voice was hoarse. 'Are you all right?'

Rubbing her eyes with a filthy hand, Lally nodded although she was shaking hard despite the mild April air and it looked as if she had been crying.

Ava felt in her pocket. Her phone was there and lit up when she flipped back the cover. 'I'll call for help.'

'No.' It was almost a shriek. Then, quieter, 'There's no need.

We're not hurt. I'll just call Brad. He can come and get us. Be here really fast.'

Ava looked into the wood behind them. The car was completely clear of the road, buried deep in the trees. 'But, we hit something, didn't we? What was it?'

Lally's face was a dirty oval amidst an explosion of black curls. 'A branch. Right across our side of the road. Just after the bend so I didn't see until too late. Had no chance to avoid it.'

Ava squinted back down the lane. It was quiet and still. The pale April sunshine filtered through the bright green flutter of spring leaves. There it was, just as Lally said. A thick branch straddling the road and now she began to shake too, realising how much worse she could have been hurt. When she first got into the car she'd found she couldn't fasten her seatbelt. Hadn't liked to mention it.

Lally kept shaking her head. 'I only drove the other way half an hour ago. It definitely wasn't there then.'

Ava said, 'We have to alert the police before the same thing happens to someone coming along now. They won't see it till they're on top of it.' As she stood, her legs threatened to give way. Everything hurt.

Lally's 'No' was quiet this time, but firm. 'It would take too long. Better if one of us stays this side and the other goes back round the bend to warn anyone coming that way.' A shaky laugh. 'We don't want the fuzz poking around in the car.'

Ava had smelled weed as she got in, so she could see why Lally was anxious. And she was right that it would be quicker to alert drivers themselves and get the branch moved. There was no need for an argument; no need to get off on the wrong foot before she even arrived and met the rest of the group. 'OK, you stay here and call Brad. I'll go round the corner.'

She headed down the lane as quickly as she could, her legs so weak they felt like liquid. She was aching all over, but the pain in her chest and knee had eased. No real damage done. It would be all right.

It seemed a long walk to the branch, but when she got there, she saw a piece of red metal that must have been ripped away from the car, the tarmac scattered with glass. How they had managed to skirt round the side and avoid hitting a tree right away was a mystery. But they were safe and that was all that mattered.

She tried to push the branch back onto the grass verge, but it was too heavy and even with Lally's help she didn't think they could shift it.

As she reached the bend in the road, she heard Lally talking into her phone.

And she froze.

Lally's voice had become loud, trembling with anger and with something that sounded like fear. 'No, Brad, it wasn't just an accident,' she said. 'I'm telling you, someone did this. It was deliberate.'

Chapter Two

She wanted to go back and ask Lally what she meant. But then she thought of other cars coming along and knew she had to keep going. When she turned the corner, she could hear a bird singing and an early butterfly flitted past. She sat beside the road, trying to slow her breath and steady her heart. She longed to message Will, but she couldn't do that. He would want to come and get her. To take her home and tell her yet again that she didn't need to do this. She could stay in London. He was earning enough for both of them. They could still make it together.

She shook her head, aware of a dull throb she hadn't noticed before. Her finger hovered over her mum's number. But then she flipped the cover back and stowed the phone in her pocket. She wasn't hurt, but she'd probably cry if she heard Mum's voice and after the way they'd parted she needed to be calm when they next spoke. Anyway, she had to keep both ears free to listen for traffic. To be ready to jump to her feet and flag them down.

There was nothing to do but wait. And think. To wonder what Lally had meant on the phone when she said the accident was deliberate. It must have been hysteria. The woods here were thick. The trees looked old and they'd had some high winds recently so it was likely the branch had just cracked and fallen. Even if Lally was right, it could have been pushed into the road by kids thinking it would be funny to set up an ambush and not realising how dangerous it would be.

But something about Lally's reaction made it difficult to pass off. She had sounded so scared.

Ava shook her head again. And that throb was still there. Maybe she should ignore Lally and call an ambulance. People died from head injuries that seemed minor at first. And Lally's strange reaction might even be because *she* had concussion.

A car engine. She stood and flagged it down. The driver's window slid open as she hobbled over. 'There's a branch across the road ahead.' He got out, middle-aged and strong-looking. He reminded her a little of her dad. Made her feel safer somehow – for a moment at least. His passenger, another man who looked to be the driver's son, jumped out and together they walked towards the corner. When they came back, the driver nodded, looking at her with concern. 'We'd better get that thing moved. You sit down again, darling. You don't look well to me. Have you called for help?'

'Yes, someone's coming for us.'

The son gave her a smile that told her his dad was an old worry guts, and they headed away.

It was only a few minutes before they came back, walking round the corner, chatting to two other men. One of them she recognised as Brad. He was with a tall, strikingly handsome guy with reddish-brown hair pulled back into a pony-tail and a neat beard. They must have arrived in time to help shift the branch.

Brad ran to her. 'Ava, are you hurt?' She could only shake her head as she struggled to stand and he must have seen she was close to tears because he gathered her into a hug. She wanted nothing more than to lay her head on his shoulder and cry. But she hardly knew him. So she pulled away and managed to choke out, 'I'm fine, just a bit shaken, that's all.'

And was glad she'd fought off the tears when she saw the expression on the other man's face. They'd never met, but if they had she would have been sure he disliked her. She must be misreading him. How could he dislike her? He didn't even know her.

The other two men were already back in their car, the driver calling, 'Thanks, fellas, and you take care of yourself, my love.' With a toot and a wave from the son, they were gone. Brad put his arm around her again, to help her along the road, as his companion strode ahead.

Leaning in close to her ear, Brad whispered, 'Don't mind Paddy. He'll get used to you.' She didn't have the strength to let herself wonder what that might mean.

As they rounded the bend, she saw that Paddy had run ahead and was helping Lally climb into a large brightly coloured van. The back was painted with the name of the group, Chimera Theatre, and as they came round to the side she could see it repeated. This time with the group's logo – a curling mythical creature, part snake, part lion, with a human face. It was beautifully done, if a bit sinister-looking.

The van's sliding doors were open and Lally was sitting on the long seat behind the driver's as Paddy walked into the trees towards the crashed car. Looking at the high step into the van, Ava hesitated, wondering if she could make it. Lally reached out a hand and Brad spoke softly to her again. 'Poor you. What a welcome. Let's get you home now to a nice hot bath and something to eat and drink.' He shook a lock of dark hair away and his grey eyes smiled into hers. Then his hands came under her elbows and he hoisted her up onto the step. His hands were so warm and strong, the words so kind, that tears filled her eyes.

Shuffling over on the seat beside her, Lally put her arm around her and leaned close for a moment, their heads touching. She seemed kind too. She had run to help at the station as Ava struggled out with all her bags and her unwieldy guitar case. Unbelievable to think that must be little more than an hour ago. What a start. But they were all right. It was going to be fine.

Brad went to join Paddy and they came back carrying her luggage. As they stowed it in the back she said, 'Oh, thank you. I'd forgotten all about it.'

A nod and a grunt was all she got from Paddy as he climbed into the driver's seat and slid his door closed. Brad said, 'Not to worry. I don't think anything's damaged. Can't say the same for the car. We can get the garage to pick it up, but I don't hold out much hope. Rose's mum's not going to be pleased.' Then he settled in the passenger seat and twisted towards her. 'Ava, this is Paddy. Paddy meet Ava, our newest member and, as we told you, a really brilliant actress. Just wait until you see her in action.'

Ava tried a smile. She knew Paddy was one of the founders of Chimera. He directed most of their shows. But he didn't look at her. Just turned on the engine as he put the van into gear. She felt Lally, beside her, squeeze her arm and when Ava looked at her, she raised her eyebrows and pulled a face at Paddy's back. Perhaps he was just in a bad mood or upset about the car, which was obviously a write-off.

No one spoke as they drove through the trees and out into open countryside. Ava put back her head and closed her eyes, trying to relax. Her headache was easing and although her knee was still sore, she felt much better. As Brad said, a hot bath or shower would sort her out.

She tried to ignore the twists of anxiety that kept jabbing at her insides. The nagging voice that said perhaps Will was right and this was all a mistake.

Chapter Three

But she had to get away. Things had been going wrong with them for a while. And apart from everything else, she was fed up with being just his bit of arm candy. Not even that a lot of the time because too often it was Mariella Boyd who stood on the red carpet smiling with him. Ava believed him when he said he and Mariella were just friends. She liked Mariella and understood that, as on-screen lovers in the soap they starred in, they had to be photographed together at award ceremonies and so on.

But, if it was hard to be sidelined so often, it was even worse to know that while Will had stepped almost straight from drama school into a lucrative job, Ava had managed to secure just one small part in a play that folded before it got to London and a couple of adverts in the nearly two years since she left. He said she should relax and the parts would come, but she wasn't convinced and, in her worst moments, she wondered if he even wanted that to happen.

So, when the audition for Chimera came up, she couldn't resist. And it happened by chance. In a way that made it seem meant to be.

They were at a party in Mariella's flat. As usual, the younger cast members from the soap were talking shop and she had been drinking too much, standing by a window pretending to look out and feeling like a spare part, when a good-looking guy with lovely gold-flecked brown eyes and a sweet smile handed her a glass of wine. 'Hi, I'm Joel. Looks like neither of us know many people here.' For some reason she didn't mention Will, just asked Joel how he came to be there. 'I know one of Mariella's neighbours, came with him, although he seems to have bailed.'

It was impossible not to feel relaxed under his smiling gaze and she said, 'It's good to talk to someone who isn't an actor for a change.'

He raised his eyebrows. 'Sorry to disappoint, but I'm in the business too.' He laughed as she looked away, knowing her face had flushed, and muttered some kind of apology. When his hand touched her bare arm, the tiniest tingle that she tried to ignore passed through her. She saw Will glance over, his eyes flitting from her to Joel and back again. She took a sip and smiled at him. But he didn't smile back, just gave a questioning look at Joel, then turned away. She gulped at her drink and thought, *Fuck you, Will.* She was entitled to enjoy herself too.

'I'm resting at the moment, so don't be embarrassed if you are too,' she said to Joel with a laugh. Then leaning close, reckless after too much wine, she whispered, 'And *Factory Family* is hardly the Royal Shakespeare Company, is it?'

When Joel said, 'It's work, though, and I'd rather work than not,' it felt like a telling-off and she could feel the heat rising in her cheeks again.

She buried her nose in her glass with a muttered, 'Of course. Wouldn't we all?'

'I *am* working as a matter of fact, although with none of the fame and fortune that lot gets.' He gestured to Will and the rest. By now Will had collapsed on the sofa, long legs stretched out, his arm across the back, almost but not quite touching a girl who'd only just joined the show. Will said she was a bit of a cow, but the way he was smiling at her suggested he might have changed his mind. Or else his acting had improved.

Ava stepped closer to Joel and spoke softly, 'So tell me about it,' almost laughing as she realised how that sounded. She didn't care.

But Joel's reply was serious. 'We're called Chimera Theatre and we're based in Gloucestershire. The group was started by some really talented folk who wanted to get performance to people and places that don't have much access to that kind of thing. Places like the Forest of Dean. Don't make a lot of money, but we get the odd grant to help keep us going.'

He explained that they mostly wrote their own stuff, composed the music etc. and that he'd only been with them for a few months, replacing someone called Dominic. Dominic was mainly a musician, but acted some of the smaller parts, and was good with the technical side. 'I'm like that, not the music, but the tech. Took a lighting and sound course.'

By now Will was looking over again and she saw him point at his watch and then at the door. She nodded and he went to collect their coats. While he was out of the room, she and Joel exchanged phone numbers. She told herself she was networking, but felt like a naughty little girl. It was a good feeling.

Will didn't speak in the taxi going home and when they were in the flat – his flat, although he always called it theirs – he went straight to bed without another word. He had gone to work when she woke in the morning without bringing her a cup of coffee, which he nearly always did. They were in for one of his periods of frosty silence. She told herself she didn't care. He'd get over it and she wasn't likely to hear from Joel again in any case.

When she did, a couple of days later, she took her mobile into the bathroom and locked the door, expecting a flirty chat that would be fun but end up going nowhere. But Joel launched into something unexpected. 'You know the group I told you about? Well, it happens that one of the women is pregnant and we're going to need a replacement very soon. If you fancy auditioning, I can mention your name. No guarantees, of course, but the auditions will be in London so you won't need to travel far.'

She didn't mention it to Will and almost forgot about it. It was a month before Joel rang again with a date and place. A rented space in Brixton. There was no need to tell Will. The chances of getting the job were slim – Joel wasn't even going to be there.

The audition was with two of the founding members, Brad and Rose. Rose was smiley and round-faced with sleek blonde hair in a neat plait and sporting a small bump. She introduced Brad as her partner. They told her they were auditioning other people, but Ava could tell she'd made a good impression and she had the feeling Joel had done a job of selling her.

And it was he who called to give her the good news, even before her agent got in contact. She accepted right away, knowing Will would be unhappy. Most of all because he'd known nothing about it beforehand. They had always discussed that kind of thing in the past.

They were in their tiny kitchen, making dinner, when she told him. He said, 'I don't understand why you had to keep it secret. I could have helped you prepare for the audition. Though I can see you didn't think you needed me.' He slammed the knife so hard through the potato he was cutting, it made her jump. Ava resisted the obvious reply and, twisting towards her, he asked, 'So how long will you be gone?'

'Just a few weeks initially. They want me to fit into the two plays they're doing at the moment. After that they plan to take a month's break to work on the next shows because they write all their own material, including the music.'

'What does that mean – initially? You're not contemplating burying yourself out in the sticks for any longer, I hope.'

'Why not, if I enjoy it and they want me to stay? They've lost one of their musicians so I might be able to write some stuff for them. I'd love to try that. And I had the impression that the other musician might be going soon too, so who knows.'

She went to the sink, pouring some water into a glass. Needing to avoid his eyes.

Will threw down the knife. 'Have you thought what this might do to us?' When she didn't answer, he turned away. 'Of course you have. Well thanks for sharing that with me.' Then he pushed back the chopping board, put on his coat and went out. As she cleared up and put the half-prepared food in the fridge, she knew she'd done it all wrong. But at least it *was* done and she wasn't sorry about that.

And suddenly a very different feeling shot through her. For the first time in ages she was excited and, above all, she felt free. Free from them all.

Chapter Four

Ava must have dozed off because she was aware of Lally moving and that the van was still. They were parked in a narrow lane opposite a small cottage. Rose and Brad had told her the whole group lived here together and that there was room for her. She could stay rent-free. Even in her befuddled state it was difficult to believe there was space for seven adults.

She stumbled out of the van, grateful again for Brad's supporting hand. Paddy was already heading across the road with her guitar and one of her bags and Brad took the other. As she walked over, with Lally holding her elbow, the front door opened and Rose rushed out. 'Oh my god, are you two all right?'

Lally nodded and Ava was relieved that, when she did the same, her head no longer hurt. 'Well let's get you inside and cleaned up.' Rose held the narrow door as wide as it would go for them. The two men were carrying the luggage down a little path that must lead to the garden and back entrance.

The front door opened straight into a living room where,

despite the sunshine, an open fire gave off warmth and the scent of burning logs. On the wide stone windowsill stood several little jars of wild flowers. A squashy sofa covered in a brightly patterned throw and a couple of similarly draped armchairs surrounded a battered oak coffee table. On it sat a half-completed jigsaw, a box of dominoes and a small pile of books. It was a homely scene and for some reason it forced Ava to fight back the tears again.

Paddy and Brad came through an open door that seemed to lead to the rest of the downstairs. They were carrying her luggage and she was surprised when Paddy opened another door in the corner of the room and she saw a steep flight of wooden stairs right behind it.

Lally collapsed on one of the sofas. 'I'm knackered,' she said. 'And, I'm sorry, Rose, but the car's totally fucked. Blame it on me when you talk to your mother.'

Rose spoke very quickly, sharing a glance with Brad as he headed up the stairs with the bags. 'Never mind about that now. You're both safe and that's all that matters. Sit down, Ava, you look fit to drop.' She gestured to a soft chair and Ava sank into it. Rose's bump was noticeably bigger and she ran her hands over it as she asked, 'OK, what first, tea, bath, or something to eat?'

Lally looked at Ava. 'I'm guessing a bath might be your priority. I can have a quick wash in the kitchen sink and my bath afterwards, if you like.'

That sounded perfect and she would be glad of the chance, not only to clean up but to have a few minutes alone to think. As Paddy ran back down the stairs, Rose went to the bottom and called to Brad to fill the bath. 'You go on up now, then. Brad will show you your room.'

At the top of the stairs was a small square landing with four doors around it. Brad was standing by the only open doorway. 'This is me and Rose.' She glanced into a sunlit room with a view of some distant trees and a rumpled bed, covered in what looked like a patchwork quilt. He flung open a door opposite. 'And here's you.'

Her bags were on the floor and although it was so small that there was only space for a single bed, a small chest and a free-standing mirror, the room was lovely. On the deep stone window ledge stood another jam jar of wild flowers and behind them the view was of wide fields rippling away down to a river or canal at the bottom of a valley.

She turned to Brad. 'It's gorgeous.'

He said, 'I'm afraid it's only a single bed.' There was an awkward pause and she picked up one of her bags and started to open it as he carried on. 'And there's another disadvantage that I hope you can put up with.' He gestured to a door in the corner she'd assumed was a cupboard. 'That leads to the attic, which is now Mel's bedroom. I'm sorry, it's not ideal, but she promises to disturb you as little as possible.'

There was nothing to say to that. Ava had never met Mel, although she knew she was one of the original members – they'd all gone to university together – and that she was the remaining musician of the group. Brad was back in the hallway opening another door, steam pouring out as he did so. 'OK, then, I'll leave you to it. Bath should be nice and hot.'

When he'd gone she dared to go to the mirror. Her face was as dirty as Lally's and there was a piece of fabric attached to the side of her nose. She pulled it away, telling herself no one had been looking at her that closely. Her jacket would need cleaning and there was a big rip in her jeans. She looked haggard, more like forty-two than twenty-two. At least her hair, when she ran a brush through it, looked all right. It was heavy and fell to the middle of her shoulder blades – so dark it was almost black, the legacy of her Indian grandmother. It took ages to dry and she'd washed it this morning, so she pinned it up.

As she did so she could almost feel Will running his hands through it the way he always did and she swallowed down a lump in her throat. She'd been with him for what seemed like forever, had gone almost straight from living with her parents to living with him, so it was bound to take time to learn to be on her own. But it was what she wanted. To be independent. She still loved Will, but things had been wrong with their relationship for a long time.

She hung some clean clothes over the hook on the back of the bathroom door and looked for the bolt. There wasn't one. Sitting on the edge of the bath, stirring the water with her fingers to foam up the bubble bath Brad had obviously added, she ran her other hand over her flat stomach, thinking of Rose downstairs smiling as she rubbed her bump. Will had suggested that it was Ava's miscarriage that had damaged their relationship, but they both knew that wasn't true. It, and the brief pregnancy, had just helped to show that they were looking for different things, at least in the near future.

He had been thrilled at the idea of a baby, but Ava had been terrified. It was unplanned: something Ava hadn't even imagined happening for years yet. And while Will couldn't stop talking about it, she had retreated into a weird state of disbelief. It didn't help that her parents, who had always supported her, obviously had their doubts. Felt it was much too soon for her to settle down.

When she miscarried, she could tell that their expressions of sympathy were tinged with relief – and she had to admit to feeling the same. But Will was keen to try again right away. Said, that with his steady job and prospects of even more work in the future, they were in a perfect position to start a family.

She was still hormonal and teary when she shouted at him, 'But that's just it. I'm not ready for it. I want to get my career going before I even think of tying myself down. I don't want to be just your other half.'

It wasn't what she'd meant to say, but it was true and they didn't speak for days, which gave Ava time to think. When things went back to a kind of normal, he said he understood what she was saying. They were still young and could leave it for a year or two. But even that frightened Ava. He seemed to have their whole future mapped out and the fact that he seemed determined not to see that something wasn't working made her doubt their whole relationship. And, although she never actually put them into words, she couldn't hide those doubts. It had made the past few months really hard.

If only she'd been able to confide in her parents, but things had gone wrong there too.

She hoped that time away from all of them might be just what she needed.

Chapter Five

It felt weird getting naked and climbing into the bath as she listened to the voices of strangers below. She had only met Rose and Brad at the audition and Lally for the first time today. She still had to see Mel and could hardly call the fleeting interactions with Paddy meetings. She wondered where Joel was today.

Still, the rest of them knew she was here so she put her head back and tried to relax, determined not to let the accident replay in her mind. Of course, that meant she began thinking about Will again.

After his angry flounce out of the flat on the evening she'd told him about the job, he had come back with a Thai takeaway of all her favourite dishes. They'd had loving sex that night and he had been extra nice for the whole time before she left. But they hadn't talked about her coming back or about him visiting her while she was away. She guessed that, like her, he was afraid of what they might say.

A tap on the door and, before she could speak, it opened

and a woman she didn't know poked her head round the door. She must be the remaining musician in the group and her, 'Hi, Ava, I'm Mel,' confirmed it. 'Rose made you some tea. I hope you take it with milk and no sugar.'

Sinking down in the water, Ava said, 'Yes, thank you, that's lovely.' When Mel put the chunky mug on the shelf beside the bath, she expected her to go, but she plonked herself down on the toilet in the corner. Plonk was hardly the right word for someone so tiny and dainty-looking. Dressed in workmen's-style dungarees and a striped sweatshirt, the sleeves hanging over her hands, she resembled a pretty elf with her short, spiky hair. It was such a bright red it must be dyed, but her face was very pale and scattered with freckles so she probably was a paler kind of redhead. Her eyes were lost amongst a dark halo of makeup. It was odd, but somehow it worked.

She pulled at a thread on her sleeve, staring at Ava with unembarrassed interest. 'So, they tell me you're a musician too.'

Ava laughed. 'Hardly, I play mainly flute and guitar with a bit of piano, none up to your standard, I'm sure.'

'There's a piano downstairs. An old upright, but it's been well looked after. Used to belong to Rose as a kid, although she doesn't play anymore. I use it, so feel free to do the same.'

Pulling herself up in the bath, Ava was glad of the bubbles covering her as she picked up the tea. Mel showed no signs of leaving, but she seemed as friendly as Rose and Lally. As soon as she was dressed, Ava decided she would message Will to say she'd arrived rather than calling him. Letting him know she was fully occupied with moving in and getting ready for rehearsals, so she couldn't talk. After all, there was nothing much to say. She had no intention of telling him about the accident.

Mel pulled her knees up to her chest. She seemed so flexible Ava guessed she was a dancer as well as a musician. 'I'm sorry I'll have to come through your room to get to mine. I was going to give the attic to you, but I've got so many instruments up there as well as all my other stuff, there wouldn't be space for half of it down here.'

'It's fine.' What else could she say? She swallowed the rest of the tea and reached for the towel, wishing she'd put it closer, but the water was cooling and she was aware that Lally might want a bath. Mel looked at her steadily as she climbed out and Ava grabbed the towel as fast as she could, telling herself Mel was just a laidback kind of person. There was no reason for her to want Ava to feel uncomfortable.

Finally, Mel stood and went to the door, still with that steady look. 'I hope you know how much Rose and Brad rate you. They think you might be the best thing that's happened to the group. And of course you were a real hit with Joel.'

Securing the towel around her, Ava could only mutter, 'That's nice to know. Thank you for telling me.'

As the door opened, a draught of cold air made her shiver. Holding it open, Mel gave a little laugh. 'In fact, when Rose is back in action they might even think you're a better bet than I am.'

She had gone, closing the door behind her, before Ava could think what to say to that. But it worried her. Despite the laugh, she had the feeling that Mel was deadly serious.

Chapter Six

She told herself she was being paranoid, but Mel's last remarks, along with Paddy's lack of welcome, were disturbing. So much so that when she checked her phone and saw a message from Will – *How's it going? I'm thinking of you.* – she was tempted to call him, although she knew that would be a mistake. So she kept to what she'd intended and sent him a smiley face and an: *All good so far, but lots to do. Rehearsals start first thing tomorrow, so getting an early night.* That should stop him from getting in touch later.

As she let down her hair, brushed it again and unpacked, she was glad to be alone. But it was difficult to avoid being aware that Mel could come in again at any moment. That was something she was going to have to get used to.

When Ava heard someone run up the stairs, she found herself tensing, but the bath water began running and she guessed it must be Lally. Sounds came from the room next to hers, presumably where Lally slept. Rose and Brad had the other bedroom. The bathroom accounted for the fourth door off the landing. So, with Mel up in the attic, she wondered where Joel and Paddy slept.

A voice from the bottom of the stairs. 'Dinner in fifteen minutes, everyone.' It sounded like Rose and when there was a muffled answer from the bathroom Ava also called out a *Thank you*. Her phone rang. *Mum*. They knew she was starting a new job in the country and her mother had asked her to call and let them know when she got there.

She should have done it right away, before her bath, but she'd been in too much turmoil then. Needed time to calm down. And it was too late now because she wouldn't be able to chat for long and her mum would read all kinds of things into that.

If only they could go back to the way they used to be. The three of them in their cosy little family. Before all the harsh words and the accusations she'd levelled at them. And, in any case, this wasn't the time for a nice little chat. They had to clear up a lot of shit first.

Feeling suddenly weak, she sat on the bed. Was all the trouble she was having with Will and with her parents down to her? Or was she finally seeing clearly after always being determined to view her life through rose-coloured spectacles? This job was an escape, not just from her problems with Will, but it was time to rethink all her relationships.

Chapter Seven

The phone pinged. Her mum leaving a message. Knowing it was probably a bad idea, she listened to it. 'Hi, baby, how's it going? Send me some photos when you get a minute. And I know you'll be busy, but ring us soon. Your dad's dying to talk to you too.'

There was no hint of the tensions that were so often between them and she knew her mum just wanted their relationship to go back to the way it had been when she was young. Ava wanted that too, but she wasn't sure it was possible.

Even so, and although it was ridiculous because she was a grown woman and hadn't lived properly with her parents for four years, just hearing her mum's voice made her feel homesick.

A tap on the door and Lally, hair wet but still springing with curls, saying, 'Dinner should be ready.' She had to swallow before she could look up and smile, but she was grateful for the excuse to put away her phone. She would think about all that later.

They went down the narrow stairs together and Lally headed through the cosy front room to a big rustic kitchen.

Like the rest of the house it was a bit run-down. Her dad would have been keen to redecorate and do something about the broken quarry tiles on the floor while her mum might have said it needed a good tidy-up, but Ava loved the lived-in look. A huge wooden table stood beside a set of French windows and Brad was carrying a large casserole dish from the ancient-looking Aga. Lally squeezed onto a long bench wedged between the table and the roughly plastered wall and patted the cushion next to her. Ava sat as Paddy appeared with plates. Mel, Rose and Brad followed and when they were all seated, Brad began pouring wine.

He raised his glass, the red liquid shining in the steel shaded light suspended over the table. 'No idea where Joel has got to, but I can't wait for a drink any longer. Can you all join me in welcoming our new member, Ava.' He leaned over and clinked his glass against hers and she heard a chorus of *welcomes* and *welcome, Ava.* She couldn't hear if Paddy had spoken, but told herself it didn't matter. Rose was beaming at her, while Lally nudged her with her shoulder and gave her a sweet smile.

There was the sound of a motorbike in the lane and, a minute later, a door at the back was flung open and Joel burst through. He looked straight at Ava with an expression she couldn't quite place and she was surprised by the wave of pleasure that went through her. She was conscious of her face growing warm and glad that everyone seemed to be focused on filling their plates.

There was a place free at the end of the table next to her and Joel bounced into it giving her a huge smile, 'Hello, Ava.' Simple words, but he had an intimate way of speaking, those glowing eyes looking deep into hers. When he kissed her cheek and gave her hand a squeeze, she heard a little chuckle from Lally on her other side. Paddy, who had seemed intent on eating, looked up at that and his eyes went from Lally to Joel, but he said nothing. In that moment he reminded her of Will during one of those silences she hated. Silences that were more deafening than an angry tirade would have been.

But the food was lovely and Ava began to relax. Leaning back against the rough wall with Joel and Lally on either side providing a friendly warmth, both physical and emotional, she sipped her wine and ate a huge dinner.

Afterwards they all sat in the living room. There was just room for the whole group, although she was squashed onto the sofa with Lally and Mel with Brad sitting on the arm. Rose and Paddy took the chairs while Joel grabbed a book and a cushion and, moving the jars of flowers aside, used the wide window ledge as a seat. Lally, Mel and Brad began a game of dominoes, but when they asked her to join in, she felt a weight of exhaustion descend on her. 'I think I need to get some sleep.'

Brad said, 'Good idea, rehearsals first thing tomorrow.'

Paddy stood. 'I'm off now anyway.' And he headed through the door at the back of the kitchen. The garden doors were at the side next to the table so Joel must have seen Ava's puzzled look. 'We guys get exiled to the garage. Not properly housetrained, you see.'

Rose laughed and said, 'Don't listen to him. It was converted into an annex, a little apartment. There's a power shower and everything.'

The domino players started another game, trying to persuade Ava to join in again, but she said her goodnights and went up to her room. She was hoping to be in bed, if not asleep, when Mel came through. Mel had told her to turn off the light when she wanted, she'd be fine in the dark. So she did that.

The bed was comfortable, but she expected to lie awake for ages. However, she must have slept because she was suddenly awake, knowing something wasn't right.

Lying totally still, afraid to move or even breathe, she listened. Someone was in the room with her. It must be the early hours of the morning.

Then she relaxed. Of course, it would be Mel going to the attic. She must have paused thinking she might have woken Ava. After a moment, heavy footsteps began moving stealthily across the floor. The door to the attic opened and closed again. She checked her phone. It was past 3 a.m. Mel had stayed up very late.

But as she put down the phone she thought about those footsteps. Surely they were too heavy to be tiny Mel? Just then, she heard a small squeak that did sound like Mel. It could have been surprise, but might be alarm and she sat up in bed, listening hard now.

But the murmur of voices overhead reassured her. The man – and one of the voices was definitely male – must have woken Mel, but she'd obviously only been shocked for a moment.

Ava lay down and pulled the covers over her ears, she didn't want to listen to them. But, although she could hear no actual words, it was obvious this was an intense conversation. Trying hard to ignore it, she was glad when the words died away.

But when a loud creak broke the silence, she became alert again.

And heard the tell-tale rhythmic squeak of bedsprings.

Chapter Eight

Amazingly, she must have slept and woke to sunlight and a dawn chorus of birds louder and more full-throated than she had ever heard. For a moment she lay, completely relaxed, before recalling last night. Surely Mel's visitor would have crept down by now. She certainly didn't want to see him coming through her room this morning.

Jumping out of bed, she made as much noise getting her things together as she could before heading for the bathroom, carrying her clothes. She'd get dressed in there and if he was still upstairs he would have plenty of time to make his getaway. As she washed, dressed and put on a sliver of makeup, mainly to stop herself looking as if she was still in shock, she wondered about him.

It had to be Paddy and if he and Mel were an item, why be so surreptitious about it? Mel had sounded surprised to see him so maybe they had argued, or they were only occasional lovers. And he shared the converted garage with Joel. It might be even less private than Mel's room. As she dabbed some concealer on a spot that was coming out on her chin, she stopped and stared at herself, wondering why she was so certain it had been Paddy when it was just as likely to be Joel.

Downstairs, Rose was in her dressing gown at the table, a mug in front of her. She looked tired and with her hair hanging down instead of neatly plaited, her face seemed older. She looked up when she heard Ava and gave a bright smile. 'Hi there. Did you sleep well?' Ava nodded. She would probably have to get used to those noises in the night.

Rose pointed towards the kitchen area. 'We sort ourselves out for everything except dinner, so take anything you like. There's a pot for the kitty in the top right-hand cupboard, but you get your first week free. Just buy anything special you want.'

There was coffee brewed on the Aga and she poured herself a mug. When she called back to Rose, 'Can I make you some toast or anything?' Rose's 'No thank you,' was so low she could hardly hear it. She hesitated, wanting to ask if there was anything wrong, but just then the door to the annex opened and Joel, looking bright and cheerful, came through.

'Making toast, Ava? Don't mind if I do.' He poured himself a mug of coffee and put some spreads and a tub of margarine on a tray with plates and knives. A beaming smile at Ava as she checked the toast. 'I'll take this if you can manage that.' Hearing movement overhead, she popped in another four slices of bread.

When she turned back to the table, she saw that Joel was sitting beside Rose. They had their backs to her and Joel's hand was on top of Rose's. She heard him whisper something to her.

As she piled the toast onto a big plate, Paddy came in from

the annex and Lally and Mel appeared from upstairs. It might have been her imagination that Mel looked happier than she had yesterday, her pale face tinged a delicate pink, but there was no sign from her nor from either of the men to suggest which was her visitor.

Lally was dressed in biker's leathers and stayed on her feet, grabbing a piece of toast and slathering it with peanut butter. She said, 'Right, guys, I'll see you later.' Ava knew she did the admin for the group. She had been at university with the rest of them, but doing a different course. Talking to Rose, she said, 'I'll go to the garage and check on the car when they've had a chance to pick it up. I'll call you later with the news. But first I want to try and drum up a few more dates for us.' From somewhere behind her in the living room she grabbed a motorbike helmet, saying to Ava, 'Our old Harley's perfect for scooting round the villages, so I use it most of the time, but if you can ride, you're welcome to borrow it when I don't need it.'

Ava shook her head with a smile. 'I think I'll give that a miss, thanks.'

Lally rubbed Rose's shoulder. 'I'll hand out those flyers for the show next week as well. Your last hurrah for a bit, eh.'

Rose laughed, looking more cheerful, but Ava noticed she hadn't eaten anything and had only sipped at her coffee. Morning sickness, perhaps. And if the car belonged to her mum, she might feel bad about that.

Just as she was wondering where Brad was, he bounded through the front door. 'Come on, folks, time to go. We need to get Ava up to speed. Rose is staying here; she's been overdoing it and thinks Ava will be better trying to make the parts her own without her watching.' He kissed the top of Rose's head, his hands resting on her shoulders. Ava swallowed the last of her toast and moved away. His voice was low and intimate, but she couldn't avoid hearing him say, 'You should go back and have a sleep. Don't let it get to you.'

Rose looked into her mug and said nothing.

Chapter Nine

The group rented a space above a pub just down the hill from the house for rehearsals and some performances. The pub wasn't open at this time in the morning, but the room could be accessed from the fire escape stairs at the back, so the landlord had let them have a key. The space was perfect; big and empty and there was a piano in the corner. They didn't need a stage because they always performed in the round, with the audience seated at the same level as the actors. Before they began, Joel chalked a rough oval on the floor, to mark what would be the front row, rubbing out an area at each end for the exits and entrances. 'Obviously we have to adapt these according to the shape of the venue, but you'll soon get used to that.' He looked at Ava and laughed. 'You probably know all this, anyway.'

Actually she was grateful, because she hadn't performed in very many different spaces. Rose had emailed her a copy of her own scripts as soon as they gave her the job so that she could learn the parts she was taking over. She was as prepared as she could be, but with all the others so used to the movements and timings, it wasn't easy.

They started with the series of sketches that they took to secondary schools, designed to get kids interested in Shakespeare. They involved snippets, mostly comic, from various plays interspersed with invented monologues from a character supposed to be Shakespeare himself, played by Joel. There were sections where groups of children could be encouraged out of the audience to play crowd scenes, which Ava thought might be daunting for her.

She was playing lots of small parts as well as Titania in a scene from *A Midsummer Night's Dream* and Rosalind in a snippet of *As You Like It*.

She thought the whole thing was well done and could imagine the children loving it. Paddy directed, commenting on her performance in a calm and simple way that was really helpful. There was no warmth, but nothing harsh when he pointed out mistakes or suggested new ways of doing something. When it worked he would say, 'Fine, let's move on now.'

As actors they only interacted in the Dream, where he played Oberon, but the characters were at a distance and having a quarrel so his coolness suited the scene well.

By the time he called a break, she felt almost elated. It was so good working again and she noticed Brad give Joel a look that said, *We were right, she's good.* Then Paddy surprised her by saying, 'After Ava's accident we shouldn't work too hard today. So let's call it a day, shall we? Take the afternoon off.' She hoped that meant he was warming to her, but she didn't want to stop.

There were original songs in both the group's current

shows and, although Rose had included the music, it had been difficult to rehearse at home with only a guitar. And she hadn't liked doing it when Will was around. Some of the music was written by Mel, although the songs Ava really liked were by Dominic who had left and been replaced by Joel. Ava had to take over one solo from Rose and provide backing for a couple of others.

'If the room is still free this afternoon, I wouldn't mind using the piano to have a go at the songs,' she said. Mel was quick to come in with, 'Brilliant. I'll stay and help you. We can call for a lift or walk back.' It would be much better to have Mel's help, but after last night, and not just what she'd overheard but what Mel had said in the bathroom, she felt awkward alone with her when the others had gone.

They tried the solo first. Mel played piano beautifully and with a lot of feeling and when they'd gone through the song a few times she shook her head and smiled up at Ava. 'It's probably just as well Rose isn't here. You're a much better singer than she is.'

A clap from the doorway made them both jump. It was Lally, still in her biker's leathers. 'That's true, if nasty, Mel,' she said with a laugh. 'Maybe I won't give you the sandwiches she made for you, to teach you a lesson.' She had stopped off at the house for her own lunch and told them she was on her way to check on the damage to the car now. 'Everyone else was stuffing their faces with never a thought for you. So I offered to bring something.'

'Any news on the car?' Mel asked.

'No, but it's not going to be good. Rose rang her mum while I was there and I explained what happened. To say she isn't happy is an understatement. She thinks I ought to have called the police, but I was hardly going to do that. There was some coke as well as weed in the glove compartment. Paddy managed to prise it out, thanks be. So there won't be any trouble from the garage.'

Mel lowered the piano lid. 'No point in telling the police anyway. Even if that log was put there deliberately, they wouldn't be able to prove it.' She took a sandwich and, holding out the bag to Ava, said, 'We tried them when the van was vandalised a couple of weeks ago. They gave poor old Chimera a huge cock and a pair of enormous boobs. Cost a bomb to get it redone. The cops said there was no CCTV outside the village hall where it was parked, so they couldn't do anything.'

Lally shook her head, her lips pursed. Her, 'Don't get me started on that,' was bitter, but she just picked up her helmet and strode to the door. Ava looked a question at Mel as they heard the Harley start up outside, but Mel shrugged and started playing the next song.

As musicians they had a real rapport and were soon laughing as Mel tried to sing a solo meant for Paddy, in a silly deep voice, so that Ava could practise the chorus. It was a fast and furious song and, when Mel finished with a flurry of dramatic notes and a flourish more suitable for a maestro at the Albert Hall, they both burst into laughter. 'Right,' Mel closed the piano lid. 'Do you fancy a drink downstairs? I reckon we deserve it.'

The pub was one large room divided in two by an open fireplace. In the early afternoon it was empty apart from the barman. Mel insisted on buying them beers and when they found a seat in a sunny alcove, Mel clinked her bottle against

Ava's. 'You're going to be fine – more than fine – and Paddy will get used to you eventually.'

At that a rush of anger surged through Ava that she didn't try to hide. She was absolutely fed up with people saying things like that and she didn't care what Mel thought. 'But what is his problem with me?'

Mel's smile was very sweet. As if she was pleased to have provoked a reaction. 'It's not really you. He didn't want us to take on anyone else. Thought we could work around Rose or rewrite the shows.'

'Was it the money?' That at least would make sense.

'He claims that's it, but I doubt it.' As she ran her hand through her spikes of bright hair, Ava noticed a tattoo on her wrist. Words she couldn't read. 'I think it's because he sees us as his family. Not so much Joel, who's new, but the rest of us. You know we all met at uni?' Ava nodded. 'Well, he had a bad time when we were there. His parents basically disowned him. And since then, we're all he has.'

'But I still don't see why that should make him resent me.'

'I know.' Mel took a long drink. 'But he had a lot of trouble accepting Joel too.' Leaning back, Ava drank some of her beer, feeling better. At least it sounded as if it wasn't personal. Mel went on, 'He was hit really hard when Dominic left. Apart from everything else, it was the first change to the group after all the years we've been together. Maybe this reminds him of that time just when he was starting to get over it.'

'Was he particularly close to Dominic?'

A laugh that Ava thought sounded just slightly malicious. 'You could say that. They were an item. Right from when we first set up the group and Brad, who already knew Dominic, persuaded him to join. Seems it was love at first sight for him and Paddy. That's why Paddy's family rejected him. They're very religious and couldn't take it when they found out he was gay.'

She took a long swallow from her bottle, smiling at Ava over the top.

Chapter Ten

So, it hadn't been Paddy upstairs with Mel, which meant it must have been Joel. Ava drank her beer, trying to keep her face from showing what she was feeling, even though she didn't actually know what that was. She was sure Mel was looking for a reaction and equally sure that what she had said was a message of some sort.

Still, it was best to get things clear and when Mel suggested walking back to the cottage, she knew it was the perfect opportunity to find out more about the whole group. The sun was still shining when they left the pub, but there was a chill in the air. It was only April after all. The walk was uphill along a little footpath between trees and then across the fields.

'The car? Rose's mum owns it, does she?' she asked. She wasn't that interested, but it seemed an easy way into getting Mel talking about the others again.

'Oh, yeah, I bet she's apoplectic,' Mel answered, sounding rather pleased. 'She's a stuck-up bitch. Lives in a posh little town too close for comfort. On the local council, runs the

Women's Institute, leading light in the Conservative Association, that kind of thing. She hates the way Rose lives. I think Rose only took up acting to annoy her. She's not that good and she knows it.' Again that touch of malice and Ava, who liked Rose, bit back on the comment that sprang to mind.

'Is she happy for her car to be used by the group, then?'

'Not much she can do about that, is there? Same with the cottage.'

It took a moment to process that. 'So Rose's mum owns the cottage?'

Mel stopped to retie the laces of her trainers. 'Oh yeah, she bought it when Rose finished uni. I think she hoped it would persuade her to settle down. Find a nice job and a nice young man. That backfired spectacularly, but what can she do? And we get to live there free.'

They had reached a farm gate and Ava could see the cottage not far ahead. As they went through, she closed the gate and then leaned on it, looking back down the valley, hoping to slow their progress and get more out of Mel.

'So, what about your family?' Mel asked. 'Are they as dysfunctional as ours?'

The river glinted below under the slanting evening sun and Ava focused on that, glad that the breeze whipping her hair across her face gave her a moment to breathe as she pushed it behind her ear. The answer should have been obvious. Her parents were lovely and she'd had the perfect childhood. And nothing had really happened to change that. The trouble was it was no longer so simple.

So she said, 'I'm an only child, so I guess I was spoiled.' Mel's look made her realise she had to say more or it would be odd. 'Well, my mum's really my stepmother, but my real mum died when I was tiny so I've known no different.' Wanting to get off the subject and back to the group, she said, 'And you?'

Another of those gestures, hand raking through the spiky hair, and Mel was off up the path again. 'Oh god, don't ask. My dad's a bishop, would you believe, and poor mum's the little woman at home. Gave up her career as a violinist to take care of his parishioners and further his career. Now he's got to the top and worn her out along the way, he treats her like a combination secretary and housekeeper, while he plays the field – the bastard.' A low almost-chuckle. 'And talking of bastards, I know for a fact that he's got more than one out there.'

They didn't speak for a bit. The going was steeper, they were both breathing heavily, and talking about her own family seemed to have taken the sparkle out of Mel. But after a few minutes she looked over at Ava with a smile. 'As you can tell, we've all been pretty much fucked up by our mums and dads.' Another sidelong glance and one of those quirky little, not quite friendly, smiles. 'Apart from you, it seems.'

'I didn't say my family's perfect. We've had our share of difficult times.'

Mel turned to face her. 'Oh, do tell.'

Cursing herself for blurting out something so revealing, Ava shook her head. 'Oh, just the usual teenage tantrums from me and overprotectiveness from them, I guess.'

Mel looked as if she knew there was more to find out when she said, 'So why didn't they have any more children, then?'

This was getting more and more difficult and before she could answer she had to turn away and hurry on, afraid Mel would see her expression. 'I don't know.' It sounded too curt, so she added, 'I would have liked a brother or sister.'

'Have one of mine by all means.' Mel's laugh was impossible not to warm to. 'Anyway, since you seem so interested, here's the run-down of the rest of us misfits. Rose's dad did a runner, and who can blame him, but her mum likes to give the impression she's a widow. Lally's got a huge family; seven brothers and sisters. She's the oldest and I think her parents, who have money but are like old hippies, basically left her to bring up the rest. They were always on the move and she couldn't wait to get away. Says she doesn't even know where they're living now.'

Ava kept her voice casual. 'What about Brad and Joel?'

There was a pause as they climbed over a low stone wall. Sitting on the wall, Mel seemed to be having trouble with her shoe again. 'You'll have to ask Brad about his lot,' she said. 'He never talks about them.' And she jumped to her feet and headed towards the house.

When Ava caught up with her, Mel continued as if there had been no break in the conversation. 'As for Joel, he hasn't said much, but I think he was the darling only child of older parents, which explains why he's so well-adjusted.' Another glance, eyes glinting. 'Like you, I guess.'

Ava was oddly pleased to be able to correct her. 'My parents aren't older. My dad was only twenty-two when I was born and my stepmother is a year younger.'

The last few yards were steep going and they stopped by a gate that opened into the lane beside the cottage. They were both breathing hard and Mel said nothing until she'd gone through the gate. Then, with another sidelong glance at Ava, she spoke over her shoulder.

'Maybe I'm wrong about Joel too, then. I'm only going by the photos he has beside his bed.'

Chapter Eleven

The house was quiet when they got in. Mel offered to make some coffee, but Ava needed time alone and took a glass of water up to her room, wishing yet again that it was completely private. The door to the attic was open; Mel must have left it like that in the morning, so Ava closed it and her own door, hoping Mel would stay downstairs with her coffee.

She didn't know when Will would be free to talk. It depended on how rehearsals or recordings were going, but she clicked on his number. When it went to voicemail, she couldn't deny the feeling of relief and left a quick hello, promising to ring back later.

Although they'd got on better after he'd accepted that she was determined to take up the job, and that she wanted some time apart, things were still tense. On the last morning he told her he'd taken a couple of hours off to drive her to the station and she blurted out, 'But I already organised a taxi,' regretting it as soon as the words were out of her mouth.

His, 'Thanks, Will, that was really thoughtful of you,' was said on a small laugh that wasn't at all amused.

'I'm sorry, I'm just so anxious about it all. You know what it's like.'

His look said he didn't. The job was just a petty little thing that would do nothing to help her career. Or maybe that was her interpretation of the look. Because when she came back from her shower, he had laid the table beside the living room window with a lovely breakfast that he must have run down to buy at the gourmet deli along the street.

She wasn't really hungry but said, 'That's wonderful.' He gathered her into his arms and when he kissed her, it was so sweet and familiar she stayed with her face pressed into his fresh-smelling shirt, wondering if she was making a huge mistake. When they were sitting down, she called to cancel the taxi, thanking Will once again as she bit into a bagel. But when she looked over at him, about to say something about how delicious it was, she had the feeling he was suppressing the urge to tell her to stop overdoing it.

They hardly spoke on the way to the station. The traffic was busy so he had to concentrate and she couldn't think of anything to say. Above all, she was worried that the longer than usual breakfast might make her late for her train. Someone from Chimera would be at the other end to meet her and keeping them waiting wouldn't make for the best start.

In the end, Will couldn't find anywhere to park and she knew her voice sounded curt when she said, 'Please, just pull up anywhere and let me out. I can manage my bags.' Without a word, he did just that.

A quick peck at his cheek through his window was all she could manage and that was it. Except that, as the train pulled out, she saw him run onto the platform and raise his hand. Just too late for her to wave back. She didn't know if he'd even seen her. Or if he knew she'd seen him.

She shook her head. That was over for now. Nothing she could do about it. Instead, she needed to focus on making a success with Chimera. To show herself, if not him, that she had made the right decision.

She needed that coffee now and downstairs the old-fashioned percolator on the Aga was nearly full. As she poured herself a mug, she heard a rumble of voices coming from the annex. They sounded very like those she had heard in the middle of the night. She was sure one of them was Mel, and although the other could be Paddy she realised it was far more likely to be Joel.

She didn't want to hear what they were saying and took her coffee to the piano, at the other end of the room. Far enough from the annex door to make her feel she wasn't eavesdropping and to let them know she was there. Soon she was lost in the music.

It must have been about twenty minutes later when Mel came out, pink faced and smiling to herself. 'You really are good,' she said. 'I'll definitely have to watch out when Rose is back in action.'

No sure what to say, Ava decided a simple, 'Thank you,' was her best option, but she must have glanced at the door as Mel closed it because she said, 'I was looking for Paddy. Joel doesn't know where he's gone. You haven't seen him, have you?'

'No, I haven't seen anyone.'

'I expect Rose is lying down. She needs her afternoon naps these days.' Again, that note of malice hovered and Ava, afraid of what her face might show, flicked through the pages of her music book.

Mel headed to the living room and Ava heard the door to the stairs open and her light steps running up. The annex door opened again and Joel came in. 'Still working?' he said. 'No need to stress it. You impressed everyone this morning. That includes Paddy, even though the miserable bastard will never tell you.'

'Actually, playing the piano is the best way I know of unwinding.' She realised she sounded stilted, but couldn't help being conscious of what he and Mel might have been up to just now. It was none of her business, of course, and she told herself not to be a prude, although she knew that wasn't why she felt uncomfortable.

'Fancy a walk down to the pub?' he asked. 'A drink will definitely help you relax.' She was spared having to make an excuse by the front door opening and Lally coming in, pulling off her helmet and shaking her curls back into shape. Her, 'Hi, folks, how's it going?' was interrupted by a loud thump from upstairs.

They all looked at the ceiling and then, with alarm now, at each other as the thump was followed by two more crashes and finally, loudest of all – a piercing scream.

Chapter Twelve

The door to the stairs burst open and Mel stood there, her face chalk white, black makeup streaked down her cheeks. 'This is the fucking end. Look at this!' She held out a violin – no, too big – it was a viola, Ava thought. Where the wood was intact, it shone rich and brown, but there were great gouges across the whole surface and the strings dangled loose, obviously having been cut.

Joel rushed over, taking the viola, and, with just one shocked glance, placed it with the utmost gentleness on the coffee table. Then pulled Mel into his arms as she cried; great heart-shaking sobs.

Ava looked at Lally, frozen beside her, and seeming almost as shocked as Mel. 'What the fuck,' she said. 'I told them. I said it wasn't going to stop.'

Still wondering what she meant, Ava saw Rose come down from upstairs. Her hair was neatly plaited, but she was wearing her dressing gown again. 'Oh my god,' she said. 'What happened?'

Mel, half sitting, half lying on the sofa with Joel's arm around her, pushed him away. Her face twisted and the words came out as a croaking growl that sounded nothing like her normal voice. 'My instruments, my instruments.' As if realising what she had said, she gave a groan that seemed to come from somewhere so deep it shook her tiny frame, and she fell back into Joel's arms.

For a moment the other three stood looking at her. Then Lally ran to the stairs. Ava followed through her own bedroom and on up to the attic. Lally was standing at the far end of a long loft room lit by a single skylight. Close to the door where Ava stood was a double bed with a crumpled duvet and pillows askew. Shoes, boots and odd bits of clothing were strewn everywhere, but that could just be the way Mel lived. Dusk was gathering outside and the skylight wasn't large, so the room was dim.

Ava found a switch beside the door. There was no central light, but various lamps dotted around came on. Several had coloured bulbs giving the room a magical air, like being in a fairground. At the back was a long table or workbench covered with musical instruments. Mel had a large collection, all kinds of strings, small drums and other percussion. Then there were pipes of various kinds and two keyboards.

As Ava moved towards her, Lally held up one of those rain sticks made from hollowed bamboo. It had been crushed and the pebbles spilled out of the splintered wood onto the floor. Some colourful maracas next to it had been almost completely smashed. The seeds scattered on the table. The table itself was dented where the hammer, or whatever had done the damage, had landed. A set of bongo drums had been ruined: their skins ripped and punctured. And a small stringed instrument that looked a bit like a zither, had also had its strings severed like the viola Mel had brought down.

Lally looked at Ava, her expression so weird Ava wondered if she was going to faint. 'Who the fuck would do a thing like this?' she asked. The words were difficult to hear, breathed rather than vocalised. She pushed away some of the pebbles and seeds and half-sat on the table, looking as if her legs would no longer hold her.

Ava could only shake her head as Joel, Mel and finally Rose came up the stairs. Lally went towards Mel, her arms outstretched, but Mel moved away, shaking her head. She came to the table, picking up a little pipe that had been snapped almost completely in two and staring down at it as if she still couldn't believe what had happened.

Rose said, 'Your fiddle's not been touched. It's still in the cupboard downstairs. I checked before we came up.'

And Joel, 'I think the keyboards are OK too. It's really only a few things.'

Mel threw the broken pipe on the ground so hard it bounced. Then her hands went to her hair and, instead of her usual gesture of running her fingers through it, she clutched at the spikes of red so hard it was as if she wanted to tear them out.

Joel came to her, trying to take her in his arms again, but this time she shoved him away. 'No.' She shook her head. 'Leave me alone, just leave me alone.' Then she picked up a photo frame from the table and held it pressed tightly against her chest as she swayed back and forth. Her eyes shone with tears in the lamplight as she looked over her ruined treasures and her chest heaved with something suppressed – sobs or an outburst of rage – Ava couldn't tell.

Whatever it was, it felt too intimate, too intrusive, to look at her or even to be here, so Ava began to walk to the door. Lally, already there, opened it, while Rose and Joel looked at each other, unsure.

Then Mel rounded on them and the anger burst out. 'That's it, fuck off and forget about it, why don't you?'

They all stopped and Joel said very softly, 'We'll do whatever you want. Just tell us.'

'You could start by explaining how this happened.' She looked at Rose, her eyes clear of tears and burning with anger. And something more than anger. 'You were here all day. So go on, tell me.'

Rose staggered and sat on the bed. It was almost as if Mel had struck her. 'I'm sorry, Mel, but I was fast asleep all afternoon. After everyone had their lunch, I was so tired. And we don't lock the doors, you know that.' She turned to Ava as if pleading for help. 'People are always coming and going, half the time without taking a key. We don't even have enough for everyone. Someone could just have walked in.' She looked back at Mel, her voice shaking, 'And I was wearing ear plugs. I'm sorry, I'm so sorry.'

'So it was this so-called prankster again, was it?' She spat out the word. 'Isn't that what Brad called him – or her?'

Lally said, 'Mel,' and went to her, touching her arm, but Mel jerked away.

'But this isn't a prank or a joke. It's someone who wants to hurt me. To hurt me personally.'

Rose said, 'You surely don't think it's one of us?'

Mel stared at her for a long moment and when she spoke

her voice was as hard as her eyes. 'I don't know. What do you think, Rose?' Lally made a small sound of protest or of attempted comfort, Ava wasn't sure, and Mel flashed a look at her. 'Oh, just get out, will you. Get out, the lot of you, and let me clear up.'

Chapter Thirteen

Downstairs, Brad was in the kitchen stirring something on the stove. He didn't look up, just said, 'About half an hour until dinner. OK, all?'

Rose said his name so breathlessly Ava was surprised he could hear. But he turned, taking in their expressions, his own smile dropping away. 'Jesus, what's happened?'

Rose sank onto the sofa and Ava, feeling more of an outsider than ever, perched on the wide window ledge so the other two could take the chairs. Brad, rubbing his hands on a tea towel, came to sit next to Rose, squeezing her knee. She leaned over, resting her head on his shoulder.

Lally spoke, 'Someone got in and destroyed some of Mel's instruments.' Now it was Lally who sounded angry.

Brad smoothed Rose's hair. 'Oh my god, were you in the house?'

Rose looked up at him. 'Yes, but I was asleep. I think Mel blames me, but I didn't hear anything.' She sounded about to cry.

Ava glanced over at Joel, expecting him to speak, but he just picked at something on the arm of his chair. Of course, she kept forgetting that he was a relative newcomer too. The atmosphere was so awkward she said, 'I'll keep an eye on the dinner.'

On the Aga something tomatoey was bubbling and she gave it a stir. There was a French stick on the chopping board, with a pottery bowl beside it, so she began cutting thick chunks of bread. Then looked in the cupboards and brought out a packet of spaghetti. From the other room she heard Brad say, 'I'm phoning Paddy to come back. We need to talk about this all together.'

Joel, perhaps feeling as out of place as she did, came behind her and asked, 'All right? Why don't we go outside for a minute? Get away from it.' He called out, 'I'm turning off the sauce. We can put on the pasta when Paddy gets back.' Then he opened the door that led to the garden.

He was right. It was a real relief to get away. They crossed the strip of grass. Although it was dusk, it was lighter in the garden than in the low-ceilinged rooms of the cottage; the sky the palest translucent blue edged with pink at the horizon. The garden was a narrow shelf on the hillside with grassy fields, studded with tiny white, yellow and blue flowers, dropping steeply away from it. When they sat on the low wall it felt almost as if they were on a ship sailing a tranquil green sea.

'Bloody hell, that was intense,' Joel said.

'I know, poor Mel. Who would do something like that? Destroy things rather than steal? That viola must have been worth a lot of money.'

At that Joel said, 'Just a minute, don't move,' and dashed back inside, returning almost immediately. Lowering himself down beside her, he shook his head. 'I just checked the kitty. We don't keep a lot in there, but it hasn't been touched and you're right, it wasn't a thief. I mean, Brad's laptop is sitting there on the table and even an idiot would know that a viola could be valuable. They would have taken it, not broken it.'

If things had been different, it would have been pleasant sitting in the cool twilight with him, overlooking the pretty valley. If they could have talked about ordinary things. Maybe flirted a bit. Got to know each other. But after what had just happened to Mel, it would have been callous to talk about anything else. Above all Ava was conscious of those noises she had heard in the attic last night and the mumbling from the garage earlier today. If Joel and Mel were in a relationship, they seemed to want to keep it secret. So if she said any more about Mel she was afraid she might mess up. Instead, she just sat listening to his breathing beside her and a distant blackbird singing its heart out.

The door behind them opened and Paddy strolled out, drinking from a bottle of beer. 'I've just put on the spaghetti. So, dinner won't be long. Brad's upstairs with Rose and Mel's hiding out in her room. Much as I feel sympathy for them, I'm also starving.'

Lally came out too, also with a bottle of beer. She waved it at Ava, but Ava shook her head. Lally took a huge gulp and, as if it had energised her, the words burst out, 'I don't know about you lot, but I'm seriously spooked.'

Paddy patted her arm. 'No worries, love.'

She pulled away looking almost as angry as Mel had seemed. 'Have you forgotten what happened to me and Ava just yesterday?'

From his seat on the wall, Joel twisted to look at her. 'What's that got to do with it?'

'You are joking, I hope.' The scorn dripped from Lally's words.

Paddy turned away, calling behind him as he headed back into the house. 'Not now, Lally. Let's just have our dinner and talk about what we can do to help Mel.'

Joel got up and followed him, but Lally shook her head at Ava, obviously furious, before storming after them. Ava decided to stay where she was for a bit. This was between them.

But she jumped to her feet, her breath stalling as she heard Lally shout, 'No, no, it's no good pretending anymore. It's time to face up to it. And time we told poor Ava just what she's got herself into.'

Chapter Fourteen

Walking slowly into the house, Ava tried to calm her thoughts. She had no idea what Lally meant, but she was clearly very upset. She was sitting at the table leaning back against the rough wall, her arms crossed so tight across her chest, her knuckles stood out sharply. Joel was next to her and as Ava came close, he touched Lally's shoulder. She shifted away.

Paddy, carrying a bowl of pasta in one hand, and the bread Ava had cut in the other, looked at her properly for the first time and said in a calm tone, as if nothing out of the ordinary was going on, 'Could you bring the cheese and the grater, please?'

When she came to the table, Joel looked up and shook his head. He didn't want her to ask Lally anything. Before she could decide whether to ignore him or not, Paddy said, 'Let's all try to eat our dinner in peace and then we can talk. OK, Lally?' He dished out some pasta and put it in front of her, then passed some to Ava and Joel. Joel began grating cheese onto his own food and even Lally took a piece of bread. It looked as if whatever she wanted to say was being put on hold.

Ava poked at her pasta. She couldn't eat. This was ridiculous. She needed to know.

Lally evidently felt the same. She threw her untouched chunk of bread into her dish, where it slowly turned red as it sank into the sauce, and looked up. 'It's no good. We've got to talk this through properly. Not just for Ava's sake. We've all been avoiding it too long.'

Paddy put down his fork, with the commanding air that made it impossible not to wait for him to speak. 'Of course. If that's what you need. I had no idea it was bothering you so much. You know what I think, but go ahead. Just remember it could be a series of coincidences.' He turned to Ava, sitting next to him. Looking at her properly again, although his voice still had the formal tone that let her know she was a stranger. 'Lally thinks someone has been playing a series of not very funny practical jokes on us, but there's really no proof. And, above all, no need for someone who's just arrived to be anxious.' There was something about his voice and the rich brown of his eyes that did have a calming effect.

But not on Lally, it seemed. She stared hard at him. 'What say we let Ava decide for herself when she hears everything, eh?' Then she leaned across the table. 'At first we didn't connect things,' another glance at Paddy, warning him to let her go on. 'But after a while they just built up. I don't even know when it started. Weeks, maybe months ago. There was the old van. Our previous van. It broke down on the way back from a gig. The garage said the engine was pretty much shot and they thought someone had put water or maybe Coke or some other soft drink into it while the van was parked outside the venue. It would have cost so much to fix; it was cheaper to buy another one second-hand.'

Paddy, his voice steady, said, 'Don't forget we only had that local garage's word for the extent of the damage and what caused it. Rose and Brad are so gullible, wouldn't hear of it when I suggested we try elsewhere before giving up on it.' He held up his hand when Lally went to speak again. 'And even if the garage was on the level, they told us that local kids in that area had regularly been vandalising cars just like that. Big bottles of Coke into the engine. And our old van would have been an easy target. No lock on the petrol cap and they knew everyone would be inside at the show until ten or eleven p.m. at least, which meant they wouldn't be disturbed.'

Lally shook her head, her face stubborn. 'What about what they did to the new van?' She was looking at Ava again now. 'Mel told you about the graffiti, didn't she? The boobs and cock added to the Chimera picture. What she didn't tell you was what was scrawled on the back. Things like: *Fuck off back to London you perves.*'

Joel spoke to Ava. 'It, and the damage to the old van, happened in the heart of the Forest of Dean. It's quite a remote place. Not much for the kids to do. And some people there don't like strangers.'

Lally shifted on the bench until she was looking into his face. 'Shut up, Joel, and let me finish.' Her expression was so bitter, Ava saw him flinch, but when Paddy came in with, 'Steady now, we're all friends,' Lally pressed her fingers against her lips as if afraid of what else she might say.

For a moment, no one spoke. Ava certainly didn't want to. She'd heard nothing yet to prove that Paddy and Joel weren't right, but then she thought of Lally's reaction after their car accident and of what had just happened to Mel.

Lally pushed her plate aside and put her elbows on the table, her chin on her clasped hands. 'OK, I'll make it short. That was only the start. We've turned up at gigs to find they've been cancelled by someone pretending to be one of us. The posters I've put up have been ripped down or covered in the same kind of filth as the van.' A deep breath. 'We've had dog shit posted through our letterbox, which means they know where we live. And now the log across the road and Mel's instruments.' Ava jumped as Lally slammed her clasped hands down on the table, muddy hazel eyes staring into hers. 'So what do you think, Ava? Am I paranoid, like they keep saying, or are we being targeted by someone who hates us?'

Chapter Fifteen

No one spoke. Ava had no idea what to say. All she knew was that Lally's expression and the way her breath seemed to have choked in her throat were convincing. She must believe what she was saying and Ava's own heart had begun to beat very fast. She looked at Joel, but he was staring into his plate. Paddy had hardly eaten anything either.

Her phone buzzed in her pocket and began to play its familiar tune and she expected it to be her mum, but when she saw who it was, she knew she had to answer. 'I'm sorry, I have to get this. It's my dad and he hardly ever rings me.' Although the garden was dark by now, it seemed the best place to go. Mel and Rose were upstairs, obviously both very upset.

Her dad was a man of few words and at the best of times he hated talking on the phone. As soon as she answered he said he knew she was probably busy and he wouldn't keep her, but her mum was very anxious because she hadn't called. After that he ground to a halt, obviously having no idea how to say what he needed to.

She rescued him. 'I'm sorry, I've been really busy, getting settled and starting rehearsals.'

'That's good. How's it going, then? Enjoying it?'

'It's fine, hard work of course, but the cottage is lovely and the group have been very welcoming.' She knew it was stilted, but it was the best she could do.

'That's good, Ava love.' A pause, which in the past she would have been able to fill. Why was that so difficult now? He gave a noisy breath, obviously dredging his memory for something he'd planned to say. 'Send us some photos, when you get time.'

'Yeah, I'll do that as soon as I can.'

'That's good. Well, I won't keep you chatting. Just wanted to know you were OK. Daisy wants to speak to you. Is that all right?'

'Of course, put her on.' Ava wished she could ask him to stay, to go on talking in that croaky voice she had always loved, but there was no point. Conversations with him were always short and after their recent arguments she couldn't fill the gaps with chatter the way she used to. She was still saying goodbye when she heard a small click as he put his phone down and went to get her mum. She must be in another room, probably fearing Ava would say she didn't want to speak to her.

While she waited, she turned back to the house. The kitchen and dining area were brightly lit, the living room almost dark. Lally was still seated at the table, her head in her hands, with Paddy by the sink washing up and Joel moving away from the window where he'd been standing. She had the feeling he had been looking out at her. Lally said something she couldn't hear and the others turned, Paddy waving a hand to tell her to keep her voice down. It was clear they were still arguing.

As Ava watched, their faces seemed to distort. Paddy must have put on the main strip light and it was too harsh. Or it could have been the old glass in the windows that had faults and ripples running through it. Whatever it was, they looked different, ugly, almost cruel – as if they were wearing masks. Or – she felt a small shiver inside – as if they had taken off their masks.

'Hello, sweetheart.' Her mum's voice, normally so vivid, sounded almost as hesitant as her dad's had been and Ava felt another pang of guilt. She wanted to answer, but couldn't seem to speak. Daisy went on, 'I stayed out of the room hoping it would make Dad talk a bit longer, but you know him. I think he's got so used to me chattering away all these years, he doesn't know how to do it.'

Ava couldn't bear it. Wanted things back the way they used to be, at least with her parents. 'Look, Mum, I'm sorry for the way I've been lately, please tell Dad that too. Part of it was to do with the way my career was going nowhere and part was because I realised Will and I were grinding to a standstill.'

There was a little gasp from Daisy, whether relief or anxiety, Ava couldn't tell. Probably she just realised how careful she had to be to stop the conversation descending into another misunderstanding. 'Like I said, my lovely, we've always wanted what's best for you. What would make you happy.' Another deep breath. 'And sometimes we got it wrong. We know that now.'

She hated hearing that sorrowful note in her mum's voice. 'Let's not talk about it anymore, Mum. I overreacted, that's all.'

Knowing it would make her relax and be able to talk more

naturally, she asked about Daisy's job. She was a teaching assistant in an infant school. Loved it and always had a fund of funny stories to tell. This time she suspected that her mum had come to the phone with a few anecdotes prepared and, as she talked, her voice lightened and became almost as lively as usual.

Only half listening, Ava saw the main striplight in the kitchen turn off. Lally, Paddy and Joel were still in there, but the spotlights dotted around were kinder and they were all standing with their backs to her. It looked as if Lally was making coffee, while Paddy took glasses from a cupboard and Joel rooted in the fridge – a pleasant domestic scene that suited the story her mum was telling about some cooking she'd been doing with a group of five year olds. In the middle of the anecdote Ava saw a flicker of movement in the dark living room as the door to the stairs opened and a shaft of light shone down.

Then one of the small lamps came on and she saw Mel and Brad in the far corner where they couldn't be seen from the kitchen. Mel was in Brad's arms, her head buried in his chest, but when she raised her face to his and kissed him, it was a passionate lovers' kiss. Certainly not just a gesture of comfort. They must have heard a noise on the stairs because they stepped quickly apart, Mel rubbing the back of her hand across her lips as Rose came through the door.

She wasn't sure when her mum had stopped talking, but all the animation had gone from her voice when she said, 'Ava? Are you still there?'

'Yes, Mum, I'm here.'

A little laugh that managed to sound deeply sad. 'I thought for a minute you'd hung up on me.'

'I wouldn't do that.'

'Well please just tell me you're all right. And that we're all right again.'

'I'm fine and we're fine too. Of course we are.' It wasn't true and her mum had always been able to tell when she was lying, but she hoped that not being able to see her might make it more difficult.

It seemed not. 'I know you're still angry with us, but we love you so much. Please remember that. And remember we're here whenever you need us. You'll always be our baby girl. The most important thing in our world.' Her voice wobbled.

It was hard to say goodbye and the tears threatened as she did so, all too aware that her mum was struggling too.

Afterwards, the silence of the garden felt heavy in her ears. She groped for the low wall and sat on it again. The longing to see her parents, to be back with them in the house she still thought of as home, was almost overwhelming. But things could never be the same even there.

And, as she looked at the strangers in the lighted rooms in front of her, she had never felt so lonely.

Chapter Sixteen

When the group in the kitchen headed to the living room, Ava followed them. Brad on the sofa with his arm round Rose glanced up at her and she wondered if she had imagined the hint of warning in his eyes. But she told herself he could hardly have seen her out in the dark garden. The kiss had only lasted seconds and maybe she had misinterpreted it. After all, she knew very little about these people or their relationships with each other.

Joel was carrying a tray of glasses and a bottle of brandy. He placed them on the low table alongside the coffee pot and mugs Lally had put there. 'Help yourself, guys.' He looked at Ava and waved at the bottle. 'Present from an elderly gentleman who's a bit of a fan of ours. Used to be an actor himself, apparently. I think we need it tonight.'

Brad said, 'Mel has called the police to report what's happened.' A glance around at everyone. 'The break-in and damage to her instruments.'

Lally, her voice still harsh, 'And what about the rest of it? All the other things.'

'Well, they already know about the two incidents with the van, so they're bound to look for a link.'

Mel spoke from where she was sitting on the window ledge, 'And it wasn't a break-in. The door was open.'

Brad leaned forward to pour himself a brandy and pointed to the coffee pot to ask if Rose wanted some. As he did so Lally, who, like Ava was still on her feet, made an exasperated noise. 'I'm going to bed. Make sure you lock all the doors before you come up.'

Paddy touched her arm. 'I do that every night.' When she'd gone, Mel got up, grabbed a glass, filled it to the brim with brandy, and followed her without a word. Ava took her place on the window seat, watching as Brad kissed Rose's hair and she nuzzled into his chest. Paddy sat drinking brandy and staring ahead.

Once she guessed Mel was safely in the loft, Ava went up too. Although she was feeling drained it was too early to hope to sleep, but there was no chair in her tiny room so she undressed and got into bed with a book. She had meant to go through the script for the other play – the one for adults, called *Dark Matter* that Chimera performed in village halls and pubs etc., but she knew it wasn't a good idea; she wanted to get away from thinking about the group. From thinking about anything.

However, she couldn't concentrate and was tempted to call her mother back; to talk the whole thing through again. She thought about the last words Daisy had said on the phone. *You'll always be our baby girl, the most important thing in our world.*

She knew it was true, but her parents' reactions to her miscarriage had deepened a rift that had been growing since Ava was a young teenager. That was when she began to realise that things were not as simple as she'd imagined and that her mum and dad had secrets. Some of them very dark.

When she married Ava's father, Daisy had taken two-year-old Ava into her heart as completely as if she had been her birth mother. Her dad had told her that, although they'd introduced her stepmother to her as Daisy, she soon began calling her Mummy. When she was a teenager, she asked him if he had minded. Was it difficult to see his first wife, her real mum, replaced so completely? His face went red with embarrassment and he turned away before muttering, 'How could I? It made you both so happy.' And by then of course it was clear to Ava that Daisy was the love of his life.

It helped that Daisy had been a close friend of Ava's actual mother, Jane, and always talked about her; telling Ava how lovely she had been, how proud she would be of her daughter. Still, it was difficult to think of her as a real person. Her death had been sudden, so she hadn't been able to leave any messages for her baby daughter. The photos that were still around the house showed a woman who looked very like Ava, but as a child she was never more thrilled than when people who didn't know the situation said she resembled Daisy. They would laugh together over that because it wasn't true. Daisy was short and round while Ava was always tall for her age and skinny. Although they were both dark, her stepmother's hair was a wavy chestnut nothing like Ava's dead straight rope of almost black.

But the things both her parents had said when they found out she was pregnant and their reactions to the miscarriage had brought up all sorts of thoughts in Ava that had caused her to be so angry with them she couldn't hide it.

She knew Daisy's first marriage had been not just a disaster, but the worst kind of nightmare. Something she had never been able to properly recover from, so it made sense that she would be worried about Ava rushing into a commitment with Will too young. When Ava snapped that she was older than Daisy had been by several years, her dad said, 'But she wouldn't have settled for him if she hadn't been pregnant.'

This was a sore point between them because it had been years before Ava had found out that Daisy had actually had a child during her first marriage. And she had only discovered that inadvertently. Another secret they'd kept from her.

It made her so angry that, just days after the miscarriage, with her emotions all over the place, she had blurted out to her dad, 'And what about you, Dad? Wasn't Mum, my real mum, expecting me when you got married? And she was younger than I am. Is that what you're thinking about?'

The expression on his face told her everything.

And although Daisy tried to tell her how much Ava's parents had loved each other and how devastated her dad had been when her mother died, Ava hadn't been convinced. It wasn't fair to be angry with them, but she couldn't help it. Not yet anyway. Even though she knew part of that anger was with herself for loving Daisy more than she could ever love the shadowy figure of her real mother.

She tried to go back to her book, but couldn't concentrate. She was hungry and regretting that wasted pasta. Wishing too, that she had brought up a glass of brandy. She threw the book on the floor, turning off the light and trying to sleep.

But that only made her think of what was happening in the here and now. She had been certain it was Paddy upstairs with Mel. When Mel told her he was gay, which was surely done deliberately to disabuse her of the idea that they were lovers, she'd assumed it must be Joel. But that secret kiss with Brad in the corner of the living room changed everything. And Rose had obviously been upset about something in the morning. If she knew Brad had sneaked out in the middle of the night to be with Mel that wasn't surprising. There certainly seemed to be no love lost between Mel and Rose – at least as far as Mel was concerned.

She must have slept because she was woken by her phone ringing on the window ledge beside the bed. A stab of panic went through her until she saw that it was still only 10.30. It was Will. She'd forgotten her promise to ring him tonight.

'I'm sorry, I was about to call you earlier on, but Dad rang and after dinner I was so tired I came to bed and fell asleep right away.'

'On your own, I hope.' It was said with a laugh and she could have been imagining the hint of something else in his voice.

She laughed too. 'Of course, although,' she spoke as softly as she could, 'it's not very private. One of the women in the group has to come through my room to get to her own.'

'When I come to see you I'd better book a hotel room then.' If her laugh sounded more uneasy than excited, he didn't spot it or decided to ignore it. 'You're not doing any shows for a while, are you?'

'It won't be long. Rose's last one is next week and after that I should be ready to go.'

'Well I've got this weekend free so I can sort out a nice

room for us in Gloucester. I've never been there so I'll enjoy a look round.'

'I don't know. I think they expect to rehearse with me every day and it's a long way for you to come for just a few hours.'

'Don't you want to see me?' There was definitely a touch of ice now.

'Of course I do. Look, I've been asleep so I can't think straight. I'll find out what the plans here are and let you know.'

'OK, you do that. Let me know when you have time for me.'

Her, 'Will, don't be like that,' was too late. He had already gone. She lay back in bed wanting to cry, but knowing she might be heard through the thin walls of the cottage.

And as if responding to her thought she became aware of Mel crying softly in the attic above her.

Chapter Seventeen

Everyone was subdued the next day, but as planned they drove to the rehearsal room above the pub and started on the second play in the present repertoire – *Dark Matter*. It was an original script by Brad, and Ava had loved it the first time she read it. Each time she had come back to it the impact was greater. Brad was a really good writer.

The theme was mankind's destruction of the earth and the damage being done to the planet's natural resources. But it was handled with the lightest touch and plenty of humour. Appropriately, for a play that was being performed in the heart of the English countryside, it was also about the ancient myths that, according to Brad, were still very much alive. The gods and goddesses, faeries and demons, ghosts and apparitions that people continue to half believe in. These elemental spirits, according to the play, were distraught at the damage being wrought on their special places. In one of the most powerful scenes a river goddess came out of the water to drown a man.

There was original music by Mel and Dominic again. Folky

tunes, many of them comical and a bit bawdy, that she was sure would appeal to unsophisticated audiences, but a couple of beautiful laments and ballads too.

As they worked – she played the river goddess – she forgot everything and revelled in being part of such a wonderful creation. Brad was enthusiastic about her performance. He played the man she drowned: a landowner who wanted to divert the river that was home to the goddess, and she loved acting with him.

The *river* for the rehearsal was marked by a couple of pieces of rope laid parallel on the floor and even when they performed it would be nothing more than long lengths of blue and green fabric. With the clever lighting and sound effects that Dominic had designed for the scene, they all assured her it worked brilliantly. 'The magic of theatre,' Brad said with a grin.

They were both sitting on the floor beside the rope river, tired after the scene. It was quite physical and Ava could see that it wouldn't be good for pregnant Rose to carry on any longer. Brad said, 'Rose does some really clever stuff with the fabric, so that it seems to ripple, then swirl and grow angry. At times it looks like part of her costume, which is made of the same stuff. You'll see when you watch the performance next week.'

He lay back on the floor next to her, his hands behind his head. Although he was slim his tight T-shirt showed off well-defined muscles and when he looked up at her, his grey eyes glinting in the light from the tall windows, she could see why Mel might find him difficult to resist.

As if guessing her thoughts, he smiled a slow smile. 'Of course, you can adapt once you feel comfortable with the movements. Make it your own. Rose weaves green ribbons and glittery what-nots through her hair.' He reached for one of her brown-black strands, twisting it through his hands. 'But do what you think works best for you. With your dark complexion and this amazing stuff,' he gave her hair a tiny tug, 'I think you'll fit the part even better than she does.'

She jumped as Mel began thumping out one of the fake folk songs on the piano. 'Once more for this one, guys, then I need to go.' She was bashing out the notes of the song so loudly she had to shout as she went on, bouncing on her stool. 'Rose just messaged me to say that the cops are at the cottage. They're looking at the scene of the crime and then want to speak to me.'

Paddy put his hands on her shoulders. 'OK, but go easy on that instrument. It's done nothing to you.'

They rehearsed the song quickly then Mel asked Brad to take her back to the cottage. 'Paddy said he wants to go over a few things that Ava does on her own, so they won't need us for a bit.' Joel said he would go with them. He wasn't needed here and had some replacement parts for their sound system to pick up.

Once they had gone the room felt very empty and left alone with Paddy, Ava grabbed her script and began studying it. When, in that emotionless soft voice of his, he suggested a tea break she wished they could just do what they had to do then get away from each other. But it was impossible to say that, even though he probably felt the same.

At least making the tea – there was a tiny kitchen area in one corner and they'd brought their own supplies of tea, coffee and biscuits – kept him busy while she looked at the lines she already knew inside out and picked out a few notes on the piano. What did people call it? Self-soothing? Well, just touching a piano or guitar did the trick for her.

She felt so much calmer by the time Paddy brought over their mugs that she surprised herself by saying what she had been thinking while she played. 'I'm not surprised Mel's distraught about what's happened. If someone damaged my guitar or flute, I'd be desperate.'

He sipped his tea, nodding. 'Yeah, I get that. My ex-boyfriend, Dominic, would have killed anyone who ruined one of his precious instruments, but I think Mel's mean even more to her.'

Ava felt a tiny twist of pleasure. He had spoken with so much more ease than usual and to mention his ex must mean he was beginning to accept her. She knew though that it was best to leave Dominic's name alone and stay with Mel. 'Does she have insurance?'

'I guess so, although some of the stuff is irreplaceable because she picked it up on her travels. But her father paid for the trad instruments, the violin, viola and keyboards etc., so I think he would have made sure she was covered. You know he's a bishop? Well I gather they keep a baby grand in the bishop's palace for her. Of course, they had hopes she'd become a concert pianist.'

He swallowed the last of his tea and put his mug on the top of the piano, muttering almost to himself, 'Another one with a disappointed family.'

Chapter Eighteen

When they finished rehearsing, the others still weren't back. Paddy messaged Brad, but Brad told him Mel was furious and had gone out for a walk to calm down. Apparently, the police interview had been so rudimentary she guessed they were just fobbing her off. Joel was still not back from town with the van so they might as well start walking back.

Although it had been fine working with Paddy and their conversation over tea had been much more relaxed, Ava didn't relish spending extra time with him. 'You made the tea so I'll wash up if you want to go on,' she said. 'If we're done for the day I might walk down and have a look around the town.'

He rubbed her shoulder. 'Don't worry, there's a few things I want to do before I leave anyway and the cups won't take a minute.' She almost flinched. It was the first time he had touched her and alone like this it felt oddly intimate. The tiny smile and the crinkle of his dark-brown eyes as he looked down at her made her sure he'd seen the flush come to her face.

She looked away, but his hand had dropped and he was striding to the door. 'If you come downstairs now I'll point out the way you want to go. It's easy to take the wrong direction and end up in the middle of a farm. I did it once and they have a load of half-wild dogs roaming around their yard.'

Before she could thank him, he was running up the stairs again. She shook her head, still embarrassed by her reaction to his touch. And even more by the fact that he'd obviously noticed. But she told herself he'd soon forget it and at least it was good that he seemed to be warming to her.

The idea that she might stumble upon a pack of savage dogs didn't make the first part of the walk relaxing, but once she was out of the trees and could see the path snaking down to the river at the bottom of the valley and the little town just over the bridge, she began to enjoy it.

She took her time. There was nothing she needed in the town. It was just a relief to be completely alone and she realised how tense she had been, not only since she got here, but before that when things had been so difficult with Will and with her parents. One of the reasons she wanted to be away from everyone else was to be sure she could phone Will without being interrupted or overheard. It was Thursday and before the rehearsal Paddy had suggested they all take the weekend off. It would be their last opportunity for a while because they had most Saturdays booked after that. So, it would be best to do as Will wanted and let him come up right away. She needed to make him see that this had to be a proper break and she could only do that face to face.

She stopped on the bridge, but, instead of calling him, she

stood for a long time looking down into the river, at the tendrils of green waving back and forth as the clear water washed through them. And she wasn't thinking about Will, but about her real mother, Jane, again.

Jane had been on her mind a lot recently and rehearsing a play where she had to drown someone made it impossible to avoid thinking about her death. Because her mother had died by drowning. And drowning in a river. In fact, when she first read the *Dark Matter* script she remembered thinking it was one of those coincidences that feels as if it must be something more than that.

Ava wasn't sure when she'd first been told about the accident. She must have been very young, because she'd always felt vaguely resentful of Jane for doing something as dangerous as swimming in a river when she had a young child. She'd assumed Jane had been alone and thought her reckless. But when she was a teenager, she'd found out that the truth was very different.

She was fourteen and, after a childhood that apart from Daisy's occasional episodes of depression, was close to idyllic, she had begun to rebel a little. Her first boyfriend had come and gone leaving her upset and blaming her parents for restricting her time with him, not letting her stay out late or wear the kind of makeup and clothes she wanted.

Inevitably she began to wonder if things might have been different if her biological mother had survived. More than once, when Daisy tried to discipline her, she recalled shouting, 'You can't tell me what to do. You're not my real mum.' Afterwards, she always felt terribly guilty because she knew how much it hurt Daisy.

But she became obsessively fascinated by Jane. In photos

her mum remained young and pretty: never had the chance to age. It was easier to identify with her than plump and unglamorous Daisy. Where once Ava had been thrilled when people said she looked like Daisy, now she convinced herself that she was just like Jane.

One evening, while her dad chuckled over a terrible TV comedy in front of the electric fire that flickered with red and orange lights in a bad imitation of a log burner, she'd taken down some of the old photo albums they kept on a high shelf. Coming in from the kitchen Daisy said, 'If you want copies of any of those to keep in your own room, we can have some made.' She pointed to one that showed Ava and her mother on what must have been her first Christmas, telling her Jane had shown the photo to her soon after it was taken. 'She was so excited because it was the first time you sat up. You must have been about six months.'

It was a good picture and Ava could see the delight in her mum's face and the way baby Ava looked up at her with absolute love and trust. And for the first time she could remember she felt a real pang of loss, which quickly turned to anger. 'She shouldn't have gone swimming like that all on her own.'

Daisy gestured for her to come into the kitchen and said she couldn't understand how Ava had misunderstood. 'She wasn't alone. We told you that years ago. Told you exactly what happened. Surely you remember?'

Ava shook her head, not just confused, but feeling breathless – as if the whole world, the whole past, had somehow shifted.

Chapter Nineteen

The story came out slowly, with Daisy insisting several times that they'd told her it all long ago and she must have forgotten. Her mum hadn't been alone after all and she hadn't done anything daring or reckless. She had just taken a dip, after a picnic on a hot summer day, in what should have been a safe part of the river. It seemed she must have become trapped in a tangle of underwater weeds. By the time anyone realised she was gone, it was too late.

And her husband, little Ava, and her friend, Daisy, had been there too, sitting on the bank.

When the whole story was told, Ava heard Daisy's soft voice coming from far away, telling her again, 'But you knew all this from when you were tiny.'

Shaking her head, breathless with rage, Ava said, 'No. You and Dad told me she was on her own. I know you did.' For some reason she was desperate to believe that was true.

It was Daisy's turn to shake her head and her voice was as trembly as Ava's. 'Perhaps you were too young to take it in.

And you seemed fine.' An odd little gasp. 'Maybe we should have talked about it more often, but it was so upsetting. Can you imagine how hard it was to know we were right there and didn't see what was happening?'

Ava's arms were crossed so tightly over her chest it almost hurt. 'I needed to know it all. You should have made sure I did.' She wanted to scream and stamp like the stubborn little girl she'd been not so long before.

'I'm so sorry, but it was incredibly painful for me and your dad. I suppose we couldn't bear to go over it again and again.'

When Daisy reached for her, she kept her arms crossed and moved away. Couldn't bear to look at her anymore and went upstairs to lie on her bed. Next morning, she left for school without her breakfast and didn't speak to either of her parents for a couple of days.

Why it had upset her so much she didn't know. When she talked about it with Will, he asked if she thought Daisy was lying and that they had deliberately deceived her, but she didn't believe that. More likely, just as Daisy said, they had told her when she had been too young to properly comprehend. After that they had been glad to let it go. But even now she couldn't help feeling that her wonderful childhood had been built on a falsehood. One of several.

Another thing Will suggested was that she was so upset because she suspected her dad and Daisy of having an affair before her real mother died. She couldn't bear to think so, but knowing how much they eventually came to love each other she wondered if they had been so happy sitting on that river bank together that they had been oblivious to what was happening to Ava's poor mother.

Or – and this is what she wondered, in her darkest

moments – had her mum seen how close her husband and her friend were becoming and decided she no longer wanted to live? Did she really care so little for Ava that she could abandon her?

She wouldn't, couldn't, let herself think that, but being near water always made her feel apprehensive as if, in a moment of madness, she might throw herself in. It was ridiculous, she was a good swimmer – her dad had made sure of that. But she guessed she must have some dim memory of the accident even though she had been under two years old. Perhaps she had been the only one aware of her mother's struggle.

When she was young, she was plagued by terrifying nightmares, many of them featuring dark and threatening water. But even though they often had to come to her room to comfort her when she woke, crying or screaming, she was sure her parents had never suggested that there might be a connection.

But then, she told herself, drowning must be one of the most elemental fears, which was what made her scene in the play so powerful.

A movement on the hillside caught her eye. A couple of big magpies swooping out of the thick clump of trees she'd come through on her way down. The pub was visible to one side of the little wood, but she couldn't make out the cottage higher up.

It was no good, these were all delaying tactics, and, taking a deep breath, she clicked on Will's number. He answered straight away with a curt, 'Hello.'

'Is this a bad time?'

'It depends what you want to say.'

It was the closest he could get on the phone to one of his

sulky silences and she found herself smiling – a smile of irritation rather than amusement. He was so predictable. 'I was calling to tell you I'll be free this weekend if you still want to come over.'

A pause. 'I'm not sure now. I may have to go to a thing.'

A thing? It was so feeble she didn't even try to hold back a small laugh. 'OK, well if you find you can get away just let me know, but it will be the last chance for some time. We're fully booked at weekends from now on.'

'It's *we* now, is it?' he said, which was so ridiculous she didn't answer. A tiny figure came round from the back of the pub heading up the hill and she wondered if it was Paddy leaving. If it was, he had been a long time. The silence stretched on and Will must have realised she wasn't going to speak. 'I was talking to Mariella about that guy at the party. The one who got you the job.'

She wanted to say it wasn't Joel who had done that. It was her performance at the audition, but there was no point so contented herself with an, 'Oh yes.'

'She says he must have gate-crashed. No one seemed to know him.'

'That's because the guy he came with was just a neighbour she'd invited. Mariella probably didn't know him either. Just asked him so he wouldn't complain about the noise.'

He must have been looking things up online while they were talking and he spoke more cheerfully. 'There's a decent-looking hotel in Gloucester we could try. Can you get there easily from where you are, or do you need me to pick you up?'

'No, I'll be fine.' She smiled; glad he couldn't see her. 'But what about your thing?'

'I'll get out of it. You're more important.'

She didn't respond to that, just said she'd be fine getting to Gloucester on Saturday and he signed off with a much happier, 'Can't wait to see you.'

Her answer, 'Me too,' was as warm as she could make it. Whatever Will thought, she knew it wasn't going to be an easy weekend, but there was no point in thinking about that now.

Chapter Twenty

Crossing the bridge, she walked into town. It was one of those classic English places with a market cross surrounded by a square full of stalls selling mainly fruit and vegetables, cheap clothes and knickknacks.

Nearby was a signpost for the railway station, which was a relief. Lally had picked her up straight off the London train in Gloucester, so when she'd told Will she could easily get back there she really had no idea if that was true. She didn't want him coming to the cottage. He would be charming of course, but when they were alone, he would make it clear that he despised the whole group and thought the way they lived was pathetic. 'Still not moved on from being student posers.' He'd said that before about some friends of theirs who had put on their own, spectacularly unsuccessful, show at the Edinburgh Fringe Festival.

She knew it was partly bravado and, as she walked up the little lane to the station, she told herself he was embarrassed by the success that had come to him so easily. He was only too aware that many of the people they knew from university thought it was mainly due to his good looks. What had happened to him was very different from what they'd planned. They had all aimed to get as much varied experience as possible in theatre, radio, TV and film, knowing none of it would be high profile or pay well, but would help them develop their skills. What they didn't say was that they all also dreamed of the big break and resented him for getting his when most of them were still out of work.

She kicked a stone down the lane too hard, so that it went further than she meant and bounced into a puddle, almost splashing the shoes of a man hurrying ahead of her. He glanced back with a frown, but had looked away again before she could give an apologetic wave. Slowing her steps, to avoid any chance of catching up with him, she went back to thinking about Will. Wondering if things between them would be different if he was still struggling like her.

Another reason she didn't want him turning up at the cottage was that she hadn't told any of the Chimera group that she was with him – someone they would probably recognise even though the TV in one corner of the living room of the cottage had never yet been turned on and looked to be gathering dust. After this weekend of course it probably wouldn't be necessary to talk about Will at all.

At the station she checked the trains to Gloucester on Saturday. It wouldn't be a problem getting there. After wandering around the market for a bit she found a café and bought herself a wrap and some coffee, enjoying being on her own as she leaned back in her seat, watching people walk by. Then she saw a mop of brown hair moving between the market stalls and recognised Joel. He saw her and waved, coming into the café and sitting opposite. Although she had been relishing the solitude, she was pleased to see him. Maybe because she had met him first or because he was also a relative newcomer to Chimera, he felt more like her own friend. And he was easy to talk to and – she couldn't deny it – easy on the eye.

He ordered a coffee and said, 'Paddy called to tell me you'd come down. Thought you might like a lift back. Not to worry if you'd rather walk.'

'No, a lift would be good, thank you.' She was feeling tired and knew tomorrow would be a hard day. They were going to rehearse both productions and Rose would be sitting in for the first time, so Ava was quite nervous about how she would react.

Joel wasn't just easy to talk to, he was also easy to sit quietly with. They both watched the stall owners beginning to pack up. 'The market's much livelier at the weekend. Lots of fabulous food stalls,' he said. 'Why not come down on Saturday? I can show you the best pub if you like.'

A stab of disappointment that she tried to ignore. 'I can't, I'm afraid. As it's my last free weekend, a friend is coming down to Gloucester and we're meeting up there.'

'Ah, say no more.' The sunlight picked out the gold flecks in his eyes. 'Is it the guy you left the party with? The one from *Factory Family*, Will Carew?'

It annoyed her that she kept flushing when she talked to him, but she took a gulp of coffee. It was best to be honest. 'Yeah, we've been together since uni, but we won't be seeing much of each other after this. We decided we need a break.' She told herself she had only revealed that to him because it might mean he didn't mention it to the rest of Chimera.

His smile somehow convinced her that he completely

understood what she was trying to say even if she wasn't clear herself. Looking out at the market square again, he said, 'You didn't happen to notice a tall fair-haired guy with glasses in town while you were wandering around, did you?'

She was grateful for the change of subject and remembered the man she nearly hit with the stone. 'There was someone like that walking up the lane to the station. Why?'

He stared into his coffee looking puzzled. 'That sounds like it was him then. I thought I must have imagined it.'

'Who do you think it was?'

'I might be wrong, but I could have sworn it was Dominic. You know, Paddy's ex. But he's supposed to be in Bristol. Wonder what he could be doing here.'

'Perhaps he came to see Paddy or one of the others.'

A nod, still looking doubtful. 'Maybe, although it all got pretty nasty before he left. I think it's best if we don't say anything to the others. If he came to see one of them it might not sit well with the rest. And I might be wrong about seeing him.'

'Of course, I won't say anything.' They finished their drinks then headed to the van. It was a longer route along the roads than the walk down the footpath and as he drove, she couldn't resist asking. 'I didn't realise you knew Dominic. How did you come to join the group?'

'Like with you, it was coincidence more than anything. Although you could say I stalked them.' When she glanced at him, he laughed. 'I came to one of their shows and really loved what I saw. My grandparents live in the Forest of Dean and I was visiting them. Well, there's nothing much to do there and, knowing I was what my granddad calls *a theatrical*, they suggested seeing the show. I thought it would be amateurish rubbish, but we went and I was blown away.'

'Dominic was still with them?'

'Yeah, this was about a year ago and of course I talked to the cast after the performance and found out he was responsible for the fantastic lighting and sound effects, which is something I'd studied. I was out of work so I offered to help out, just hoping to get more experience. Not long after that it all fell apart with him and Paddy.' He pulled up outside the cottage and raised his hands above the steering wheel. '*Eh, voilà,* I was the obvious replacement when he left. The way they live and work together, it's important that new people are compatible.' She remembered what Will had said about Joel getting her the job and felt a twinge of disappointment. He obviously wasn't far off beam. The fact that Joel had met Ava before the audition, and liked her, must have given her an edge.

Paddy came out of the house. Tall, serious-faced and elegant as always, he was incongruously carrying a bright-blue plastic pail in one hand and a mop in the other. The pail was full of cleaning products. Brad followed with a large paint can and an armful of brushes. At first Ava smiled because the effect was quite comical, but then she saw their expressions. And knew something was very wrong.

Chapter Twenty-One

Ava climbed down from the van, while Joel poked a head through his open window. 'Something wrong?'

'I should say there's something fucking wrong.' This was from Brad as Paddy, his face grim, began loading the things he was carrying into the back of the van.

Mel, holding a long paint roller and a pile of rags, shook her head, her expression as dark as the men's. 'Can you believe it? Those arses, whoever they are, have got into our rehearsal room and messed it up. The pub landlord's raging. Says unless we get it cleared up now, we can forget about using the room again. Apparently, there's graffiti all over the walls and God knows what other damage.'

Brad, at the front of the van again, said, 'He's blaming it on us of course.'

Joel asked, 'But why would we want to wreck a place we need?'

The others looked at Paddy. 'He says whoever did it, we're

responsible. And he's right. He trusted us with the key. Says I must have left the room unlocked today.'

Joel responded, 'I bet you didn't.'

A tiny smile from Paddy that was more like a wince. 'I was sure I'd locked up, but I was on my own and could have been distracted.'

Ava could feel rather than see Joel looking at her and she remembered the figure she had seen outside the pub when she was talking to Will on the bridge and then, with a jolt, the tall man heading to the station who just might have been Dominic. They had agreed not to mention him and if Joel didn't say anything it wasn't her place to do so. After all, she'd had only a glimpse of the man and didn't know what Dominic actually looked like. Instead, she said, 'I'll come and help.'

But Brad touched her elbow to move her away from the van. 'Thanks, Ava, but the best thing you can do is to stay here and go over your stuff with Rose. Ask her to show you her moves with the fabric river and how she does her hair. She shouldn't be on her own either.' It made sense so she didn't argue, just stood and watched as Joel drove away, regretting the sandwich she had eaten because her stomach was churning.

Inside, Rose called to her to come upstairs. She was in her bedroom at a cluttered dressing table by the windows. The bed was covered with blue and green lengths of fabric, which must be the stuff they used for the river. That strangely intimate smell of other people's bedrooms lingered in the air, although one of the little windows with their old-fashioned catches had been pushed open.

As Rose stood, she held up more lengths of fabric that must have been draped over her knees. 'This is my costume. I'll show you how I wear it. There's not much room in here, but I can give you some idea of how to move it and use the stuff for the river. We can do it properly down at the pub tomorrow.' She tossed the thick blonde plait over her shoulder. 'That's if they'll still let us use it, of course.'

Ava had the feeling she didn't want to say any more, but she couldn't resist asking, 'How do you think they got in?'

Rose was straightening the costume, presumably trying to find space for Ava to get her head into it, although it still looked more like a heap of cloth than anything someone could wear. 'Well, the main way in is up a staircase from the pub itself, but the door at the top is supposed to be locked when we're rehearsing. I don't suppose anyone in our group checked it because we always come in through the fire escape at the back and that's the only door we have a key for. So the landlord or one of the cleaners might have left the other one open.'

'Who do you think did it?'

Rose sighed. 'No idea. Of course, Lally will assume it's all of a piece with what happened to Mel, but honestly I think these things are just coincidences. A run of bad luck.' She gestured to Ava to take off her sweatshirt and when she went to unzip her jeans, she waved a hand. 'That's OK, I wear green footless tights underneath, but you'll be fine with your jeans for now.'

As she pulled the costume over Ava's head and helped her find the armholes she said, her voice muffled by the fabric, 'Anyway, if there is someone out there who wishes us ill you needn't worry. It all started before you came so they can have nothing against you.' She pulled Ava's hair from the neck line and let it slip down behind her, standing back to take a long look. 'Yeah, that fits pretty well and I don't think we need do any alterations.'

They practised with the costume and the fabric river for a while, laughing as they bumped into each other in the cramped space or trod on the fabric. At one stage Ava got it so twisted around her legs that she could only fall on the bed laughing as Rose, almost overwhelmed with giggles, tried to extricate her. But Ava soon felt confident that she'd get it right when she was in a bigger space with more room to manoeuvre.

'OK, sit by the mirror and try out some of the ornaments I use in my hair,' Rose said, lowering herself onto the bed with a big sigh. She sounded tired.

After all the laughter, Ava was still smiling as she tried different things with her hair, but when she looked at Rose's face, reflected in the mirror, it was serious, almost grim. She was probably just concentrating. All the same, it was unsettling and Ava couldn't help thinking back to the way the faces of Lally, Joel and Paddy had seemed to become mask-like when she'd looked at them in the kitchen from the dark garden.

Rose, still agile despite her bump, and with her energy recovered, jumped up and leaned over Ava's shoulder. She picked up a glittery slide and looped a hank of Ava's hair through it, then dangled a long green earring beside Ava's cheek. Somehow, with her cheekbone exposed and glittery shadows playing on it, her face took on a mysterious quality and Ava could see that, with the right makeup and lighting, the effect would be quite sinister. Perfect for a vengeful goddess.

Head to one side, Rose studied her as Ava fiddled with a piece of green chiffon, trying to tie it at the back of her head. Then she came closer, resting her own warm cheek close to

Ava's, their eyes next to each other. Rose's pale blue-green gaze was unblinking, her voice so soft it was almost a caress. 'You look beautiful. Hardly need any of this and I know all the others are impressed. Brad hasn't stopped talking about you.'

As Ava dragged her eyes away and moved back on the little stool Rose smiled, a preoccupied smile, her voice still the almost-whisper that felt hypnotic. She picked up a twist of Ava's hair, just as Brad had done, and held it out to one side, dancing her fingers along its length. 'And Brad is right. This lovely stuff is perfect for the goddess.'

Ava's breath had caught in her throat. Something was going on here that she didn't understand. Then Rose gave a huge laugh and fell back on the bed, her bump sticking up as she lay there laughing as if she had said something hilarious. 'Your face,' she said. 'You should see your face.' Ava turned to her and Rose pulled herself upright, grinning hard. 'Did I spook you? I was channelling my goddess persona. That's how I do it, only louder for the audience, obviously. It's a shame we aren't filming instead because I think *sotto voce* or even a whisper would be much more effective.'

Ava pulled all the slides and ribbons out of her hair and nodded. 'I can see that, but I'm sure it works brilliantly anyway.'

Rose began rolling up some of the fabric. 'Well, you'll see when I perform it next week. I'm actually quite nervous about what you'll think.'

Feeling silly after her overreaction, Ava managed a laugh that she hoped sounded genuine. 'I bet you're not half as nervous as I'll be tomorrow when you come to the rehearsal.'

The usual warmth was back in Rose's voice. 'No need for nerves at all. I've heard such good things, I know I'm going to be impressed.' She stood and put her hands on Ava's shoulders. Their eyes met in the mirror again. Rose's really were an unusually pale greenish-blue. 'I do hope we're going to have the chance to act together one day.'

Then she turned away and headed for the door. 'Come on, let's see what we can sort out for dinner.'

Chapter Twenty-Two

There was a strong smell of paint in the room above the pub next morning and they opened all the windows because Rose in particular found it difficult to bear. 'I'm sorry,' Brad said, bringing her a chair where she could get the best view of Ava in the first rehearsal. 'There was no other way to cover up the graffiti.'

Apparently, Paddy had told them last night, the landlord was rather pleased when he saw how they had cleared up. 'The walls were in a pretty bad state already. Badly in need of a coat of paint. And the rest of the mess was mainly over the floor – all our tea break supplies tipped out and thrown everywhere.'

Lally, when she'd arrived back at the house, had been as upset as Rose had predicted, especially when Mel had blurted out that the graffiti used all their names and consisted of some obscene cartoons of various members of the group. 'Only Ava escaped, which is understandable, but she probably won't get off so lightly next time,' she'd said, swallowing down a glass of brandy and scrubbing a hand across her eyes.

Brad said he'd been onto the police and really believed they were taking things seriously this time. 'When I sent the pictures I'd taken of the graffiti, and it was obvious they were personal attacks on us, they said it sounded as if it might be linked to what happened to Mel. I think something will start happening now.'

Although Paddy's expression as he ate steadily didn't suggest he was convinced, and Joel raised an eyebrow at Ava, it seemed the others had decided to let it go for now. And they all had an early night, Mel coming through Ava's room before she was in bed and giving her a little peck on the cheek. 'Sorry it's all so shitty,' she said. 'Believe it or not things used to be really good.' At the door to the attic her encouraging smile was belied by the black smudges of makeup under her eyes.

But the rehearsal next morning for the school performance worked so well, everyone became quite buoyant. They were wearing their costumes for the first time and using the lights and sound effects, which made it feel more real. For schools these were kept minimal to make it easier to set up and perform in a hall or a gym. Lally had come to watch, along with Rose, and she acted the part of the audience enthusiastically, laughing and even whistling a couple of times until Paddy told her it was distracting. 'Not at all, I've watched at schools and seen the reactions. Definitely heard the odd whistle,' she said.

When they broke for coffee, Ava pulled up a chair next to Rose and away from the others, nervous to hear what she thought. She needn't have worried, Rose beamed at her, 'You were great and it'll be even better with a proper audience.'

They ran through the adult play afterwards, trying it exactly as if for a real performance. The props and effects were far more complex than those for the school show and Ava was amazed, when the main lights were cut and only the acting space illuminated, at how brilliantly the lighting and sound worked, especially during her big scene.

It was the first time she had worn the costume to rehearse and the first time she had tried out the manoeuvres with the fabric river in a realistic space, and it was difficult to remember everything she had practised with Rose at the cottage. She had to come on in darkness, arranging herself amongst the fabric that served as the river so that with her costume of the same material she, hopefully, wouldn't be noticed until she moved.

Dominic and Joel had worked out the perfect way to make the lights suggest ripples and sparkles of light on water, managing to make it beautiful and sinister at the same time. Together with the eerie music, which was accompanied by some ethereal wordless singing from Mel, she imagined the effect would be spine-chilling. And straight afterwards the launch into a brightly lit and bawdy scene would make a wonderful contrast.

Ava was so caught up in the play that she forgot to be nervous. It was only when the lights came up and she saw Rose looking at her that the anxiety kicked in. She was also tired after two energetic performances, so told herself it was no surprise that her knees felt weak. But when she sat beside Rose she was very aware of the hard, almost painful beat of her heart and how hot she was under her multi-layered costume.

First she had to listen to Paddy complaining that, although nothing had actually gone wrong, everyone had been lacking in energy. 'We don't usually do the two performances one right after the other,' Mel said.

'I know, I know, and I think we should stop for today. Except I'd like to go over her goddess moves with Ava and then run that scene again with Brad.'

Rose turned to Ava and her translucent greenish gaze was kind. 'It was good, but you can't act that scene with as much power as it needs until you're really confident with the moves. I can stay as well if it won't put you off.'

'No, stay, please. I want your help.'

At that Rose leaned close, with a little chuckle. 'Very wise. Between us we can make sure Paddy doesn't browbeat you the way he used to with me.'

Lally had ordered sandwiches from the pub and when the others went down to eat, she, Paddy and Rose stayed in the rehearsal room talking through both performances as they ate. When they tried Ava's moves, Paddy left most of the directing to Rose. At the end he said, 'That's good. You ought to do more directing, Rose. Let's call Brad up for a proper run-through of the whole scene. Then call it a day.'

Paddy worked the lights and they used just the recorded sound without Mel's voice and somehow Ava found it more difficult than with everyone involved. It felt awkward being so intimate with Brad when Rose was their only audience. The goddess, although she killed him in the end, began by seducing him. When they finished, Rose and Paddy didn't speak, the only sound breaking the silence coming from Brad lying on the floor with his eyes closed, his breathing loud. Ava found she was stifling her own breath, and untangling her legs from him and the clinging fabric, she jumped quickly to her feet.

Finally, and it seemed to take forever, Rose spoke, and she too sounded breathless, 'That was wonderful. With Mel's live singing to add even more atmosphere it'll be spectacular.'

Paddy gave a small laugh. 'Of course, you've never seen it before, have you, Rose? It certainly is a powerful scene.' Then he clapped his hands together, standing to put his chair with the others against the wall and coming back for Rose's. 'Well done, Ava, you're almost as good as the original.' Rose stood and let him take her chair, smiling and giving him a little thank-you nudge with her shoulder, although her gaze was on Brad, still stretched out on the floor.

Chapter Twenty-Three

The others had all stayed in the pub and were sitting together looking very happy, a couple of bottles of wine in front of them. Rose said, 'I'll drive back if you three want to have a few drinks. You deserve it.'

The pub was quiet and as the rest of them talked and laughed Ava didn't say much; she was too tired for one thing, but she felt very happy. It was so good to be doing the thing she loved and to know she was doing it well. Finally she felt like a real part of the group. The pub landlord called out to them now and then from behind the bar, obviously having decided to forget about the damage to his room – no doubt helped by the fact that it looked better than before.

When they finally got up to leave Ava felt woozy, but very cheerful. Someone asked where she was going for the weekend, but she pretended not to hear – didn't want to spoil her mood by thinking about it. Rose, obviously seeing no one was capable of cooking, suggested she drive them down to town to collect some fish and chips.

Paddy insisted on doing the ordering, bouncing out of the van looking much less dignified than usual while Mel staggered after him, shouting too loudly in the quiet street that she and Brad, who were vegan, wanted chips and pea fritters.

Back at the house, Paddy handed out bottles of beer from the fridge and they took their paper-wrapped parcels of food into the living room, eating with their fingers. Ava's salty cod and chips were delicious. Someone turned on music and she lolled back on the sofa, sandwiched between Mel and Lally. At some point Mel passed her a joint.

When she woke, she had no idea what time it was, but Lally had gone and Mel, next to her on the sofa, was snoring lightly. Otherwise the room was empty, only one small light left on.

On her feet, she felt shaky; she'd had too much to drink and the joint hadn't helped. Peering out into the garden she could just make out two figures, who looked like Joel and Paddy, both holding bottles of beer. The others must have gone to bed and when she'd negotiated the stairs, she heard low voices from Rose and Brad's room.

It was one of those drowning dreams. The water dark and cold as she thrust out with her feet desperately trying to touch the bottom of the river. The trouble was, her hair was caught in the waving weeds, pulling her down and down.

She jerked half-awake, but the sensation of something tugging at her hair was still there. She was lying on her side, long strands hanging over the edge of the bed and when she pulled them behind her neck, she almost expected to discover they were caught around something at the side of the bed. But, no, they flopped free. It had just been a dream after all.

Turning over, she closed her eyes. But the dream had been so vivid she was afraid to sleep again, even though she wanted so much to be alert and ready for the difficult weekend with Will. Best to lie quietly until her mind became calm again. That usually worked to lull her into a dreamless sleep.

A sound nearby had her eyes flying open. She didn't move, although her heart was beating fast. But it began to slow when she realised it would be Mel coming up late, unless it was her night-time visitor again, whether he was Joel or Brad. A sliver of light shone through her closed eyelids and she heard the stealthy opening of a door.

She thought it was the door to the hall, not the attic, but when she woke again, what could have been minutes or hours later, she heard the bed above creaking up and down, up and down in ever-increasing urgency. Until it stopped and there was silence.

Certain she wouldn't sleep again, she lay waiting, eyes open, asking herself if she wanted, or didn't want, to see who it was when he came down.

In the end it didn't matter. She slipped back into sleep and woke to daylight.

On the train to Gloucester she got a message from Will: he would be there in about an hour. So when her train arrived she looked for the hotel, then strolled around for a bit. It was another sunny day, although cold with a biting wind, and she was forced to retreat to a warm department store, looking through racks of clothes she had no interest in buying. Checking the time on her phone, she saw she'd missed another message. *Just arrived and checking in. See you in the hotel bar.*

She didn't want to start off on the wrong foot by leaving him hanging about and the sooner they met, the sooner she could say what she needed to. All the same she went into the toilets and checked her face, put on a bit more lipstick and brushed her hair. It would get blown about again as soon as she stepped outside, but it made her feel better. Except that it brought back the memory of that dream and the trapped hair pulling her down into the watery depths.

It had grown even colder outside, a few flurries of sleety rain coming down, but the hotel bar was welcoming, managing to be both elegant and cosy. The place was quite busy – she guessed with locals in for a Saturday afternoon drink as well as residents. Will was sitting in a corner reading a book and, in the moment before he spotted her, she saw him as if they had never met.

His chair was under an art deco wall lamp and his fair hair shone in the light. He'd had it cut recently and his dark jacket and open-necked blue shirt suited him really well. He always looked good but she could see he had made a real effort. It was impossible not to feel a little flutter of attraction. When he looked up and smiled at her, she could see a woman nearby give her the *What did she do to deserve him?* look she had got used to even before he became known in the soap. She knew most women would think her mad for what she was about to do.

He stood and kissed her. One of his sweet kisses that always used to make her knees wobble. When he heard her little laugh and stepped back asking, 'What?' she shook her head. It was impossible to answer without offending him.

He had a pint in front of him and had bought her a gin and tonic. She wasn't sure whether it was nice or irritating that he knew exactly what she would want.

'So, how's it going? With the rehearsals, I mean.' It was the right thing to say, so why did she feel that spike of annoyance? Perhaps because it was so right and she couldn't actually believe he was interested. Felt he had prepared it.

Nevertheless, when she talked about the plays, she couldn't hide her enthusiasm and he began to ask questions that seemed genuine. Brushing back his hair in a gesture she always used to love, he said, 'Yes, I've looked up some of Chimera's old reviews and it sounds as if their stuff is really original. I'm sure the writer…'

He paused and she supplied, 'Brad.'

'Yeah, Brad, seems to have something. He needs to get his work seen more widely, but that's not easy.' When she nodded, he asked, 'What about the music? Do they still have songs written by Dominic Bennison?'

'You've heard of him?'

'So have you – don't you remember Matt at uni? He never stopped playing that album. The guy produced just the one when he was something like sixteen then had a major breakdown and disappeared.'

That explained why the Chimera music had sounded vaguely familiar. 'Yes, they still use his songs, but he's left now so there won't be any more. It was all a bit messy, I gather.'

'Another breakdown?'

She shrugged and didn't mention the relationship with Paddy, just asked about his week but, unusually, he didn't seem keen to talk about it. 'Oh, you know, same old, same old. To be honest I'm getting fed up with it. Need to be moving on soon, I think. My agent says I should stay another year, but I don't know. When I see people like you all fired up and doing exciting new things, I feel like I'm wasting my time.'

He looked depressed and she put her hand on his. 'Of course you're not. *Factory Family* is going to open lots of new doors for you.'

'Is it? I wonder.' He gave her fingers a little squeeze before moving his hand to pick up his pint, swallowing it down in one then looking straight at her. His blue eyes glinted in the light. 'And I'm losing you too, which doesn't make it any easier.' When she didn't speak, he shook his head. 'Honestly, I can't blame you. I'm not the guy you fell in love with.'

She was speechless. This was so unlike him. Her throat hurt, remembering how wonderful it had been at the start. The urge to tell him he was being silly – they could still make it work – was very strong. But she knew it wasn't possible. 'Oh, Will. I'm so sorry. It's not just you, I've changed. We've both grown up, I guess, but we can stay friends.' She couldn't blame him for shaking his head on a tiny laugh and almost laughed at herself. 'I know that's easy to say, but I want us to try. It's not your fault or mine. We were just too young.'

Always before, he would have argued. Told her she was speaking with her mum's voice. She could almost hear him saying as he had so often, 'Just because your mum's first marriage was a disaster doesn't mean every couple that get together as teenagers are doomed to fail.' It was true that Daisy, although she tried to hide it and said she liked Will, clearly thought they'd got too serious too young.

But today Will just nodded. He seemed to have come to

accept the inevitable. Maybe he knew it really was best for both of them. And as she looked at him, she was overwhelmed with a wave of feelings. Sorrow, compassion and also love.

They sat for a few minutes, hand in hand, before he gave his brilliant film-starry smile. 'Do you think we can still use the double room I've booked, though?'

Her grin had him grabbing her bag from under the table and heading towards the stairs, bounding up so fast they were both breathless when they got to their door. And once inside it was so inevitable, and so natural, that they would fall together onto the bed.

Afterwards she lay with her head on his chest as he played with her hair, the way he always did. 'If that's what happens when we break up, we need to do it more often,' he said.

It had been lovely and she hoped they could end like this, rather than the way things had been with them recently. As he began to fidget – he could never lie still for long – she moved to her own pillow. He propped himself on his elbow, still holding a strand of her hair, saying, 'Sit up for a minute.' His voice no longer sounded sleepy, but puzzled and when he said, 'Turn around,' she did as he asked.

'What's the matter?'

'Your hair.'

'What's wrong with it? I only washed it this morning.'

'There's a chunk missing. Looks like a bit's been cut off.'

Chapter Twenty-Four

The rest of the weekend didn't go as smoothly as those first hours. Will had found a lovely restaurant for dinner and they talked about anything but their relationship, both keen to keep the mood of the afternoon from fading. But as they walked back to the hotel, he took her hand. 'This is the way it should always be with us.'

It was hard to keep to what she knew she must do when she could feel him so close to her. She swallowed. 'But you know it doesn't last. When we live together, we don't get on.'

He dropped her hand and turned away; his shoulders hunched. 'I can't understand why you keep saying that. I know things haven't been easy for you, but if you'd just let me help you it could all be different.'

They had been over this so many times. At first she had been only too happy to take his advice. Going to auditions he suggested and missing those he said would be a waste of her time. When she started ignoring him, he would get cross and go into one of his sulks. It didn't help that she knew she was losing confidence and it was showing when she did try for a job. In the end she'd started taking temp work in offices and shops, but he kept telling her she didn't need to work. He could keep them both.

They were walking as far apart as the pavement would allow and when she saw the hotel ahead, Ava said, 'Please, Will, I just want to make a success of this without any emotional distractions. I need it.'

Inside he stopped in the foyer. 'I'm going to the bar for a drink.' She didn't follow and he didn't look back. She must have been asleep when he came up to their room.

Next morning, she woke to find him looking down at her. 'I'm sorry about last night, but I don't think you realise how hard this is for me. I had no idea you were so unhappy with us.' She wanted to say that was because he never listened when she tried to tell him, but it was too late for that. He lay down beside her again. 'I understand if you need a break to think things over and to try and make a go of it with this Chimera, but can we just call it a break rather than an ending?'

She couldn't help sighing; wishing this could be easier. 'I don't think it matters what we call it, but I don't want to think things over. All I want for the moment is to make this job work. And you should be free to get on with your own life.' They were silent for a long time, then she said, 'Anyway, I wouldn't be surprised if you get a big offer soon. You said your agent is putting out feelers in America. If something like that happens you won't want to be thinking about me.'

His, 'All right, I get it. You've made up your mind,' was gruff, but he kissed her forehead very gently.

She swallowed. 'What about all my stuff at the flat? I can't get back for a while.'

He stroked her hair. 'Don't worry about it. I'm not planning to move anyone else in right away.'

She went down to the hotel car park with him. Standing beside his beloved old BMW sports car, he said he wanted to come and see one of the shows. 'I'll just turn up some evening. Won't make a fuss or any demands, but I'd love to see it. And I know it's going to be good.' Then he gave her a warm hug, but didn't kiss her, whispering, 'Better start as we mean to go on.' He sounded almost relieved. But as she watched him drive away, turning back at the exit for a final wave, the tears she hadn't realised were going to come, bubbled over and she had to stand with her face close to the hotel wall, hoping she couldn't be seen.

On her train, however, she wasn't thinking about Will himself, but what he'd said about her hair. He had repeated it just now before they said goodbye. 'You know I've been looking at your hair over the weekend and you're wrong. It *has* been cut with scissors. The line's too straight to be anything else.'

She had an answer ready for him. 'It must have been Rose. She helped me style it for the show with lots of ornaments and slides. I think one of them got stuck and she took it out. Didn't realise she'd used scissors.' It was a lie, but she couldn't have him worrying.

But it was very worrying for her. Unless she was going mad and had chopped at her own hair, someone else must have done it while she slept. Surely it couldn't be connected with the spate of cruel tricks being played on Chimera? If it was, that must mean the pranksters, whoever they were, had access to the house and that they were targeting her too.

That was chilling, but it was just as frightening to think it might be a member of the group and she felt sick at the thought of one of them leaning over her with a pair of scissors while she slept. Sick and angry. And her first instinct was to tell everyone as soon as she got back to the cottage and demand an answer.

But presumably whoever had done it had wanted to upset her and she wasn't sure she could ask the question without showing that it had done just that. Because she couldn't deny they had succeeded. Even thinking about it made her shiver and what a laugh the evil bastard would have if she broke down and cried when she talked about it.

She wondered about confiding in Joel: asking him to try and find out who it was. She felt most at ease with him and he could talk to everyone else more calmly than she could. But she had to face the fact that it might be him, especially if he was Mel's nocturnal visitor. Paddy seemed the least likely contender simply because he slept in the annex and they'd had very few interactions outside rehearsals. But then she remembered how cold he had been at first. And he was still aloof, which could hide any amount of resentment.

Then there was Rose's odd behaviour when they were working on her hair. She had to be a suspect. In fact wasn't it possible she had done it while they were playing about with the ribbons and slides? It could have happened much like the story she'd told Will, but surely Rose would have told her what she was doing? She couldn't help remembering that strange hypnotic voice and wondering if she could have been so lost in the moment, she could have missed her hair being cut.

She shook her head. It was no good trying to narrow it down because any of the others might have a secret agenda or have been playing a not very funny joke, expecting an indignant Ava to start shouting about it next morning. After all, no real harm had been done.

All the same, she knew she would find it difficult to sleep in that room again.

It was growing dark as she walked back from the station. Her bag wasn't heavy, but it was uphill most of the way and the cold wind had returned, blowing into her face and straight down into her lungs. She had to stop for a moment when she got to the pub. Warmth and light wafted through the open door and she heard a burst of laughter. For a moment of paranoia she imagined all the members of Chimera were in there, talking and joking about what they had done to her.

Taking in a punishingly cold breath, she hurried past. It was ridiculous, but if any of them were in there she didn't want to see them and she certainly wasn't in the mood for socialising.

Chapter Twenty-Five

When she reached the cottage, she still hadn't decided what to do, but felt calmer, as if the answer would present itself. Rose, making tea in the kitchen, smiled and asked how her weekend had gone. Brad was at the table working on his laptop, looking up to give her a quick, 'Hi, Ava,' before tapping away again. When she asked if everyone else was back, Rose said Lally was away until the morning while Joel and Paddy were down at the pub. Mel was in her room.

That was when she knew what she had to do. Running upstairs and on up to the attic, she tapped on Mel's door, then tapped again. When there was no answer, she took a breath and pushed it open, knowing she had to do this now, before thinking about it made her decide it was a bad idea. The room was in semi-darkness, lit by only two of the coloured lamps. Mel sat at one of her keyboards wearing headphones, which explained why she hadn't heard. She looked surprised, but took off the headphones and smiled. 'Come in, come in, sorry about the mess.'

Ava noticed the photo frame she had clutched so tightly after her instruments were damaged, sitting next to her on the table. It held a picture of a woman with red hair in a shiny bob, smiling as she held a violin. Looked as if she was on stage after a concert. Mel's mum, she guessed, with the same elfin prettiness.

Beside it sat a glass of brown liquid, which must be brandy. But Mel seemed sober enough, although her eyes looked strange. They were a mottled kind of grey or blue, like smooth pebbles and the lids were red as if she had been crying. But the effect was most likely caused by the reddish orange light from the lamp next to her and the fact that, for the first time since Ava had met her, she wasn't wearing her usual black makeup.

Another deep breath, then she launched into it. 'Mel, I'm sorry, but I'm having problems sleeping. I know you have to come through my room to get up here and, like I said at the start, that's fine.' She was finding it difficult to speak now, her breath coming in little gasps. Mel looked at her, expressionless, giving no clue as to what she expected to hear; giving no help.

'The problem is, I didn't realise there might be someone else passing through as well. Coming through in the middle of the night.' There was a flash of expression that Ava couldn't interpret in Mel's eyes, but she had to plough on. 'The thing is, it's really disturbing being woken like that with someone creeping back and forth and I can't sleep afterwards, or if I do I have nightmares.'

The orangey light gave Mel's pale face a weird glow and when she smiled, her eyes seemed to disappear. 'And I suppose you hear noises from up here too?'

Ava smiled too, 'Well, yes, that bed does squeak quite a bit.'

Mel laughed, taking a swig from her glass, holding up the bottle that must have been beside her on the floor, and pointing to a glass on the bedside table. It would be more relaxed if they were both drinking so, although she didn't like brandy, Ava poured herself a little and took a sip, sitting on Mel's bed.

Mel came over and sat next to her. 'You know who it is, don't you?' When Ava shook her head, she chuckled and lay back on her pillows. 'But you've guessed?'

Embarrassed, Ava shook her head again, 'No, how could I?' She was very aware of Mel watching her with an odd calculating look that she couldn't interpret and the silence went on for so long she felt forced to say something. 'It's none of my business anyway.'

As if making a decision, Mel sat up, sitting with her arms wrapped tight around her bent knees. She was gazing into a gloomy corner of the room and the name came out as a whisper. 'It's Brad.'

Ava knew it was wrong to feel that ripple of relief. It would surely be better for everyone if it was Joel rather than Brad. Poor Rose. But she told herself it might be an arrangement they were all happy with. Some people didn't rate monogamy. The words came out before she knew she was going to speak. 'Does Rose know?'

'I imagine so. After all, I was with him first.' She held out her arm and, in the dim light, Ava could just make out the tattoo on her wrist – fancy intertwined letters, B&M.

That was a surprise and it must have been obvious in her face. After one long look at her, Mel closed her eyes. 'We were together for two years before Rose made her move on him, but he still can't keep away from me. And there's nothing she can do about it except pretend it isn't happening.' Her voice was sleepy, sounding half-drunk.

It was difficult to know what to say. 'How did you break up in the first place?'

'Rose looks so sweet and innocent, but she set out to get him and she managed it for a while, but now he feels trapped and knows it was a mistake.'

Ava had thought Brad was all right, but at this moment she despised him. Still in that sing-song voice, Mel said, 'She's trying to get me out. That's why they wanted you. Someone who can take over the music when she gets rid of me.'

That explained her strange remark on that first night. A reason perhaps to make her resent Ava and to do something spiteful, liking cutting a chunk from her hair, to frighten her away. Well it wouldn't do that, but she wasn't prepared to put up with being scared to go to sleep. So she said, 'Well I can promise you I won't be taking over from anyone who doesn't want to leave, so you can relax about that. But, Mel, it just isn't fair that I have to lie there while people creep through my room and back in the middle of the night. Like I said, I can't sleep and I won't be able to work if I don't get enough rest.'

Mel sat up, suddenly alert. 'OK, you take this room then and I'll have yours. I'll move the instruments that are too big downstairs. There's a walk-in cupboard that used to be a pantry and most of them should fit in there. We can do it right away if you want. I can finish taking away all my stuff tomorrow.' She jumped to her feet looking completely sober and full of energy.

It was the best solution for Ava, but she paused. 'Are you sure that will work?'

A smile spread slowly from Mel's lips to her eyes. 'Yeah, no problem. Just knock if you want to come through when you think I'm not alone. Lally won't care if she hears noises in the night.' Then the smile grew wider. 'Are you thinking about Rose?' When Ava didn't answer that smile seemed to falter. 'I can see you are, but there's no need. Rose is a lot tougher than she looks.'

Chapter Twenty-Six

It was odd being up in the attic, with evidence of Mel all around her. She had changed the bedding, but Mel had only taken her mum's photo and her keyboard down so far. The drawers and the wardrobe were still full of her clothes, Ava's own stuff was in her bags on the floor.

Even when Mel's things were gone, she knew she wouldn't like it as much as the pretty little room downstairs. She had exchanged the view of the wide fields for a patch of sky that she could only see by lying on the bed. And there was a musty smell that she knew would be difficult to shift without windows to open.

Although she was sure she would hear anyone coming up the stairs and should feel safe, she couldn't relax until she had wedged a chair in front of the door at the top. Even then she found the dim corners of the room with their shadowy beams disturbing and she doubted she'd be able to sleep tonight until she was completely exhausted.

At least she wouldn't be performing or rehearsing for the

next couple of days. Just watching Rose do her last shows. So she didn't need to be particularly alert. To tire herself out she fired up her laptop, deciding to find out what she could about Dominic Bennison.

The first picture she came upon could have been a younger version of the man she'd seen heading to the station, but it was impossible to be sure. He was certainly blond and wearing dark-framed glasses, but he was just a boy, a nerdy-looking boy hunched over a piano. The Chimera website still featured him rather than Joel. They obviously hadn't got round to updating it and from the way the rest of the group looked, the photos were quite recent. But there were none with him in spectacles, which made it difficult to link him to the guy Joel had asked her about.

Continuing to search, she found a few articles about him. They were all around ten years old. From the time of his brief moment of fame. Apparently he was at a school for musical prodigies, expected to make a splash as a concert cellist or even a conductor. But he had abandoned his studies to produce an album of his own composition, playing many of the instruments himself.

The later articles mentioned his breakdown and then there was nothing. When she looked up the reviews for the Chimera productions that Will must have checked out, they were from much less prestigious publications, either local newspapers or online blogs. Nearly all mentioned the music as a highlight of the shows, listing Dominic Bennison and Mel Gower as composers, but it was only *The Stage* that referred to his past moment of fame – *some may recall Bennison's album,* Myriads, *written when he was only sixteen. It's good to see he's back working after disappearing for so many years.*

When she ran out of things to read about Dominic, she found herself looking up stuff on *Factory Family*, lingering on pictures of Will. One showed her with him and she smiled because they looked so happy together. There were more with Mariella looking as much like a couple in love as did Ava and Will. She knew it was acting and, anyway, it shouldn't matter to her now, but she felt a pulse inside that was almost painful; wondering how she would feel when there was a real new girlfriend beside him. It wasn't healthy doing this and she switched off and lay down, closing her eyes and trying to ignore the tears that welled from under her lids.

She woke from a deep sleep to a silence so profound it felt suffocating. When she turned over to look out of the window a wave of confusion went through her and she sat up staring into the dark. Then she remembered, she was no longer in the pretty bedroom where grey light always filtered through the curtains, but in the windowless attic. Staring up through the skylight she saw a hazy moon and a few stars.

And then she heard what must have wakened her. A series of low whistles coming from somewhere outside, but close by. It was nothing, probably just someone walking along the lane next to the cottage, but she switched on the bedside lamp to check that the chair was propped against her door.

It was still there, but she regretted turning on the light. It had a blue bulb and spread a cold halo over and around the bed, leaving the rest of the huge room with its black beams and high, high ceiling in gloom. Switching it off again she shivered and pulled the covers close, wondering if she would have been better staying in the room downstairs.

And of course, now she was awake, she needed the toilet. One thing she hadn't thought about was that she would have to pass where Mel was sleeping to get to the bathroom. She didn't turn on the light again, but opened the door at the top of the stairs and stood listening. There was no sound from downstairs, so she crept down to the other door and, holding her breath, slipped through the room keeping her eyes away from the single bed.

Once inside the bathroom, the light almost blinded her and with eyes adjusted to the brightness, it was tricky getting back to her room and she had to grope her way up the stairs. But when she was in bed again her mind began whirling. She'd been so focused on getting through Mel's room without disturbing anyone that it was only now she registered how silent it had been. Not a hint of movement. Or even of breathing.

Mel wasn't there.

Next day, in the bustle of getting breakfast and loading everything into the van for the show, no one commented on the fact that she and Mel had changed rooms. Perhaps none of them had noticed. Ava had slept badly after her bathroom visit and she was angry with herself. The room swap should have helped, instead she was making it into another problem, which was ridiculous. It didn't matter what Mel did. Whether she stayed up late, roamed around in the middle of the night, or crawled into someone else's bed, it wouldn't affect Ava anymore. And she would get used to the different sounds that carried into the attic and through the shadowy spaces up there. As soon as she could get to town again, she'd buy new clear lightbulbs.

Lally wasn't back by the time they all piled into the van, presumably making a leisurely return from her weekend because she wasn't needed at the school. As Ava wasn't performing today, the only thing she could do was to help to set up the rudimentary scenery in the school hall, while Rose discussed the organisation of the morning with one of the teachers. As the kids and the rest of the staff filed in she found a seat where she would be able to see exactly what Rose did. It was strange being back in a school hall for the first time since she'd been a teenager herself and she knew she'd be horribly anxious when she came to actually perform. For today she would try to enjoy the show and to pick up as many tips from the way the rest of them interacted with the kids as she could.

Rose, in particular, was really good with that aspect; somehow making it impossible for the youngsters to feel embarrassed or to refuse to do what she asked as she guided them through their small roles in the scenes. She was made for working with kids – Ava wasn't sure the same applied to herself.

While they loaded the van afterwards, Rose stayed in the hall talking to a couple of the teachers. Ava came back to tell her they were ready to leave and as they left the hall together, Rose wiped her eyes.

Chapter Twenty-Seven

Back at the cottage, Ava felt restless. They would be doing the other play tomorrow evening, the adult one – *Dark Matter* – with Rose performing again, so there were no rehearsals. Mel was clearing the attic room of her stuff and said she didn't need any help, and although Ava had offered to cook the evening meal, it was too early to start on that.

No one was around downstairs and when Lally, who had been working up in her bedroom, which also served as her office, came down for a break Ava suggested she help with some of the routine office stuff. 'Otherwise I'll go out for a walk. The weather has turned so nice again.'

Lally looked into the sunshine-filled garden. 'Actually, I'm about up to date with everything, so, if you want company, I'll come with you.'

It was what she had hoped. Apart from Joel, Lally was the one she felt most able to talk to, maybe because she seemed a bit disconnected from the rest of the group. As they left the cottage, Lally pointed along the lane in the opposite direction to the pub and the town. 'Let's go this way for a change.'

The lane was quiet, clumps of Spanish bluebells sprouting beside the hedgerows. After a while they climbed over a gate and headed along the side of a field, the earth in dry ruts that were almost painful to walk on. A gap in the fence at the end took them onto another lane. Lally said, 'So you've swapped rooms with Mel, have you?'

'Yes, I wasn't sleeping well where I was.'

Lally stayed silent, as if she understood completely but Ava, hoping for more, said, 'She told me, she and Brad were together before he and Rose became a couple.'

At the end of the lane they came to a grassy space dotted with a few benches. Lally had looked at her with surprise when she mentioned Mel and Brad and it crossed Ava's mind that Mel might have been lying. She shouldn't have said anything.

But Lally headed for a bench and sat down. This area was considerably higher than the cottage and although there was a similar view, it was made more spectacular by the height. The fields stretched all around and down to the tiny blue strip of river and the little grey boxes of the town at the bottom. 'Yes, Mel and Brad were a thing for a couple of years. In fact,' she glanced at Ava, 'I went out with him for a while too. That was before Mel and before I realised I preferred women.' A smile at Ava. 'I guess you could say Chimera is just a tiny bit incestuous.'

She knew she needed to be careful now, but had to ask. 'But Rose and Mel get on all right, don't they?'

A snort of laughter and a touch to her forearm. 'Well, Mel can be a bitch and I think she resents Rose for everything. The fact that she's got Brad, that she's having his kid, but also the fact that everyone loves her. But that's just Mel and if you accept that she doesn't seem to want to be happy, then she's OK.'

It was impossible to ask outright if Lally knew whether Brad was still sleeping with Mel. And thinking of Mel's calculating look, she wondered again if that was actually true. It could still have been Joel going up those attic stairs.

Lally jumped to her feet. 'There's a nice little café over there if you fancy some tea and cake.' Without waiting for an answer, she walked on.

When they were sitting in the café, with tea in a flowered pot and two huge pieces of chocolate cake in front of them, Ava was relieved when Lally said, 'While we're on the subject of our incestuous little group, I might as well fill you in on the Dominic debacle.' She forked a chunk of cake into her mouth, chocolate staining her teeth as she talked. 'I hadn't thought of it before, but it's Brad we all have in common – apart from you and Joel, of course.'

'I thought everyone met at university.'

'Most of us did but Brad is really the common denominator. I went out with him before he met Mel and then moved on to Rose, but he and Dominic already knew each other. They were at some posh private school together as kids. Dom was younger than Brad and I gather Dom left early. His parents thought he was getting corrupted or something. I suppose because he was just coming out as gay. So they put him in that hothouse school for young musical geniuses and he had the first of his breakdowns.'

'But he wrote the album too.'

'Yeah, although when I met him, if anyone asked about

that, he usually denied any knowledge. We were into different kinds of music anyway so no one cared. And he was such a sweet guy he was really popular, although I don't think he realised. Good-looking too and I always thought he and Paddy were made for each other.'

She tucked into her cake with so much gusto Ava couldn't help smiling. It made her feel hungry too and they ate for a while without speaking. Like Joel, Lally was easy company. When she pushed back a black curl that had fallen into her eye and left a smudge of chocolate on her forehead, Ava laughed and pointed to it. Lally rubbed it with her fingers, but they were so chocolatey she made it worse. Handing a paper napkin to Ava, she almost choked on a crumb as she waved her hand in front of her mouth. 'For fuck sake do it for me, will you?'

When Ava had managed to get rid of most of the mess, she sat back. 'What happened with Paddy and Dominic then?'

Although she'd eaten all her cake, Lally scraped at the mess of chocolate on her plate, her voice soft and low. 'Honestly, I hardly know. It was just so awful; so sad. Dominic got the idea Paddy was playing around, which I'm sure wasn't true. And he became completely paranoid. Of course with Paddy being bi and always having dated women before Dominic, Dom was jealous of everyone.'

Ava focused on brushing crumbs from her lap, avoiding Lally's eye. Mel had made a point of telling her Paddy was gay. She wondered why.

Lally was still talking. 'Then one day Dom just upped and left. Went back to his parents in Bristol. The parents he claimed to hate.' She swallowed the dregs of her tea and pulled a face because it must have gone cold.

As they left the café Ava asked, 'Had these weird things started to happen before he left?'

When Lally swung round fast towards her, Ava stepped back because she looked so angry, dark eyes flashing. 'Oh, no, don't even think it. Dominic would never do anything like that. If he wanted to hurt anyone it would be himself.'

Feeling almost scared, and regretting the way the whole mood had changed, Ava swallowed. What a clumsy idiot she was. She touched Lally's arm. 'I'm sorry, that wasn't what I meant.' It wasn't true. That was exactly what she had been thinking, but she regretted upsetting Lally.

Lally rubbed her face with her sleeve. 'It's all right. You don't know him. It's just that, although there's never been anything remotely romantic between us, I really love the guy. We were always the best of friends. There were times when I think we were closer than he was with Paddy.' Her voice disappeared into a sob as she shook her head. 'Oh, Ava, I'm so worried about him. I've tried to contact him, but he doesn't reply.'

Ava stood helplessly, not knowing what to do. But Lally solved the problem by clutching her arms around herself and striding away. When Ava caught up with her, she muttered, 'I'm sorry about that, but I just miss him so much and I worry about what he might do.'

Chapter Twenty-Eight

The next couple of weeks passed quickly and Ava enjoyed working so much she felt happier than she had for ages. Will messaged her a few times just to ask how things were going and she replied in the same way. They didn't speak and she tried not to let herself think about him. It wasn't difficult during the day. Even in the evenings she was fine because Chimera always ate together, then there'd be games of dominoes or cards or trips down to the pub. She would never like the attic room much, but with a bit of a clean and some new lightbulbs it felt less grim. Most importantly, she was sleeping better.

Rose only came to the occasional performances and Ava could feel herself growing in confidence with each show. The others were all enthusiastic about how she was developing her roles. Even Mel told her she was brilliant and Paddy's nods and grunts felt like huge compliments coming from him. Rose, getting larger all the time, seemed genuinely pleased that she was a success.

On a rare day when there were no performances, she walked down to town with Joel and Lally. It was pleasant chatting with them and she felt she could really call them friends now. They all had stuff to do and agreed to meet for lunch in Joel's favourite pub. When she got there Joel was already sitting in a little courtyard at the back. He held up his phone. 'Lally just messaged me, we're not to wait for her, she's at the opticians getting new glasses and might be a while.'

They ordered food and ate in friendly silence. Then Joel said, 'You seem to have settled in very well. Do you think you might stay on when Rose comes back to work?'

Although she'd thought about it, she shook her head, 'I don't think Chimera will need me.'

He chewed for a bit then took a gulp from his pint. 'Unless Mel moves on.'

'Is she likely to?'

A head movement that was neither a nod, nor a shake. 'Well, she's clearly not happy about Brad and Rose. And everyone really likes you.'

That stupid flush of heat rose into her cheeks again. There was something about the way he was looking at her; something about his golden-brown eyes that she found really attractive. And was this his way of telling her there was definitely nothing between him and Mel? She said, 'But Mel's been with Chimera from the start. The group obviously means a lot to her.' A careful sip of her drink, fearing she might do something stupid like choke on it. 'And now those pranks have eased up, things seem so much nicer all round.'

Sitting back in his seat, Joel gave a little laugh. 'Although Mel isn't happy that the cops seem to have done almost nothing.'

Even Ava would have felt better if the police had found out who had been behind it all. Because if the car accident on her very first day was one of the so-called pranks then that was a real concern. But of course they hadn't reported it to the police. Without stopping to think, she found herself blurting out, 'I don't suppose it could be connected, but when I was sleeping in the little bedroom below the attic someone cut a chunk from my hair.'

Almost as soon as the words were out, she regretted them. For one thing she didn't want to think about the incident and she had determined never to mention it to anyone in the group. Joel had put on his sunglasses, but now he took them off, throwing them onto the table with a click of plastic against glass. 'What the fuck. When did this happen? I mean, was it when you were in bed asleep?'

She nodded. 'Yes, but it doesn't matter. I'm sure it was just a joke. I shouldn't have said anything.'

His eyes creased, the gold sparkle seeming to darken. 'Jesus, that's horrible. No wonder you wanted out of that room.' He put his hand over hers and squeezed for a moment, letting go and moving back in his seat as Lally appeared through the door.

They all walked back together. It was warm and sunny, a perfect day to be in the country. As they came out of the town and onto the path leading to the river, Lally put her arm through Ava's on one side and Joel's on the other and told them, 'I'm really glad you two have joined the company. We've all been together too long, needed some different people to spark us up.'

Joel said, 'But you were very upset when Dominic left.'

Instead of reacting as Ava had expected, Lally just made a noise that could have been a laugh or a snort. 'Yeah, well I might have picked different if I'd had a choice about who should go first, but it brought you to us so I'm not complaining.'

Standing on the bridge Ava looked into the water, those dark weeds making her sway with them. Lally grabbed her arm. 'Are you all right?'

'I'm fine, just went a bit dizzy. It happens to me sometimes when I'm on a bridge.'

Lally put a warm hand on her back, 'I get that too. The feeling that you might somehow be forced to jump in. But it must be worse for you with your mum drowning like that.'

Ava's breath caught in her throat. She couldn't recall telling anyone in Chimera how her mum had died, but Joel was saying, 'That must have been awful. Losing a mother so suddenly.'

Lally started walking ahead. 'It might have been a good thing in my case.'

They glanced at each other as they followed her and Ava guessed Joel was thinking the same as her: that it was strange for Lally to be so tactless. She touched his arm and spoke so only he could hear. 'I was so young it didn't really make much impact on me, and my dad married again when I was only about two and gave me the perfect stepmother.'

Joel squeezed her fingers and nodded, his smile saying more than any amount of sympathetic words. Then he ran ahead and said to Lally, 'OK, so what's your story?' Ava knew he was diverting the conversation to avoid any chance of her being hurt. It wasn't necessary, but she was grateful. And she tried to ignore the tingle in her fingers from his squeeze.

She heard Lally say, 'Oh god, don't get me started. I can't stand my parents. They had me, then a new baby every year. All girls until the sixth, their precious boy, came along. My mum never looked after any of them either. That was all down to me. And they wondered why I left home for good as soon as I could.' She was walking fast and realising they had lagged behind her, she turned to wait until they caught up, pulling up a long piece of grass and holding it to her lips to make a whistling sound.

Then she shook her curls and threw the grass to the ground. 'Chimera is my family now. And screw anyone who tries to damage it.'

Ava could feel rather than see Joel trying to catch her eye, but she looked down at her feet. As they passed the pub, no one spoke for long minutes, the only sound their breath as they climbed higher.

Finally, Joel said – and Ava could tell he was deliberately making his voice cheerful – 'Well, at least all those nasty things have stopped happening. So either the police scared them off or they've decided to turn their viciousness elsewhere.'

At that Lally rounded on him. 'Oh, but they haven't stopped happening. I've had to fend off loads of abusive emails to the Chimera account and my bike seat was covered in smashed eggs the other day. Not only that, but I'm certain other people are keeping things to themselves. Nothing big, but upsetting. And if nothing has happened to either of you two, it's because you're newcomers.'

Ava didn't dare look at Joel, just hoped he'd understand

that she didn't want the hair-cutting incident brought up. Thankfully he said nothing about it, but rested his hand on Lally's shoulder. 'I'm sorry. I thought it was all over.'

Lally trudged on and her voice was low and depressed. 'It's not over at all. And I'm really worried. Worried that they're just biding their time. Working towards something big. Something big and dangerous.'

Chapter Twenty-Nine

Maybe it was because Lally's words had scared her more than she would admit that Ava slept badly that night. Or maybe it was because her ears had tuned in to listen for that soft whistle coming from out there in the darkness. When it did come it brought her completely awake even though it was so low. She knew it was likely to be the same harmless person: someone who lived nearby, coming home from working late or leaving for an early shift, but that didn't stop her lying rigid, listening for it to happen again.

When after three or four notes it stopped and there was silence, she lay watching through the skylight as the shadows of grey cloud moved across the black of the sky.

At least that was the whistle done with, but if she was to sleep again she knew she had to persuade herself that Lally was being alarmist. And she couldn't really believe that the branch in the road had been put there deliberately. It was of a totally different order from the graffiti and the other small acts of vandalism.

But then the damage to Mel's instruments was different again and Mel was right that it seemed personal, as did Ava's hair, although that was nowhere near as serious. Perhaps someone in the group was using the other *pranks* as a smokescreen to get away with settling personal gripes. The more she thought about it, the more likely that seemed. Although why anyone would have a gripe with *her*, she couldn't imagine. Unless Mel really did believe she had been brought in to replace her, or there was more to Paddy's aloofness than just a dislike of change.

Anyway, she was beginning to think she might be able to allay their worries about that soon. Because she had almost decided she wouldn't stay on after Rose was back on form, even if they asked her. Although she liked some of the group, there was a strange vibe that she still found uncomfortable even now she had more or less settled in. No doubt the sense of something not right with the dynamics was heightened by the nasty things that had been happening, but, as Lally said, there was also something unpleasantly incestuous about the general atmosphere.

There was no denying that Brad was a talented writer and she loved being in *Dark Matter* so she would see out her agreed contract. It was very good acting experience and she wanted to prove she could make it on her own, without Will's advice or support. But she wouldn't be sorry to move on.

Having settled that in her mind she hoped she'd be able to sleep, but it was no good, and eventually she switched on the bedside light and tried to read a book she had picked up downstairs. It was one she guessed Brad had used to research some of the ancient British myths of nature gods he used in the play and was probably not the best reading to soothe her to sleep. Many of the spirits were as vengeful and malevolent as her own character in the play and it seemed the humans who shared the forests, hills and rivers with them had to spend a lot of energy placating their anger.

She was about to put the book aside when she heard a creak close by. Although she told herself it was just Mel moving in the bedroom below, it sounded closer than that. Listening, her breath held, she heard it again and knew it came from the little staircase that led up here and nowhere else – to the attic. There was someone right outside her door.

The tap and Mel's voice, just above a whisper, let her breathe again. 'Ava, are you awake?' She slid from bed and quietly moved the chair, climbing back in before answering that *yes, she was awake*. It would be embarrassing to let anyone know she had barricaded herself in.

When the door opened, Mel said, 'I saw your light. Thought you might like company if you can't sleep.' Without pausing for an answer, she curled up on the end of the bed. She was wearing a rugby shirt with wide green stripes and a turned-up collar. The shirt almost reached her knees and she scrunched her bare legs and feet under her.

Ava didn't want to talk, but since Mel was here she said, 'I keep getting woken up in the early hours by someone whistling outside, someone coming along the lane I'm guessing. Did it used to bother you when you slept up here?'

Mel chewed on her thumbnail. 'Nah, don't remember it.' But the smile, that was more of a smirk, suggested she was lying. Ava wondered why. Happy to let Ava feel spooked maybe?

But if she insisted on being here, it was worth finding out what she thought about Lally's theory. 'Have the police turned up anything about the damage to your instruments or any of the other things that have been happening?'

A head shake, her chin set as if tears might be threatening. 'They're fucking useless. Talked to me for ten minutes, gave me a crime number and filed their little report away after they ticked the boxes. When I rang for an update they told me they thought any connection with the other bits of vandalism was *highly unlikely*.' She put on a low voice with a fake West Country accent for the last two words. Together with the gormless expression that transformed her tiny face, it was impossible not to laugh. 'They said it was probably a robbery gone wrong. Apparently, burglars often damage stuff just for the fun of it and that they must have been disturbed before they could actually take anything.'

'Well Lally thinks it's all connected. And that whoever's doing everything is planning something bigger.'

Leaning her back against the end of the bed, Mel stretched her legs out alongside Ava's so she was forced to shift over. 'You and Lally seem to be getting on well.'

There was always a sense with Mel of something slightly malicious in whatever she said, but Ava remembered Lally telling her she was just a bitch who liked being unhappy. So it probably wasn't personal. 'Yeah, she's made me feel welcome.'

'Unlike some of the rest of us.' It sounded like a statement rather than a question, but Ava laughed. 'I didn't mean that at all. Everyone's been fine. I feel pretty settled now.'

'But some are finer than others, eh?' That undertone of sarcasm was definitely there, but she decided to ignore it. The bedside light gleaming on the pale skin of her legs, Mel rubbed her bare feet together, the toes painted different bright colours. Her feet weren't as pretty as the rest of her. Lumpy and with bent toes: dancer's feet. 'I hear you had a funny turn on the bridge today?'

The surprise almost made Ava come out with what she was thinking, *Why would Lally have told anyone about that?* But she guessed it was what Mel wanted, so she shook her head. Let Mel interpret that however she liked. But the barb, if that was what it was, had worked, and she felt hurt, as if Lally had betrayed her.

'You must find water a bit scary. Seeing what happened to your mum.'

Now Ava was angry and the horrible feeling she'd had more than once – that they might all be bitching about her behind her back – was there again. Swallowing it down, she tried to keep her tone neutral. 'How do you know about that?'

Mel was chewing another nail now. 'You told someone, didn't you? Lally? Or Rose and Brad at your audition. Them, or maybe it was Joel.' A shrug and a casual smile. 'I don't know.'

She searched her memory. Even though her mother's death had been so much on her mind lately, she would surely not have talked about it at a first meeting. And Joel had obviously known nothing until Lally mentioned it on the bridge. The drive from the station with Lally that first day, even before the accident, was hazy so could she have said something then? She was tempted to tell Mel to go away and leave her alone. Instead, she clenched her teeth and looked down at the duvet cover, running her finger along one of the wavy blue lines winding across the white cotton.

Arms above her head as she yawned, showing tiny white teeth and the tip of a pink tongue, Mel seemed perfectly at ease. 'Do you remember your mum at all?'

The image of a river with dark weeds swirling came flashing into her head, but she forced it away and then forced a smile. Mustn't let Mel see she had struck home. 'No, and my stepmother is perfect. So I'm not complaining.'

'Shame for your mum, though: to be replaced like that.'

'She wasn't. Both my dad and my stepmother talked about her all the time. There were pictures of her around the house and we visited her grave a lot. She and my stepmother were friends so she could tell me stories about my real mum that even my dad didn't know.'

Why was she feeling defensive and why had she blurted all that out? Mel was the last person she should be confiding in. But she was too tired to care and when Mel just swung her legs down and with another enormous yawn said, 'Ah well, we'd both better try and get some sleep,' she told herself it didn't matter. After all she had nothing to hide.

All the same, when Mel was gone, she still couldn't sleep. Each time she closed her eyes that image of dark water with coils of green churning through it came back. The reminder of her night terrors as a little girl. Had those nightmares really been fuelled by dim memories? It would surely have been impossible to know, at less than two years old, that an arm flailing in the water might spell tragedy and the overthrow of her world. And she probably hadn't seen even that, because no one else had noticed a thing.

She remembered seeing a painting by Breughel called *The Fall of Icarus*. The canvas is busy with everyday life, people ploughing the fields, or on board a sailing ship. It's only when you spot a tiny white leg in the sea that you realise it shows a boy drowning: young Icarus fallen from the sky. W. H. Auden wrote a poem about the picture because he was impressed by

Breughel's wisdom. The way he understood that individual deaths make no impact on the lives of most people. Her mother's last struggle against death had been like that. No one looking as she lost her hold on life.

Not for the first time she wanted to cry for the grief she had never really felt; for the guilt at having supplanted her mum so completely with a more perfect replacement. She wondered if her dad ever had the same feelings.

Chapter Thirty

Next morning she felt drained, but tried to hide it, especially from Mel, whom she was glad to see yawning over breakfast. It was going to be a long day. For the first time they were performing both plays, using a school hall for the kids' performance in the afternoon and the play for adults in the evening. There was nowhere else locally that was suitable and the headteacher was very happy to host them, providing part of the takings went into her depleted funds. 'There's so little of any kind of culture around here and many of these families don't even get to Gloucester very often, let alone London,' she said.

During the journey to the school, along winding country roads, Ava began to doze, jerking upright when her head touched the cool window on one side or Joel's shoulder on the other. But she must have slept because she was jolted awake by Rhianna's voice bursting from her phone. It was an unknown number so she didn't answer, but when whoever it was rang again and then a third time, she heard Brad mutter something, clearly annoyed, so she switched the phone off completely.

The first show went well and as always during a performance the adrenaline kicked in and she had plenty of energy, but when it was over, and the others followed one of the teachers to the staffroom to eat their sandwiches and have coffee, she excused herself. She was too tired to be hungry and needed to be alone.

When Rose had told her that Chimera shared a house, she had liked the idea, but hadn't realised how much she needed her own space. As an only child she was used to spending time by herself. Her parents were always there, but she could escape to her own room whenever she wanted. Even living with Will had left her plenty of time alone. But the others were always around in the cottage and Mel's visit last night showed her that even up in the attic she couldn't escape completely.

The school was on the edge of a tiny village, a hamlet really, because apart from a run-down-looking pub there was no centre. It didn't take long to get through the scatter of houses and out to the woods that surrounded them on all sides.

Stepping off the road she headed in amongst the trees. It was another warm day, almost hot, but off the exposed road the sun was gentle as it dappled through the canopy of spring leaves. Alone with birdsong and the tall silent trees she smiled, feeling totally content for the first time in so long. And when she came upon a misty sea of purple English bluebells she laughed out loud.

Walking through the flowers and down a long slope, enjoying the crackle of broken twigs under her feet, she came to a stream and sat beside it, revelling in the quiet. Even the birds had stilled. The only tiny sound was the water trickling over the shining stones in the stream. She was tempted to lie back and close her eyes, but she was so tired she didn't dare. If she slept she might miss the show. No one would know where to find her.

Folding her arms over her bent knees she looked around. This was the kind of ancient woodland she would imagine when she performed as the goddess in future.

Although she had tried to put it out of her mind, she couldn't help thinking about what Mel had said last night and feeling that stab of guilt again. The guilt at enjoying her childhood so much and hardly thinking about her poor mother. Being so glad to have Daisy in her place.

She wondered if her parents' marriage would have survived if her mum had lived. So many of her school friends had divorced parents, especially those who had married young. And her dad was so devoted to Daisy, she couldn't believe he had ever felt as much for anyone else. It did no good thinking like that. Who knew what might have happened if someone had been alert enough that day, or if her mum had managed to free herself? It was sad, but all over long ago and Ava could not have had a happier childhood, which was what counted. She jumped to her feet, brushing off her jeans.

As she turned, she heard a small crack of sound, a twig breaking, then softer still the whisper of something moving through the bracken. Motionless, she listened. She was a city girl. Had no idea what kind of animals might be in these woods: rabbits, foxes, badgers, she guessed. Creatures that would be more afraid of her than she need be of them. So the best thing was to stride forward making as much noise as possible. She couldn't remember exactly where the road was, but headed through the mist of bluebells.

That scuffling came again, this time from somewhere on her right. She veered a little to the left. But now it seemed to be behind her and she turned to look back towards the stream. No movement there and she couldn't see the stream either.

Standing in a shaft of sunlight, suddenly feeling too warm, she looked about her – all sense of direction gone. She had thought the woods silent, but now that scuffling and the cracks and rattles of brittle things being disturbed and broken seemed to be everywhere.

She hurried on, no longer sure if the rapid urgent crunches she could hear came from her own feet or from something else. The trees were denser here and she was sure she hadn't passed them on the way in. Leaning back against a thick trunk she tried to catch her breath; to get some idea of where she was.

But soon, instead of her eyes, it was her ears that were straining, almost certain she could hear those scuffling noises much closer now. But underneath them something else. Something that sounded like breathing.

A deep breath of her own to calm herself. It was either a big animal like a badger or her imagination.

Then.

A touch on her shoulder and when she jumped and yelped, it gripped her. Firm, warm and very real.

Chapter Thirty-One

She whirled round.

It was Brad. Only Brad. Smiling and saying, 'Hey, sorry, didn't mean to frighten you, but you're going the wrong way.' He squeezed her shoulder again.

Ava tried a laugh, her heart beating so hard and loud she worried he might hear it. Couldn't have spoken if she'd tried. But he smiled again and held out a hand, almost as if he meant her to take it, before turning away. 'I thought I'd better come and get you, you seemed to be gone a long time and these woods are deceiving. Easy to get confused.'

They were back at the bluebells before she realised she had been following him. 'How did you know where to find me?'

A nudge with his shoulder. 'Ah, wouldn't you like to know?' Then a laugh. 'No, I spotted you heading this way. I'd walked over here myself to make a call in private.'

By the time they reached the road, she was calm, her heart that had been beating so fast seemed to have slowed right down. *What an idiot, spooked by a few cracking twigs.* It seemed even more ridiculous when she realised how close to the houses and the school she had been all the time. Kids in uniform were streaming out of the gates and there was a steady parade of cars and buses taking others home. That explained why Brad had come looking for her. She had been longer than she'd intended.

The others were standing around the Chimera van, just outside the school hall, with the wide doors open, getting ready to set up for the evening performance. When Ava joined them Brad asked if she'd eaten, pointing to a bench nearby when she shook her head. 'Have your sandwiches now, then. We don't want you keeling over during the show.' Then he walked away saying he needed to phone Lally and Rose at the cottage.

There was less setting up to do than usual because they had left the lighting and sound equipment in the hall from earlier on. Joel normally did that, together with Brad, so this time he helped the rest of them with the scenery and props. They had finished by the time Brad joined them again.

Beckoning them all into a huddle, he obviously had something to tell them, something good by his expression. 'Lally's had a phone call to say a theatre critic from the *Guardian* is planning to see *Dark Matter*. They've asked for details of the itinerary and apparently she might turn up any evening in the next couple of weeks depending on her schedule. So this could be our big break.'

They were all excited. Brad, of course, was thinking of the play, but Ava realised it could be a wonderful opportunity for her too. She had a major role, probably the best part in the show, so this could really help her.

The performance was one of the best they'd ever done. Although Mel and Paddy didn't show it, Ava imagined they were as excited as she was and that seemed to give their acting an extra fizz of energy. Brad was a bit manic, clutching her too hard when she was trying to drown him and hanging onto her leg for longer than usual as he struggled in the fabric river. But it suited the part so it wasn't a problem. As they took their bows at the end Joel was smiling so widely, she almost laughed when she looked at him.

They stayed talking to the audience for an hour or so, as some teachers and parents served drinks, and when they finally headed to the van Ava was still buzzing. She switched on her phone again and saw three more missed calls, but this time they weren't from the unknown number. But from Will.

They hadn't spoken for a week or more and had exchanged just a few messages, saying very little, so she wondered why he was so keen to talk. Most likely it was some good news about work. He had been hoping to be up for an award. If so she was happy for him and also pleased that she could share something exciting of her own.

But now the evening was over, the tiredness she'd been fighting all day slammed into her. It didn't help that one of the fathers at the school had been very keen to keep her paper cup of wine topped up. She couldn't face talking to anyone, certainly not Will and in the van with all the others listening, so she turned the phone off again.

As they drove along the dark roads, with nothing to see but the dotted line of red cats' eyes and the shadows of trees and grey clouds above, she closed her eyes. But something was nagging at the back of her mind.

It was those phone calls, so many all at once, from the unknown number and then from Will. And Brad's news about the critic. Was that a coincidence or had it something to do with Will? She remembered him saying Brad's work should be better known. Will was very good at networking, so perhaps he had pulled some strings. He might even know the critic. It was going to be a great opportunity for the whole group, including her. But she couldn't help hoping it had nothing to do with him.

Back at the cottage, Rose had left some food on the Aga for them, but Ava had eaten too many salty snacks and downed too much wine after the show to want anything. She was also so tired she knew she would sleep as soon as she was in bed.

It may have been the whistle that woke her, but although she lay listening for a while she didn't hear it again. Her phone was on the bedside table, but still turned off, so she switched it on to check the time. 3 a.m. and almost at once the phone started beeping. Another missed call and this time a voicemail from Will. *What the hell is going on? Please phone me, I don't know what to do.*

What the hell? Her thoughts echoed his words. He sounded so strange. His voice so different she couldn't tell if he was excited, angry, or in a panic about something, but it was too late to phone him so she fired off a quick message. *Sorry performing all day so I missed your calls. What's up?*

Almost as soon as she sent it he rang, his voice cutting

through her own *Hello*. 'What the hell is wrong? You want me to call you urgently and then don't answer. I've been going mad here.'

This was so weird she couldn't speak for a moment and when she did all she could say was, 'I don't understand, I haven't phoned you for ages.'

She could hear him breathing slow and heavy, as if trying to calm himself. 'You called the studio. Left a message to get in touch with you urgently. They had to get me out of rehearsal. I thought you must have had an accident or something terrible had happened down there. When you didn't answer after I phoned you, I was beside myself. I've not been able to sleep and I was just about to ring your parents, to see if they knew anything.'

It was difficult to take in the torrent of words, but she fastened on the final bit. 'Thank god you didn't contact Mum and Dad because there's nothing wrong. Nothing wrong at all.'

A noise, something like a choke. 'Then for fuck sake why ring me at the studio? You know that's only for emergencies.'

'I didn't. I don't understand what you're talking about. Like I said, nothing's happened and I have never called the studio, today or ever. I wouldn't do that.'

For what seemed like ages she could hear him breathing and knew she was doing the same. Trying to work out what had happened. And then she realised and knew she had to tell him. 'Will, I think it must have been some kind of mean practical joke.'

The sound he made could have been a mirthless laugh, or a snort and she didn't blame him. 'You see, someone has been playing horrible pranks on people down here. On Chimera, I mean. I didn't think they would turn on me, but then there was that chunk cut from my hair…'

'I thought you said you knew how that happened.'

She bit her lip; she'd forgotten she'd lied to him about it. 'I realised it might not be what I told you, but it didn't seem important. And why ring the studio?' Even as she said it another thought surged into her mind and he was there at the same time.

'Someone must have got the number from your phone. Figured it would have more effect like that.' Although he couldn't see her, she nodded. It was the only thing that made sense because she had it in her contacts under *Will – emergency only.*

There was nothing to do, but apologise again and again to him. He told her it just wasn't on to have rehearsals disrupted. When she said nothing, his voice softened. 'Ava, it doesn't sound safe down there. Has anything else happened that you should have told me about? Are you in danger?'

The car swerving to miss the branch across the road, Mel's viola gouged with a knife, her rain stick smashed with a hammer, the shit through the letter box that next time might be a bundle of lighted rags. She said, 'No of course not. It's stupid and nasty, but not dangerous.'

'All the same. Snooping in your phone, cutting your hair. I call that more than stupid.'

'Look, Will, explain to the studio that it was a hoax call. Tell them I will never call you there so not to take messages that claim to be from me.'

Chapter Thirty-Two

After he rang off it seemed impossible that she would be able to sleep again, but amazingly she did; waking later than usual. There was no performance until the evening when they were doing the show in the room above the pub just down the hill so there was nothing to do until late afternoon. No need to get up. So she lay there thinking about the call from Will. Until she remembered what he'd said about almost ringing her parents and sat bolt upright, reaching for her phone. If someone had indeed got into her contacts list they would have been able to find *Mum and Dad* and their separate mobile numbers with no problem. It was Friday, a day when her mum didn't work, so she rang their landline right away.

'Ava, is something wrong?'

It was so unusual for her to call on a morning in the week that she could understand her mum's reaction, so she came in quickly. 'No, nothing at all. Well, just something silly that I need to warn you about.'

'Is it Will?'

She didn't have time to wonder why that question had come into Daisy's mind first. Had to make sure she was warned before she or Ava's dad had a fright like Will. 'No, well it is in a way. It's about something really annoying that just happened to him.' She could somehow hear the silence from Daisy. 'It's just that you need to ignore any messages from me that don't come from this number or where you don't recognise my voice. Someone seems to have hacked my contacts and called Will at the studio claiming to be me.'

The pause went on for a while. 'Are you sure it's not Will having a joke with you?'

'Of course not. Why would he do that?'

'I don't know. To have an excuse to call you, perhaps. I mean he's not happy that you've left him, is he?'

'It's not like that, Mum. We've decided to take a break, to see how things work out for us after a bit of time concentrating on our careers.'

'But it was your decision, not his, wasn't it? And he likes to call the shots.'

This was not the way she'd expected the conversation to turn and she couldn't keep the hard edge from her voice. 'I don't know what you mean. Will knows I need to stand on my own feet for a while. He's fine with it.'

'So long as you come back to him. I mean he's always been quite possessive.'

It sounded so bitter, so unlike Daisy, that Ava was angry now. 'I don't understand why you and Dad are always against Will. And this has nothing to do with him.'

'Of course, I'm sorry.' She could hear her mum was upset.

'Look, I can see I've caught you at a bad time. Just tell Dad what I've said. I don't want either of you to be worried unnecessarily.'

Obviously realising she'd made a mistake, her mum said, 'Of course I will, don't worry. How are things going there?'

She'd always loved chatting with Daisy, but she didn't trust herself after such unfairness to Will, who had been consistently nice to both her parents. So she answered that everything was fine, but she had to get ready for a show this afternoon, hating herself for lying.

In a way she was glad she had been annoyed by her mum because it had fired her up and made her see she had to do something about the situation. It was really affecting her now and Lally seemed to be the only one who was taking it seriously. So, when she was dressed, she knocked on Lally's door.

It was the biggest of the bedrooms, which made sense as it also served as an office, with space by the window for a desk and a couple of filing cabinets. Lally was working on a laptop, a pile of papers beside her, but she swung her office chair round and beamed as Ava peeped round the door. 'Hi, Ava, did Brad tell you the good news about the critic?'

'Yeah, it's amazing, isn't it?' As she said it she realised she hadn't asked Will if he had anything to do with that.

She gestured to the bed and Lally waved her hand to tell her to sit, swinging right round to look at her. 'Are you all right, you look worried?'

'I am – about all these jokes, pranks, or whatever you want to call them.' Lally was really listening now, her brow furrowed. 'What you said when we walked back from town about things happening to other people, well I've had a couple of experiences that might be connected.'

When she'd explained, Lally pressed her hands together as if in prayer, fingers against her lips. Her dark eyes looked almost black as she sat thinking. 'That's horrible. I'm so sorry. What do you want to do about it?'

That surprised Ava. She wasn't sure what she'd expected, but not to have it thrown back at her. 'I was hoping you might suggest something.'

'Well, my first thought was to get everyone together and talk it through. See if anyone knows anything. But you might not want that.'

Ava wondered if Lally guessed that she thought it had to be someone from the group and that she might not want to confront them, but she could think of no other option. 'That's what I think we have to do. It's the only way to find out if they have any suspicions.'

Lally jumped to her feet. 'OK, I'll go and see where everyone is. I won't say anything until I can get them all together because we don't want them to work out their alibis.' She must have seen Ava's expression because she said, 'Sorry, that wasn't funny, but you know what I mean. It will be better if their thoughts are spontaneous. You stay there and I'll call you.'

Everyone must have been in the cottage because it was only a few anxious minutes later when she heard Lally shout up the stairs. Running down she found them all squashed around the kitchen table, Brad handing out coffees. Without breakfast or a proper dinner last night she should have been famished, but she was too nervous to eat. She took a mug of coffee, glad of its comforting warmth and to be able to look down into the white swirling through the brown as she added milk.

Lally seemed to have taken charge and that made it feel

easier. She was telling them about her own recent experiences with the smashed eggs and the unpleasant emails as well as a few offensive phone calls. 'But this morning, Ava tells me she's had some horrible things happening too.'

Ava was annoyed to hear her voice sounding weak as she explained about her hair and the message to Will – she called him a friend, no need to give away more than she needed. She coughed and tried to sound stronger. 'The most worrying thing is that it must mean someone had access to my room to do those things. Probably during the night. I keep my phone on me the rest of the time, but it's beside my bed at night.'

She looked around the table. On the bench opposite, Brad was hunched forward, arms crossed on the table and looking as if he wanted to be anywhere but here. Mel, next to him, feet in bright-pink socks on the bench, her knees hugged against her chest, was smiling her usual secretive smile. Alongside them Joel turned his mug round and round on the table, listening hard. Lally was in the chair at the end, with Paddy and Rose next to Ava. Paddy was leaning back, his arms folded, mouth a hard line, his cheekbones outlined sharply by the pale light from the window.

Pulling her blonde plait over her shoulder, Rose said, 'But you also leave your phone in the dressing rooms during the shows. I know there's nearly always someone in there between their appearances, but we don't have keys to lock up when we're talking to the audience afterwards.'

That was true, but Joel had been shaking his head as she spoke. 'What about the hair cutting?'

Before anyone could speak, Ava said, 'It was definitely cut straight across with scissors.'

Rose fiddled with the pale strands at the end of her own

plait. 'But I know myself, when your hair is long you might not notice someone touching it very lightly and apparently there are some weird people who have that kind of fetish. Do it to women on buses and so on. So it's possible it happened somewhere other than here.'

Joel put down his mug a little too hard and Lally gave a tut of annoyance, but it was Paddy who, despite his grim expression, spoke in his usual measured way. 'I think we have to accept that something is definitely happening here. OK, we may be linking things where there is no link, but too much of it can only be explained by someone with malicious intentions against us.'

Brad said, 'What I can't understand is why they might pick on Ava. I mean she's only just joined.'

'If they want to ruin Chimera then everyone is fair game,' came in Lally.

So many people began speaking it was difficult to work out what they were saying. Eventually Rose's gentle voice cut through the hubbub. 'I still think you're connecting a series of random events, but perhaps it would help if we could work out a timeline.'

'The first thing was the Coke poured into the old van, wasn't it?' This was from Lally as she looked around the table.

Joel said, 'Yes, it was when I started working with you properly, rather than helping out occasionally.'

Brad looked up for the first time, nodding as if he'd worked something out. 'Around the time Dominic left us, you mean.'

Chapter Thirty-Three

Paddy's chair scraped so loudly on the quarry tiled floor as he thrust it back away from the table that it made Ava jump. His voice was still low, but he spoke with an intensity that was almost frightening. 'If you're suggesting it's Dom, getting some kind of revenge, then you're completely wrong.' One hand went to his hair, tugging hard at his pony-tail. 'My god, you know him, Brad. You surely don't think he'd want to destroy us?'

Brad reached across the table, as if he meant to touch Paddy, but he was too far away. 'I'm not suggesting anything, mate. Just stating the facts.'

Lally said, 'Please, let's try to look at this calmly,' although the quiver in her voice didn't sound at all calm. 'Paddy's right, we know Dom would never be malicious.' She was close enough that when she reached out she was able to take Paddy's pale hand in her dark one. He smiled at her, but Ava could see a glint in his brown eyes that suggested he was holding back tears.

For the first time, Mel spoke. 'I'm sure he wouldn't do anything malicious if he was in his right mind, but remember how he was in those last couple of weeks. If he's had a breakdown he might do something totally out of character.'

That made Paddy stand up, kicking his chair behind him with another scrape of tiles. 'I'm not listening to this.' His voice was a harsh croak.

Lally went to him. She was tall but, when she put her arms around him, her head barely reached his shoulder. He stood stiffly for a moment, then seemed to relax and lowered his head. She whispered something and he sat down again, still far from the table and looking angrily from Brad to Mel.

As if nothing had happened, Brad said, 'Unless Rose's theory is right, and it happened during a show or out and about, we have to face the fact that Ava has been got at here, in the cottage. Which means her hair was cut and her contacts stolen by someone who had access to the house. The same applies to Mel's instruments. To my mind that means someone from the group, either past or present.' He shrugged and sat back, looking at Paddy.

His voice gruff, but almost back to normal, Paddy said, 'We've only been in the cottage a year and the estate agent who sold it to Rose's mum must have had a key. Who knows how many people had the chance to copy it?'

Mel said, 'That's right and I've just thought of someone else.' She looked at Rose. 'I bet your mum has one, doesn't she?'

A small noise from Brad had Rose raising her hand. 'Yes, she does, in case of emergencies.'

Finally feeling she was entitled to join in, Ava said, 'Well the obvious first thing to do would be to change the locks.'

She could feel rather than see Joel smiling at her and Lally gave a little clap. 'That's right, we should have done it before now. And block up the letterbox, so we don't get any shit pushed in. We can put a box beside the gate for the postman to use instead. Better for deliveries too.'

As if everything had been settled, Brad jumped up saying, 'Let's do that. I'll pop into town and find something to use instead. You find a locksmith and get him out here asap.'

Lally grabbed his arm. 'Hang on. That's all good, but a lot has happened outside the house and stopping them getting in here isn't enough.'

'So what else do you want me to do?'

She shook her head. 'You can do what you want, but I'm going to call the police and email them too. Tell them everything and make them get a fucking move on to start protecting us.' She headed for the stairs with Mel following saying she'd give her the crime number from the incident with her instruments.

Brad said, 'Anyone want to come into town with me?'

Rose shook her head. 'I'll phone the locksmith.' She looked very pale and when she stood, she pressed a hand to her back, rubbing her bump with the other as she walked very slowly to the stairs. Brad, with a look back at Paddy, as if he expected him to say something else, went after her. At the bottom of the stairs he stroked her hair and whispered something to her.

Paddy went out into the garden, although it was gloomy and Ava could see spits of rain on the window panes. He stood, looking over the valley, one hand behind his back, clenching and unclenching.

The ideas they had come up with were good. The new locks should keep the house safe from outside attack and up in the attic, with the chair wedged against the door, Ava could feel secure from unwanted visits from inside. Even so, she still felt unsettled.

She took a yogurt from the fridge, bringing it back to the table. Alone with Joel, who was by the Aga making more coffee, she felt able to say, 'Do you think it could be Dominic who's behind all this?'

He stirred the pot, then turned to face her. 'Well, whatever Paddy wants to think, I remember what Dominic was like just before he left. I mean I only saw him a few times, when I helped out with the tech stuff around then, but it was obvious he was seriously upset. Disturbed, I'd call it. I mean, besides his conviction that Paddy was having an affair, or multiple affairs, he seemed to think all sorts of things were going on. The group conspiring against him. That they all hated him. He told me because I was an outsider, but even I could see it was mad.'

After a couple of spoonfuls, Ava regretted the cool yogurt, should have had something hot. Now everyone was gone the room felt cold, despite the Aga. Paddy had left the garden door, next to her, slightly open and she got up to close it, rubbing her arms where goose bumps were forming. Without asking, Joel poured her a fresh mug of coffee and brought the biscuit tin to the table. When he sat opposite, she took a chocolate digestive. He laughed when she dunked it in her coffee. Along with the warm drink and the sweet chocolate, his laughter made her feel better.

He said, 'The thing that makes me doubt the Dominic theory is what's happened to you. I can see why he might hate the group and even want to attack me, as I took over from him.

But why you? Paddy should have been his obvious target and nothing seems to have happened to him.'

'I know. The only reason I can see for anyone who has a grudge against the whole group to attack me is that my old room was so accessible. Easy pickings.' She lowered her voice. 'I mean if it was someone living here, they could have come in at any time. If I was awake, they'd just say they wanted to speak to me, if I was sleeping and they woke me they could claim they were heading up to see Mel.'

His eyebrows rose. 'In the middle of the night, though?' She picked up her mug, too embarrassed to speak, thinking of those footsteps in the early hours, the voices and the rhythmic creak of Mel's bed. The creaks that could have been made by Joel if not by Brad. She certainly didn't want him to know she'd heard them.

At least he didn't wait long for an answer, glancing round then leaning towards her to speak very softly. 'If it is one of us rather than Dominic or Rose's mum, which seems a ludicrous idea, my money would be on Mel. I mean she clearly resents you.' A tiny laugh. 'You and Rose and probably Lally too. But she's also scared of you. In case they want you to take over from her. When Paddy suggested we manage without replacing Rose, his idea was that Mel could double up parts, but Brad and Rose were adamant we get someone new – ideally a musician to fill the gap left by Dom as well as take over from Rose. Mel certainly felt threatened by that.'

Ava remembered Rose, at the audition, saying it would only be a short contract. *But if it works out I'm sure we could use your musical talents for the new shows.*

Of course, she had suspected Mel from the start, even if the attacks on her had nothing to do with the pranks against the group. But then Lally and even Rose could easily have got into her room as well. And if Brad really was Mel's nocturnal visitor, she knew she had slept through him coming back on at least two mornings. So he had to be a suspect as well. And when she began to think like that, she couldn't even rule out Joel himself or Paddy.

Even with the door closed there was a chill breeze coming through and a huge shudder went through her. Joel said, 'Hang on a minute,' and disappeared into the annex, coming back with a grey fleecy hoodie. 'It's perfectly clean, I promise,' he said, putting it over her shoulders and tucking it around her arms. It felt soft and soothing and she found herself looking up into his gold-flecked eyes. For a moment the silence seemed to hum in her ears and she thought he was about to lean down and kiss her. She swayed against him as he smiled a question and knew she was smiling back.

Chapter Thirty-Four

Then Paddy came through the door with a waft of cold air and a mist of drizzle. Joel stepped back and Ava pulled the hoodie close and picked up the mug of coffee. One of Paddy's eyebrows quirked upwards and his mouth curved in a little smile, but he just said, 'I guess we can all expect to be quizzed by the cops now, but I hope people don't start hurling accusations about.'

There seemed nothing she could say to that and, not daring to meet his eyes or Joel's, she carried her mug upstairs, closing the attic door and sitting on the bed as she tried to catch her breath. When she met Joel at the party, she had enjoyed being with him and had imagined they might have a mild phone flirtation that would peter out after a little while. But it was very different getting close to someone she was not only working, but living with. And that moment downstairs had felt very intense. There was something about his eyes in particular that really drew her in. Almost as if she had known him forever. It was something like the feeling she remembered having about Will in their early days.

But it was no good. She was still too caught up with Will. Still not sure if she could let him go; not sure if she wanted to. And she knew enough about Mel by now to realise she could easily have lied about her relationship with Brad. There was nothing to say it was really him, rather than Joel who had made those late-night visits to her in the attic.

Above all, she told herself, she needed to focus on work. The critic was due to see the show any day now and she was determined to perform at her best. She couldn't do that if she was distracted.

As if he knew she had been thinking of him, her phone rang and it was Will. He launched straight into an apology for being so harsh with her about the message to the studio. 'I was out of order. You did nothing wrong and there I was, telling you off.'

'It's all right. You'd had a shock. It must have been awful when you couldn't get through to me. But I'm glad you didn't actually ring my parents. I've told them what happened now so if someone has got their phone numbers as well they won't be frightened.'

'That's good. To be honest I was feeling terrible for holding off on calling them, but I know I'm not their favourite person.'

There was no point in trying to reassure him now. It was all in the past. 'They're just very protective of me.'

'Some might call it possessive, but whatever.' He laughed, but she didn't, remembering that her mum had used the same word about him.

The laughter died from his voice too. 'Look, I really am

worried about you. Are you sure you shouldn't move out of there? Get a flat on your own. I can help with the rent.'

That was the last thing she wanted; although it would be good to have her own place, she couldn't afford it and it wouldn't be her own if he was paying for it. 'There's no point, I'm only here for a bit longer. And we have a critic coming from the *Guardian* any day now.'

'That's great, really great, I'm sure you'll be brilliant. I can't wait to see you in it. It's ages since I've seen you perform.'

Trying to make her voice casual, she asked, 'You haven't been trying to get us publicity, have you? I thought you might know that critic.'

His voice became muffled and she thought she heard the sound of traffic in the background. He must be in the street. 'Sorry, Ava, I'll have to go, but take care please. For my sake if not your own.'

Dropping the phone on the bed, she told herself he hadn't cut her off because he wanted to avoid answering her question. Anyway, it didn't matter if he had mentioned Chimera to the critic. That was how it worked.

She realised she was still wearing Joel's hoodie and dragged on a warm jumper instead. Downstairs there was no one about and she put the hoodie on the back of a chair where Joel would be bound to see it and started making herself some toast. But then the door to the annex opened and he was there. 'Ava, can you come in here a minute?'

It was impossible to refuse and she picked up the hoodie, holding it against herself as if for protection. The door led into a tiny square space with a door facing her and others to right and left. Joel held the right-hand one open and she stepped inside. The walls were whitewashed brick and there was no window, but a small skylight. There was just room for a bed against the wall with a chest that also served as a bedside table beside it.

It was very neat, the bed covered in a bright-blue duvet, and when Joel closed the door, she saw a striped dressing gown hanging from a hook. One wall was covered in metal shelves that looked to be a hangover from when the annex was a garage and although there was a row of books on the lowest shelf, those higher up held the kind of things that would normally belong in a workshop: tins of paint, a rack of tools, boxes of grass seed, and various metal and card boxes that looked to contain tools or gardening equipment.

Seeing her look around, Joel said, 'A bit rudimentary, isn't it? Paddy has a much nicer room on the other side. He and Dominic used to share that and my little space was just a storeroom that we fixed up for me. So,' he pointed at the shelves of tools, 'I have to live with the previous tenants. But it's fine for now. This is nice though.' He stepped out into the hall again and opened the middle door to reveal a tiny bathroom with just enough space for a sink, toilet and walk-in glass shower cubicle: the power shower Rose had mentioned.

Ava thrust the hoodie she had been clutching towards him so awkwardly she knew she looked ridiculous, but he just dropped it on the end of the bed, sitting on top of it. When Ava turned to go, he held up a hand to stop her. 'I wanted to tell you something I haven't mentioned to anyone else.'

It was too awkward to stay standing and the room was so small his knees were almost touching hers, so she moved to the far end of the bed and half-sat on the little chest, pushing a photograph frame and a book back so she didn't knock them off.

Joel picked up his phone and said, 'I didn't tell the rest of them, but I've had some strange, not very nice, messages lately and I wondered if they were anything to do with you.' He raised his hand, 'Sorry, that came out wrong. What I meant was that the messages are all warning me against getting close to a woman. They don't name her, but I can't think of anyone else it could be.' He pushed his hand through his shiny brown hair.

'What do they say?'

He held out the phone and she moved so she could see the screen. There was a series of messages all saying more or less the same thing. *Leave her alone, you bastard. Keep your fucking hands off her or you'll regret it.* She stepped back, confused and not wanting to stay so close to him. 'But why should they be about me?'

'Apart from the fact that I can't think who else they could mean, they started soon after I met you at that party.'

In her thick sweater she felt suddenly very hot, not knowing what to think, let alone say, but finally she managed, 'There must be someone else it could be.'

He was staring at the phone and now he nodded, slowly, 'I suppose it might be Mel. We had a bit of a thing when I first met the group, but that was over before I even moved in here.' Despite her embarrassment, another guilty thrill went through her as she thought: *So it must have been Brad, not Joel up in the attic with her.* She made herself listen to what he was saying. 'Of course, it might just be a random stab in the dark to unnerve me.'

That made sense. 'Yeah, that's more likely. Another way to get at the group. They might have been sending the same kind of thing to the others, just hoping to hit some kind of nerve.'

She was very conscious of him looking at her and knew he was about to say something she would have no idea how to answer. Something that might change their relationship. And it was too soon for that. Avoiding his eyes, she picked up the photo frame. It must be the one Mel had told her about. The one of Joel with his parents – a graduation picture – Joel awkward in cap and gown. It looked like a chilly day and the man and woman were bundled up, hair blown by the wind. As Mel had said, they were much older than Ava's mum and dad. She held it up, searching for anything to change the subject. 'Nice photo.'

A crack of laughter. 'It's fucking awful and you know it.' But his smile was amused not offended. 'It bucketed down most of the day. That was one of the rare dry moments, blowing a gale instead.'

She replaced it on the chest and was surprised when he said, 'They're my grandparents. Brought me up. I'm like you, lost my mum when I was really young and Dad couldn't cope.'

'Oh, Joel, I'm sorry, I didn't realise.' She thought how odd it was that she seemed to be attracted to motherless men. Will's mum had deserted the family when he was only a little boy and he was still bitter about that.

Joel said, 'It's fine. Like you, I was so young I didn't really miss my mum and instead of a stepmother I had my gran.' A head shake and a small laugh. 'I wonder if it's acting generally or just Chimera that attracts people with iffy family situations.' She nodded, but didn't mention what she'd been thinking about Will. 'Brad's another one,' he carried on.

'What do you mean?'

'Dad's a workaholic and his mum's not really there either. Brad boarded at one of those posh public schools and spent most of his holidays palmed off on friends – had some nasty experiences there too, I gather.'

'Oh my god, poor Brad.' She couldn't imagine what that must have been like for him. Her stepmother, wonderfully vibrant and happy most of the time, was prone to depression and had even been hospitalised a couple of times, but Ava had always had her father and the interludes when Daisy was sick had been short-lived. She almost blurted it out to Joel – he was so easy to talk to – but Daisy wouldn't want a stranger to know, even someone she might never meet.

Joel obviously hadn't noticed anything because he went on, 'It's amazing he's so well adjusted, but maybe that comes from being so talented. I'm sure he channels some of the stuff he's gone through into his plays. So at least he got something positive out of it.'

She found herself smiling to encourage him to go on, although she knew she should leave, she'd been here too long. The trouble was, she really enjoyed talking to him. But he shook his head and said, 'Look, I shouldn't be telling you this. He hardly ever talks about himself and I've no idea who else knows. He spilled it all out when we got drunk together one night. The next day he kept looking at me as if he regretted it.' Another headshake along with a smile. 'You're too easy to talk to.'

It was so like what she had been thinking about him, that she felt the colour rise into her cheeks. 'Don't worry, I won't say a thing.' How odd, though, yet another man without a proper mother – another man that she had to admit she found attractive.

Joel was looking at her again in that charming way he had and she needed to get away before it was too late. 'I'd better go and have some food. I'm starving and I don't like to eat just before a performance.'

He stood, reaching for the door handle, and for a moment she thought he was going to ask her to stay, but he just opened the door and smiled as she went through. But as she came into the kitchen, she saw Mel sitting at the table with a book propped against a bowl she was eating from. She looked up and smiled her slow smile, 'Hi, Ava, how's things?'

Chapter Thirty-Five

Nobody knew when the critic might turn up, but in the familiar room above the pub, Brad said what they were probably all thinking. 'Wouldn't it be great if she came tonight. I always feel really comfortable performing here. As if we're a football team and this is our home ground.'

Their makeshift dressing room was the windowless store where the chairs were stacked when not in use. Once they'd set them out for the audience in the main room there was just enough space for them all to get changed. When Ava was in her costume, Mel helped her put on the green and blue makeup she wore for the river goddess. Mel played a small child in one scene and wore a mask for her other appearances so she didn't need makeup.

Earlier, Ava had been relieved when she was saved from saying anything to Mel about why she'd been in Joel's room, by other people arriving in the kitchen. Lally to say the police would call as soon as they could, Brad brandishing the letterbox he'd bought and Paddy silently making himself a sandwich. When Joel appeared, he was very quiet too and Ava managed to eat her own toast and peanut butter without meeting anyone's eye. It was fine because people were often quiet in the hours right before a show.

Now, taking deep breaths and doing a few loosening-up exercises, she tried to clear her mind of everything that had happened today. To focus on being ready for the play.

Lally was in the main room, selling tickets, and when she popped her head around the dressing room door and said it was time to start, Brad pointed to a metal box with a lock he'd also bought in Gloucester and they all dropped in their phones. Lally put the key in her pocket and went back out.

Waiting for the lights to go down so she could make her entrance, Ava heard a rumble of chatter, as if the audience was excited about something other than the start of the play, but it calmed down when Lally announced, 'The show is about to begin. Can I ask you to turn your phones to silent and refrain from talking,' in the tone Brad liked to call her *strict governess voice*.

Then the main lights went off, the stage lights went on and Ava felt that thump of anticipation, part fear, part excitement she always had just before a show. And they were off.

It went very well. She had a moment of terror when she nearly fell over the trailing end of her costume, but was sure no one had noticed; apart from Brad, whose eyes showed the same flash of alarm that must have been in hers. Mel was slow on her cue for her eerie singing, but again only the cast would have been aware. And it was that kind of thing that kept the adrenaline flowing and made for a more vibrant show.

The clapping at the end was loud with the odd whistle and one or two people standing to applaud, but something odd happened as they took their bows. Ava couldn't see well because of the usual barrage of camera flashes, but she heard the exit door that led to the stairs into the pub open and close; someone making a quick getaway. That was normal, but a lot of people turned towards it and several began muttering to their neighbours.

Everyone left very quickly and as they went into the dressing room Brad said, 'Thirsty lot tonight, eh? Even here we usually get someone wanting to talk, but I guess they're waiting to pounce on us downstairs.' Ava saw Mel glance over at her as if about to say something, but instead she pulled her T-shirt back on and went to help Lally who was already stacking chairs in the main room.

When Ava joined them, Lally beckoned her aside. 'Did you know you had a friend in the audience? Caused quite a stir.'

Mel turned as she added another chair to a stack almost as tall as herself. 'Bit of a dark horse, aren't we?'

Will, it had to be Will. Ava knew she had blotched scarlet and was suddenly angry. He must have been on his way when he rang her. Why the fuck hadn't he told her? 'Where is he?'

Lally said, 'I told him to go round the back and we'd let him in through the fire escape.'

As she said it, there was a tap on that door and Joel who had been rolling up some cables pulled it open. Will stood there, grinning, and for a moment Ava felt almost sick, as if her two separate worlds had collided. Then he was in front of her and before she could speak, he'd lifted her off her feet, kissing her hard as he spun round, whispering, 'I loved it, baby, and you were wonderful.' It was so funny and he felt so familiar, his arms so safe, she couldn't be angry anymore. For a treacherous moment she was even tempted to rest her head on his shoulder and ask him to take her home.

When he put her down, she saw that the others were all out of the dressing room. Will raised his arms and gave four or five loud claps. 'Congratulations, everyone, I thought that was superb and so did the rest of your audience. The writing is amazing.' He looked from Paddy to Brad, to Joel, presumably trying to work out which was the playwright. When Brad said a rather curt, 'Thanks,' he carried on as if he'd noticed nothing. 'And I thought the whole thing worked brilliantly. The music, the staging, everything.'

Paddy came forward and shook his hand, cool and polite as always. 'Thanks. We love it, but it's good to get the opinion of another professional.'

Will gave a little laugh. 'You're very kind, but I wish I had half the talent I've seen on display tonight.' Arm around Ava's waist, he pulled her close and she was suddenly very aware of Joel, although he was still fiddling around with the sound system. She didn't know how to feel. It was so comfortable being close to Will again and he was looking gorgeous. She could see Mel's eyes on him, and flicking to her occasionally with that look of disbelief she was so used to from other women. She was thrilled that his praise for the show, and her performance, was obviously genuine, but just the fact of him being here felt awkward, as if she was showing off.

Joel had propped open the fire escape and as he and Brad began to carry some of the equipment out Will stepped away from her. 'Let me help.' While they cleared up, he chatted away so easily she could feel the others warming to him. Carrying a set of lights with Brad, he said, 'I was telling Ava how much I envy her for being involved in something new and experimental like this. But you know what it's like. You have to take the work that's offered, especially, like me, when you're not particularly creative.'

By the time the room was clear his presence seemed to have brightened the whole atmosphere. When he said, 'I won't come down to the pub, don't fancy posing for any more selfies. I nearly missed the show because I got stopped on the way up,' Ava felt bad for being relieved that he was planning to go right away. Carrying some stuff down, she'd seen his BMW in the car park and she knew he liked driving through the night.

She walked over with him: they could say goodbye here. But Brad called, 'I want to get back to Rose anyway so why not come up to the cottage?'

Ava looked at Will, expecting him to say he couldn't stay, but instead he said, 'That's great. I'd love to meet Rose.' It seemed everyone was happy to go back, so the rest piled into the van, while Ava joined Will in the BMW. As he drove, he reached over and squeezed her knee. 'Are you all right? I mean I wanted to see the show anyway, but I'm worried about you. Had to see how you actually were.'

'I'm fine now. Just sorry you had to be upset like that. I've told the others what happened and we're changing the locks and taking loads of other precautions. Calling in the police too.'

He nodded. 'That's good, but do take care.' He laughed, 'And don't worry, now I know you'll be safe, I'll just have a quick drink. It would be too complicated if I slept here.'

She swallowed, it was exactly what she had been thinking:

the way she had felt when he held her close, the thrill that was there even now as she felt his hand on her knee, was still so strong. And although she was very tempted to ask him to stay, she knew it would only make things difficult. She had to look at their relationship in a cold light and she seemed to lose part of herself when they lived together. The part she had found again with Chimera.

As they pulled up outside the cottage, he turned to her. 'I really did love the show, you know and it made me realise how selfish I've been wanting to keep you with me.' He looked at her and his blue eyes shone. 'I forgot how important acting is to you.'

The tears welled into her own eyes and when he dropped a kiss on her head, his voice was gruff. 'Come on, I need a drink and I bet you do too. Then I have to get back.'

In the cottage Brad was pouring coffee, while Paddy passed around beers. Without waiting for an introduction, Rose waved a hand from her place on the sofa, 'Welcome, Will, how lovely to see you.'

Taking a mug, Will sat next to her and when Mel went to sit on the sofa with them, he smiled at Ava, as if to say, *I'm showing them we're just friends now.* She settled on the wide window ledge and Joel took a cushion and sank down on the floor beside her, leaning back on the wall, his shoulder close to her calf.

To Rose, Will said, 'I was telling the others how great I think the show is. You're all so brave to go out on your own like this.'

After that it was as if he'd always been there. He did more listening than talking, but Ava noticed that everyone was smiling when he told a funny story about his and Ava's time at uni. He steered clear of talking about *Factory Family* or anything starry at all, until Mel, tapping his knee with her fingertips, said, 'I hear you're up for best actor in a soap at the TV awards this year.'

Will took a swallow of his coffee and said, 'Yeah, and I have to be honest, I'd love to win because it might lead to other things. I mean the idea of staying in a soap for much longer doesn't really appeal, but I'm definitely an outside bet.' Then he changed the subject to ask Mel about the music in *Dark Matter*.

It was perfectly done, except when he mentioned Dominic and asked if he would be coming back to them. There was an awkward silence, until Lally said, 'We hope so, but he's working on his own stuff at the moment.' Ava remembered her saying she'd had no contact with Dominic so she was probably just guessing, but the difficult moment passed. Then Will drained his mug and stood. 'It's been great to meet you all, but I'd better get going. It's quite a drive and I have to work tomorrow.'

Ava followed him to the car. Now he was going she wanted nothing more than to take him up to her room and to her bed. It was going to feel very lonely in the attic tonight. Instead, she laughed and said, 'Well you've charmed them all.'

Hands on her waist, he pulled her towards him, his lips moving on her forehead as he spoke. 'Do you know, I was really nervous. I admire what they're doing and feel a bit inferior just spouting my not-very-original lines day after day. Thought they'd despise me. But most of all, I couldn't bear to think they might wonder what you see in me.' She was about to speak when he kissed her. It was a sweet, undemanding kiss, but she could feel the hard beat of his heart echoing her own. She whispered, 'Take care.'

Then he let go and was in the car, pulling the door closed so quickly she almost overbalanced. Engine on, he rolled his window down and leaned out. 'Goodbye, look after yourself, and…' He stopped, rubbed his face, then grabbed her hand. 'Oh, Ava.'

That was all and she couldn't say anything more either. She bent down and kissed his cheek, just as she'd done when he dropped her off at the station what seemed like years ago. But it felt so different this time. With one long look at her, he closed the window and pulled away. She watched his tail lights until they disappeared down the dark lane. Then stood for long moments, fighting back the tears.

Chapter Thirty-Six

She had got used to waking around 3 a.m. when that low whistle always seemed to sound, but this time she didn't actually hear it. Just woke with a jolt that had her sitting up trying to catch her breath. She had been dreaming and knew it was something frightening, but couldn't remember any details.

She turned her pillow over, thumping to soften it, and closed her eyes, determined to sleep again. But the churn of anxiety was still there and she was afraid the dream, whatever it was, would come back. She wondered if it had been about Will because she kept seeing those tail lights disappearing into the dark. He should be back home by now. Probably asleep, but it would do no harm to send a message.

She realised he must have contacted her right after the performance because he'd sent a photo of the cast taking their bows and the single word, *SUPERB!* She replied: *That's great, thanks, Mum's been asking for photos so I can send this one. It was so good to see you. Let me know you've got home OK.*

After she sent it, she began worrying that she hadn't got the tone right. Was it too cold or too warm? Perhaps she shouldn't have mentioned that her mum wanted a photo. Daisy's attitude to him had caused difficulties in the past and it might suggest Ava didn't care about the picture herself. She was back on the same merry-go-round of pointless thoughts.

Although she had gone straight up to bed after saying goodbye to Will, dreading any questions about him that she couldn't answer, she had lain for what seemed hours wondering what would have happened if she'd asked him to stay. At one point she had desperately wanted to do that. She thought of the last time they'd slept together. It had been so good, but that was after they'd agreed they had to break up. If only they had been as undemanding of each other when they were together, they might have lasted. But it was no good thinking like that.

She must have dozed again.

Her phone buzzed and began to play. She had no idea how long she'd slept, but it must still be very early morning and she didn't want the noise to wake Mel so she grabbed at it. It bounced off the bedside table onto the floor and she nearly fell out of bed trying to reach it.

It was Will. To ring so early he must have got her message. She was annoyed with herself. They had to become more casual or this wasn't going to work.

When she answered, he didn't speak and she thought he might have rung off. Then she heard a click and what sounded like the rustle of clothing. Finally a cough. 'Hello, is that Ava?' A polite female voice.

Not Will.

'I'm sorry to call so early, but you seem to be the last person in contact with Mr Carew. I'm Bhavani Shapoor, a police officer, and I'm afraid Mr Carew has been involved in an accident.'

Everything stopped. Only her heart beat on, so hard she could feel it in her temples. 'Where? What happened?' Impossible to say more.

'It was a car crash. He's in Gloucester Hospital.' Silence. 'Hello, Ava, are you still there?'

She wanted to speak, but had no voice. Finally she choked out a *Yes*. It was so low she wasn't sure the police officer could have heard it, but she carried on. 'If you want to see him it would probably be best if you came right away.'

Those words told her everything she needed to know. Everything she didn't want to know. She saw Will's tail lights disappearing into the black night again. Just stopped herself from screaming that she was wrong, this woman using Will's phone. It wasn't him, couldn't be him. Will was a good driver. Maybe she *had* said it aloud because that calm voice, with a slight accent she couldn't place – that hateful soft voice – seemed to answer her. 'I'm afraid there's no mistake. He was driving a BMW sports car.'

Unreal, this was unreal. Could she still be dreaming? The loft room looked bleached in the early morning light. The dark beams standing out starkly against the pale walls. Her eyes felt dry, as if she hadn't blinked for ages. There were words she should be saying. Questions she should be asking, but she couldn't conjure them up.

She must have finished the call somehow because she was out of bed and pulling on clothes and shoes, stumbling down the stairs from the attic with only a vague awareness of what she was doing. All she knew was that she had to get to Will. As she reached the door at the bottom, she took a breath. But when she eased it open, not caring if she caught Mel with someone else, Mel was sitting up in bed, wearing her striped rugby shirt, and looking wide awake. 'I heard your phone.' Ava's face must have told her all she needed. 'What's happened?'

'Will. He's been in a crash. He's in hospital.' Even as she gasped it out she couldn't believe it. Kept expecting him to ring and say it was all a mistake.

But he didn't ring.

Mel grabbed her hand, making her sit on the bed. She wanted to pull away to call for a taxi, but felt so weak she was glad to stop for a moment. It could only be a moment. Mel said, 'OK, we'll get you there.' She swung her slender legs to the floor and grabbed a pair of leggings. Ava noticed her toe nails, which had been multi-coloured, were all varnished the same navy blue or black now. *Why the hell was she thinking about that?*

They went downstairs together. In the kitchen Mel pulled out a chair. 'Sit there and I'll get the van keys, I think Joel has them.'

She went to the annex and tapped on the right-hand door, going in without waiting for an answer. Ava stayed standing and it seemed only seconds later when Joel came out. He was wearing track-suit bottoms and unlaced trainers, pulling a sweatshirt over his head and running his hands through his hair. He came straight to her. 'I'll take you. Have you got your phone?' She checked her pocket. Yes, she must have shoved it in there automatically. 'What about your bag?'

Before she could do more than look helplessly around, Mel said, 'I'll get it,' and was gone, coming back with it immediately.

Something odd was happening with time. It seemed to be speeding up and slowing down erratically and then in moments like this, as she took her bag, it seemed to freeze. Mel gave her a little push, 'Good luck.' And Joel already at the door came back for her, leading her out of the cottage and to the van as if she was blind. As she climbed in she tried to tell herself this was real and she needed to get on with it. Do what she had to.

Chapter Thirty-Seven

The roads were quiet – it was still early, but the low sun through the windscreen hurt her eyes and made the world hazy. A man walking a dog, a woman pushing a pram and stopping to check her shoe were going about their ordinary days as if nothing particular had happened and she wanted to scream at them for being so oblivious. Something terrible *had* happened. Something she was going to have to face; to get through somehow.

When Joel spoke, it made her jump. 'Will his parents be there? The police must have contacted them.'

She shook her head. The world was still unreal, but she managed to get her thoughts together enough to answer, although her voice sounded strange to her own ears. 'His mum isn't around and his dad, well, he's not around much either. He drinks and Will doesn't see much of him.' As she said it she felt as if she'd betrayed Will. Shouldn't talk about this kind of thing to a stranger. But Joel said no more.

For a moment she wondered why he was slowing the van, until she saw the hospital sign. As he drove into the car park she was tempted to beg him to go back. There was no reason for her to be here. It was all a mistake. A stupid joke.

But he parked, saying, 'Back in a sec. Wait and I'll walk in with you.'

Ignoring him she tumbled out of the high van seat and headed towards the main hospital door. Had to get it over with now. Had to know the worst. He must have run to catch her, because she felt him grab her elbow. 'Careful.' She had almost stepped in front of a car in the narrow roadway that ran past the car park.

Together, although she was hardly aware of him, they headed into the main entrance. She looked around. A little café, not yet open, a tiny shop selling papers, sweets and drinks, also closed. Signs everywhere and finally, thank god, a reception desk.

There was a small queue, an old man and a woman holding a child's hand. *Hurry up, hurry up.* But when they headed away and she was facing the receptionist she wished they'd come back again. Didn't want to know the truth.

Joel touched her shoulder and the warmth from his hand gave her a little spurt of energy. 'I've come to see Will, William Carew. He was in an accident. Car accident. It was sometime last night.' Her voice was weak, but the woman tapped at her computer, then looked up with a head shake. Desperate now to get it over she said, 'The police called me.'

'Are you sure he was brought here? Where did the crash happen?'

She couldn't bear this. 'He was on his way to London.'

'So it could be another hospital he's gone to. Have you tried any others?'

Leaning back against Joel, because if she didn't she thought she might fall down, she managed to gasp out, 'They told me he was here.'

'Well, I'm sorry, he isn't.'

She clutched the edge of the reception desk, sure that if she could just get a look at the computer she would find his name. 'Please check again, the police definitely said he was here.'

It was obvious the woman was just scrolling quickly through to shut her up. 'No, he's definitely not here and no one of that name has been admitted then released.' She opened a drawer and brought out a piece of paper. 'These are the nearest hospitals with A&E departments. You should call them. The police officer obviously made a mistake. Or the ambulance was diverted.'

Somehow she was stepping away from the desk and pulling out her phone. There were some padded benches near the doors and she was already calling the first number before she sat down. Joel's voice came from miles away and she felt him take the paper from her. 'I'll phone the second on the list.'

Waiting for an answer as the phone rang and rang on the other end, Ava felt a sharp pain in her throat, as if the tears she was holding back were covered in spikes. Somehow, when a voice answered, she asked the same question and waited, waited, for an answer, watching the shutter on the little hospital shop open and a man pushing out a rack of newspapers. The café had also opened and the scent of coffee wafted over. For a moment it covered that ominous hospital smell, making the place feel more homely. But only for a moment.

Eventually she heard the news she expected, Will wasn't there either. Joel was still waiting for a reply, but she looked over at the reception desk, almost sure they'd made a mistake and he was here somewhere. A sick feeling deep inside. Surely, surely, the woman had checked the records of the people who'd been brought in too late. Already dead.

Chapter Thirty-Eight

Her phone rang, an unknown number. Joel was looking at her, but she was afraid to answer. Finally she did. 'Glad I caught you. I've had to borrow a phone. Lost mine last night somewhere.'

She was on her feet, then sitting down again because her legs had turned to jelly. 'Will?' It was no more than a gasp.

'Yeah, I didn't realise till this morning. I've told the phone company and it'll be a few days until they send me a new one, so save this number for now.' Something must have told him her silence wasn't normal. 'Ava, is everything all right?'

All she could hear was the silence and all she could say again was, 'Will?'

'What's wrong?'

'Oh, Will.' She walked out of the doors into the chill morning air, as if that might help this seem less of a dream. 'They said you'd crashed.'

'Who said? What do you mean?'

Joel must have followed her out. He was standing in front

of her, looking a question. She turned away; too stunned to face anyone. Only conscious that Will was on the other end of the phone. Sounding just like himself. 'The police called early this morning and said I had to get to the hospital. That's where I am now. They said you'd had an accident.'

'Jesus, Ava, fucking hell.' It was him. It really was him. 'Someone must have found my phone or nicked it. I thought it might have fallen out of my pocket after I sent that photo to you. So I was going to phone the pub to see if they'd found it. Obviously not. But what a shitty thing to do. Are you OK?'

She was walking back to the car park, her feet taking her there without a conscious decision. 'I'm all right now. Just glad it's not true.'

'Look, I'm sorry, I've got to get to work. I'll call again later.'

'OK.'

'Sure you're all right?'

'Yes, fine.' But she wasn't fine. When she tried to put her phone back in her pocket it clattered to the ground. Joel picked it up and put it in her bag. He must have brought that from wherever she had dropped it. 'Sorry, sorry,' she said. Why was she crying now? He was safe. It had all been a horrible mistake. Or, a horrible joke.

Joel was muttering something about coffee and she let him lead her back into the hospital. Sitting at a table in the café she saw him at the counter on his phone. The place was empty so he was back quickly with their coffees. 'I've called Mel and told her it was a false alarm. She's going to let the police know in case whoever took the phone was the person in the accident.'

Of course, she hadn't thought of that. Had assumed it was one of those awful pranks.

Her head and her knees were shaking as if she had some kind of illness and when she picked up the cup some of the coffee slopped over the side. Joel dabbed the table with a paper napkin that was too thin to make much difference. 'Now relax for a bit. You've had a nasty shock.'

She asked, 'Do you think there really was an accident? Or did someone just want to upset me?'

His hand covered hers. 'The police will find out. Try not to worry about it for now.' A girl brought two bacon rolls and plonked them on the table and he said, 'Have something to eat and drink, then we can take a slow drive back. It's good news after all.'

'I feel as if someone has attacked me. Physically attacked me.' Her voice broke again and she gulped some coffee. It was true, she ached inside as if she had been kicked, or stabbed. His eyes were so kind, so familiar, it should have been comforting, but somehow it made her feel worse, even more alone. She suddenly thought of her mum. If only she was here. She shook her head. No, it was Will she wanted to see.

If only Will was here.

But when another thought came into her head, she shied away from it, although not before Joel seemed to read something in her face. 'What's wrong? Is there something else?'

'Nothing, I'm fine. It was just such a shock.' She wrapped the bacon roll in a couple of napkins. 'I'll take this back with me. Don't think I can face eating yet.'

He reached across the table and gave her hand a quick squeeze, drained his cup and grabbed a napkin to put round his own half-eaten roll. 'Come on then. You need to get home and have a proper rest.'

They had a school show in the afternoon, but when they got to the cottage Ava knew there was no point even trying to go back to bed for a while. The others apart from Paddy were all sitting or standing in the kitchen area with odd bits of breakfast. Lally came up and enveloped her in a warm hug. It felt good, but she had to fight to hold back the tears and when Brad did the same thing a huge sob almost burst out. She stepped away from him and covered it with a cough.

Rose called from the kitchen. 'Come and sit down. Or would you rather be on your own?'

'I'm fine. Sorry to have caused so much uproar.'

Rose pulled her down to sit beside her and, when Joel put another mug of coffee she didn't want in front of her, Rose passed her a piece of toast. She wondered what had happened to the napkin-wrapped bacon roll. Hoped it wasn't still sitting on the seat in the van. Joel said, 'I'm going for a shower. You should try to have a sleep.'

He was right. She should at least wash and put on clean clothes. And after all nothing had really happened. She just wished Will would ring again because she needed to hear his voice and to talk to him properly. Although there was nothing more he could tell her.

Mel, cutting up an orange and throwing the chunks into a bowl with some blueberries, looked over. 'The copper I spoke to said they didn't know of an accident that could fit the bill, but would keep checking.' Echoing Will's words, she said, 'If it was some kind of joke, it was a really shitty thing to do.' She took a pot of yogurt from the fridge and pulled away the lid, asking, 'So how long have you and the gorgeous Will been together then?'

Regretting the chunk of toast that had suddenly become difficult to chew and impossible to swallow, Ava said, 'We're friends, not together.'

Looking round at the others as Ava felt her face grow hot, Mel laughed. 'Judging by the way you were hanging onto him last night it looked a bit more than that to me.'

For once Rose spoke curtly, swinging her plait back over her shoulder. 'Leave her alone, Mel. It's none of our business. And she's just had a nasty shock.'

Mel laughed and tipped some yogurt into her bowl. Brad was standing next to her, drinking coffee and he muttered something that Ava couldn't hear. Mel smiled and kissed his cheek, her hand caressing his shoulder. Her voice was caressing too. 'OK, boss, whatever you say.' She stuck a spoon in her bowl, stirring as she looked up at him.

Ava saw Rose, sitting beside her, bite her lip, a nerve twitching at her temple.

There was a loud knock on the front door. Ava jumped and spilled coffee down her T-shirt. Mel ran to open the door.

Two uniformed police stood there.

Chapter Thirty-Nine

A spasm, half pain, half nausea went through her even as she told herself it was all right. Will was all right. She'd spoken to him and there had been no accident. Rose must have guessed how she was feeling because she touched her hand. 'It'll be about the report Lally made.'

Of course the police had come about those other incidents.

They wanted to speak to everyone so Lally called for Joel and Paddy. Joel was fully dressed with wet hair, but Paddy in a T-shirt, shorts and a pair of flip-flops looked as if he'd just woken up. They all headed into the sitting room.

Brad and Lally did most of the talking with Mel reminding them of her statement about her instruments. Lally mentioned Ava's hair cutting and the phone calls. They hadn't caught up with that, but took Will's name and address. She hated getting him involved in any of this.

The cops seemed happy to leave it at that and advised them to do all the things they were already planning. 'Yes, the locksmith is due later today,' said Lally.

There was no news about Mel's instruments and when they asked if anyone might have a grudge against the group, Paddy came in quickly with, 'No, no one we can think of.' The silence after that had the policewoman looking hard at them, but then standing to shake hands with everyone as the young male constable flipped his notebook closed.

When they were gone Ava went back to the kitchen to tip away her cold toast and coffee and wash the dishes. Mel picked up her bowl of fruit saying, 'As useless as the last lot. They'll just write it up and file it.'

At the door to the annex, Paddy said, 'They can hardly give us bodyguards and it looks like we're doing the right things to protect ourselves.'

Lally obviously wasn't happy, but Brad put his arm around her. 'Come on, cheer up. We'll be fine.'

Lally turned to Ava. 'Did Will have any idea who might have pinched his phone?'

Mel's voice seemed to echo in her ears. 'Or I wonder if it could have been darling Will himself trying to wind you up because you dumped him. Don't suppose he's used to that.'

All Ava could do was to shake her head because she suddenly felt so dizzy that the room seemed to go out of focus. She clutched the sink. Lally grabbed her arm. 'Sit down, you look awful.' But she couldn't move. Had to wait for everything to stop spinning.

Then a surge of cold fury swept over her that must have been visible in her face because Mel stepped back. 'Oh-oh, I'd better watch my mouth.' She stood on tiptoe to drop a kiss on Ava's forehead. 'Sorry, Ava darling. Just one of my bad jokes.'

Lally rubbed her shoulder. 'Don't give her the satisfaction.'

As Mel headed upstairs she was still laughing.

After an hour in bed, Ava felt better. She wished Will would call, but he was probably too busy. And there was nothing much to say. Like he'd already told her, someone had stolen or found his phone and decided to play a not very funny joke. It surely had to be part of the ongoing series of pranks. What Mel had said was ridiculous.

En route to the school she told herself it would all be over soon. The school performances were ending as exam season arrived and they only had three more *Dark Matter* shows to go. After that she'd be able to leave without letting the group down. It would be a relief. The trouble was that she still couldn't help feeling unnerved. And the way everyone kept talking about the critic, particularly whenever they were together in the van, added to the tension. It was obviously so important to all of them, particularly Brad.

Back at the cottage she needed to be alone and went out into the garden, sitting on the low stone wall overlooking the fields. Apart from mowing the grass occasionally it was obvious they paid the garden little attention. But the warm late spring weather had flowers springing up everywhere. Forget-me-nots and Spanish bluebells, as well as some winding plants with purple flowers that she thought she remembered her mum calling Canterbury bells. In one corner someone must have planted a herb garden because clumps of chives were beginning to sprout mauve mop heads on their soft green stems and she could smell mint mingling with the lavender from a couple of woody bushes that scented the air as the sun warmed them. She checked her phone again. Nothing.

It was weird. The whole situation with Chimera had turned

out so different from what she'd imagined. In her moments of doubt after the audition she had thought about all the problems she might have. Failing to live up to Rose's standards as an actor, or that a group that had been together so long would see her as an intruder. But, apart from Paddy and Mel, they couldn't have been more welcoming. Even those two seemed to have begun to accept her in their own idiosyncratic ways. What she hadn't expected were the peculiar and unpleasant things that were happening.

And until those two horrible phone calls, she would have felt reasonably happy about how it was going with Will. The way they had been able to part on such good terms the other night had made her think it could really work out all right. Now she was in turmoil about him. Needed that talk to clear the air; to convince herself that he couldn't possibly have had anything to do with the call. But of course she was sure of that already. She knew him too well to suspect him of anything so mean.

It was a huge relief when her phone rang. But it wasn't Will. It was her dad.

After his hesitant, 'Hello,' there was a long pause and as always she had to help him out. 'Hi, Dad, everything all right?'

'Yes, love, we're fine.' She forced herself not to speak otherwise he was likely to forget what he'd rung to say. 'It's, just, your mum thinks she might have upset you last time you spoke. Said something she shouldn't have about Will.'

It was true, but there was no point in them fretting about it. 'Tell her not to worry. It was nothing. I was in a rush, that was all, didn't say a proper goodbye.'

His agony at having a difficult conversation almost buzzed through the air at her. 'Well, if that's all. Only, don't tell her I called you, but she's been so anxious, been taking her pills again, hiding it from me of course. So if you could phone her, speak to her, set her mind at rest, that would be good.'

It was such a long speech, she knew he was really worried and she felt horrible. Always forgot how easily she could hurt her mum. And how fragile she was under the happy personality that was on show the majority of the time. 'Of course I will. I've just been busy with the show.'

His sigh was so loud she knew this conversation was really costing him, but there was something else he was clearly psyching himself up to say. 'See, Ava, you're so important to her. You've been her whole life and I think she's afraid you might make the same mistakes she did.'

They'd been over this all before and she wanted to put it behind them. So, trying to lighten things, she laughed. 'She didn't do so badly in the end though. She found you.' The silence made her think he might have gone. 'Dad?'

'I'm still here, love. But it's hard for her not to worry about your love life, because of her first marriage. It's what I blame all her problems on. I mean it wasn't just a mistake. He was a monster. Made her life a total misery. Hurt her, Ava, in ways she's never even told me about. And, of course, he took her baby from her.'

Chapter Forty

She couldn't speak for a moment. This was the first time either he or Daisy had ever brought the subject up spontaneously. 'I know and that must have been awful for her.'

It was hardly more than a croak. 'That's one of the reasons she can't bear the thought of losing you, you see.'

Hearing him so upset made her throat almost close up and she had to cough before she could speak. 'That's never going to happen, Dad. I love you both too much.'

They were quiet for a while and she listened to him breathing on the other end of the line, longing to put her arms around him. When he spoke again it was as if the words had forced themselves out. 'After their divorce he still hounded her, you know. He'd taken her child away and made sure she couldn't get him back, but that wasn't enough for him. I suppose they'd call it stalking nowadays. We even had to move because of him spying on us and what have you.'

'I didn't know.' There was so much she hadn't known and

although she was sometimes angry with them about that, she could see they had been trying to protect her.

And he rushed on, clearly regretting what he'd said. 'It was all over years ago, so don't let it worry you and please don't tell Daisy what I've said. She hates to talk about it all, but it's why she worries so much about you rushing into something too young. Something you can't get out of.'

'I know. I understand, Dad, of course I do.'

'And a few things happened not so long ago that brought it all back, you see, which makes it even more difficult to keep it from preying on her mind.'

'What?' A couple of sharp breaths that had her worrying he might be feeling ill. 'Dad, are you all right?'

'Yes, love, course I am, but, oh lord, I've said too much. Please don't mention this to your mum. She couldn't bear it if she knew we'd talked about any of it. It's just, I want you to know how difficult things are for her.' He sounded tearful again and incredibly tired, so all she dared to do was to reassure him.

After that he obviously couldn't get off the phone quickly enough.

A chill wind had sprung up and she climbed the stairs to her room for a warm sweater. Thinking hard. She was worried about both her parents. Couldn't recall ever having such a personal talk with her dad. And it had been tantalising because it made her want much more, but she knew she had to keep her promise not to ask about it. In the past she had often been angry because her parents had kept so much from her, but now she understood that there are some things you can't share with your children. And, after all, she wasn't being honest with them about what was going on in her own life.

She had found out about Daisy's lost child from her grandmother. It was when Ava was eighteen and had just left home to go to university. Daisy had a big breakdown and although her dad's story was that it was caused by overwork, Ava realised it was connected with her own departure. Unlike her dad, her nana was very talkative and the first time Ava visited her after Daisy's recovery they had sat having tea and home-made scones in her kitchen when she started talking about *poor Daisy.* 'No wonder she couldn't cope with losing you. It was bound to be hard on her.'

Ava, on her second scone and feeling not very sympathetic said, 'That's ridiculous. She's not losing me.'

Nana stirred the teapot. 'But don't forget they took her baby away from her all those years ago. That's not something you get over.' She must have realised from Ava's expression that this was news to her and grabbed the teapot, 'I'll just freshen this up.'

'Nana, what are you talking about?' So anxious to get the words out, she almost choked on the scone crumbs. 'What baby? Who took it away?'

Still fussing with the kettle, her grandmother tried to tell her she should ask her dad, it wasn't her place and all that, but when Ava said, 'You have to tell me the rest now, please. I have to know,' she sat down again and came out with the whole story.

It seemed that Daisy was pregnant when she married at only seventeen, but had her first breakdown soon after her baby was born. When she recovered, she tried to leave her husband, taking the baby with her. But he managed to get sole custody of the child, claiming she'd threatened to hurt the baby. He made it impossible for her even to see her baby after that. When Ava asked her nana if she knew what the husband was like she said, 'One of those good-looking charmers. All sweetness and light when he wants something, but turns nasty when you cross him, so I heard.'

When, shortly afterwards, Ava had tried to talk about it to her parents Daisy was so upset that she couldn't get anything out of her and Ava's dad begged her never to bring up the subject again.

Chapter Forty-One

Ava shivered and took a thick jumper from the drawer. It must have been horrible for Daisy, especially as she had been such a wonderful mum to Ava. She wondered if she'd ever tried to contact her son, who must be an adult by now.

Still with the sweater in her hand, she jumped when there was a tap on the door. Expecting it to be Mel, she was surprised to see Brad. She stood to one side to let him in and sat on the bed.

With a quick look around as if for a chair he leaned against the door instead. 'Rose wanted me to come and speak to you. She's worried about how you must be feeling.' He smiled, looking at her with gentle grey eyes. 'It's not fair this is all happening just when you've joined us. It must be very difficult.'

She shook her head. 'I'm all right. I mean nothing really serious has happened to me.'

'But today must have been traumatic, even though it turned

out all right. The trouble is you're always so calm and together, I keep forgetting that you're a bit younger than us.'

When she laughed, he gestured to the bed, to ask if it was all right for him to sit down. 'Well, I'm not calm inside at all, but I'm glad it looks like that.' Should she tell him she was planning to leave as soon as they'd done the final *Dark Matter* show? They might not have any idea of keeping her on anyway.

A light touch to her knee. 'I have to say Rose and I were quite anxious after we picked you. I mean with Paddy not sure we should even look for anyone new and Mel being so difficult, we felt it was our responsibility to choose someone exceptional.' A big smile and a pat to her knee. 'And that's what we got.'

She forced a smile too, thinking how happy those words would have made her if things had been different. As it was, she felt like crying. 'I'm glad I haven't let you down then. Rose is lovely and all this must be so hard for her, especially with the pregnancy as well.'

He crossed his arms. 'Yeah, she's not having an easy time but neither are you, so you will tell me if there's anything I can do to make things better for you, won't you?'

Suddenly embarrassed she stood, hoping he would take the hint. He stood too and she moved away to pick up her sweater. When she had pulled it over her head, one sleeve was twisted and he helped her as she struggled to get her hand through. He was just a little taller than her and she could feel his breath on her face as he spoke. 'I know Mel can be difficult and the way Lally's getting herself worked up doesn't help. I was relying on her and Rose to be your main support, but Rose is so stressed she's going to stay with her mum for a bit.'

Dragging the sleeve down over her hand, she moved back. 'Is it too far away for you to stay there too then?'

'No. Only a couple of miles – too close for comfort really. But I wouldn't be welcome there for anything more than a short visit. Rose's mother doesn't approve of me.'

Hearing him say that made her think of Will and her own mum. Perhaps it was more common than she'd thought. 'Oh, I'm sorry and you'll miss Rose, but so will everyone else. She's so important to the group and she's been really good to me.'

He touched her cheek. 'She didn't find that difficult. She really likes you. We both do.'

A sound on the stairs and Brad moved into the shadows under the high dark beams of the attic roof as a tap came on the door. 'Can I come in?' It was Mel.

Ava opened the door and standing back to let Mel in, she couldn't avoid a glance into the shadows. Mel followed her gaze, raised her eyebrows without a smile, but simply said, 'I came to apologise. Lally just gave me a pep talk and she's right. I was being mean earlier on.' A look at Brad. 'Has he been saying the same thing?' This time she did smile – at him – the same slow smile she seemed to reserve for Brad. 'I can say my own *sorrys* you know. Or did you think I never would?'

Brad laughed, perfectly at ease. 'I just came to see if Ava was coping all right after all the upsets. Don't want her running out on us, do we?'

At that Mel seemed to remember that Ava was there and she grabbed her hands, waving them up and down as she spoke. 'Of course we don't. Where would we be without her?' Those mottled eyes seemed to spark. 'You wouldn't desert us in our hour of need, would you?'

Ava laughed and opened the door again. 'Of course not.

And talking of hour of need, I promised to help Lally with the dinner tonight so I'd better go down.'

She left them there.

Helping Lally cook dinner in the quiet kitchen helped her feel calmer. But once they were all sitting down to eat, Brad kept asking Lally if she had heard anything more about when the critic might come. 'Nothing more than I told you. They're not going to say exactly when because they want to catch a normal performance. You know that.'

Joel said, 'The play's been going really well recently, so whenever she comes it'll be fine.'

Paddy, sitting next to Brad, patted his arm. 'He's right and she won't get here any sooner by you fretting about it.'

Shoving his fork into his food, Brad looked so like a sulky little boy, Ava could understand why Mel and Lally both let out peals of laughter. Joel laughed too and Brad began to eat fast and furiously. Gradually though he slowed down and nodded. 'You're right of course. I know we're gonna be fine.'

It was important to get a good night's sleep so, when Mel switched on the television, she sat down to watch, trying to relax. It was an interesting drama, starring one of her favourite actresses, and when it was over she thought she might be tired enough.

But upstairs she made the mistake of checking her phone. When there was still nothing from Will, she couldn't resist Googling *Factory Family* and then *Will Carew.* All she found was the old news that he'd been nominated for the best actor award, although it looked as if someone from *EastEnders* was tipped to win. But what did she expect? A nasty practical joke on his ex would hardly make the news.

She must have slept because it was light when her phone woke her. Will, from his borrowed mobile. At last.

But before she could answer she heard a bang, a splintering crash followed by a scream, coming from somewhere downstairs. She was out of bed, dragging a sweatshirt over her vest and pyjamas and racing down the narrow staircase from the attic before she knew what she was doing. Going so fast, she twisted her ankle and had to stop at the bottom, her hand on the wall, until the pain subsided. Mel's bed was empty, the covers thrown back and she heard footsteps and one shout followed by another.

Limping across the hall she saw Lally's door was wide open, but Brad and Rose's still closed. Downstairs the lights were all on, it was still early. Mel and Lally were standing in the kitchen area, looking towards the annex. Lally tying her dressing gown, while Mel was fully dressed in jeans and a loose shirt. Behind them Brad, in only a pair of shorts, was holding the door to the annex open. As he moved she saw Paddy, with a duvet wrapped around him just inside the tiny hallway.

She could hear someone breathing fast and heavy as Lally said, 'Oh, Jesus, Jesus Christ,' and 'What the fuck?' her voice quavering.

Where was Joel? As the thought came into her head, Ava's heart gave such a huge thump in her chest she stopped breathing. Forcing herself to move forward she heard a rattling sound that reminded her of the other day walking through the woods. But it was Paddy pushing open the door to the shower room. The sound was the crunch of shattered glass as he moved it. Behind him Ava could see that the shower screen was mostly gone, just a jagged chunk threaded with a web of shatter lines somehow still clinging to the bar at the top. It looked like a guillotine.

Joel! She wasn't sure if she'd said his name or just thought it, but then Paddy moved and there was Joel sitting on the lid of the toilet, a towel clutched round him. As if he sensed her looking, he caught her eye and smiled a weak smile. The rest of them turned and Lally said, 'Christ, Ava, can you believe it? What next?'

Although she hadn't noticed him move, Paddy must have gone into Joel's room because he handed over the striped dressing gown she remembered hanging on his door and a pair of flip-flops. 'Best get out of here and warm yourself up.' As Joel struggled into the dressing gown, Paddy helped him to his feet. 'Careful, it's tempered glass so they're thick chips, not that sharp, but look at this.' He held up his own foot and pulled a small squarish chunk from his heel. Lally let out a little yelp as blood dripped onto the glittering mess on the floor.

Joel limped out and Brad pulled a chair away from the table for him. He collapsed onto it, leaning his elbows on his knees, head in his hands. His voice was shaky. 'I'm all right. Not hurt at all. Look after Paddy.'

Paddy had disappeared into his own room and came back in T-shirt and shorts hopping on one trainer with the other foot still bare and dripping blood. Lally grabbed his arm and helped him to a chair next to Joel. Mel handed him a long strip of kitchen roll and he held it to his heel, shaking his head. 'I thought a bomb had gone off, or something.' His voice wavered just like Joel's.

Ava hadn't been able to move, but she was suddenly aware

of Rose behind her, warmth radiating from her. Her voice was very quiet. 'Brad, get the first-aid box out. It's under the sink.' He obviously couldn't hear and she moved in front of Ava, hand pressing the small of her back. Her hair hung in a tangle down her back. Raising her voice, but seeming unable to say the whole thing again she pointed down at the cupboard. 'The first-aid box.'

Everyone bustled about, Mel wiping the trail of blood Paddy had left, then making coffee. Brad kneeling in front of Paddy to dab at his foot and put on a plaster. Lally grabbing a broom and beginning to sweep up the glass in the annex hallway. Rose sighed and said, 'If everyone's all right I'll go back up.' It was almost a whisper and Ava turned to smile at her, but she didn't look back.

By now Lally had a pile of shards in a heap in front of her and Ava found a dustpan in the corner cupboard where Mel's instruments fought for space with the hoover. Kneeling so Lally could load it with the glass, she held her hands as stiffly as she could, knowing that if she relaxed them, they would begin to shake. The hallway and the floor of the shower room clear, Lally began to sweep out the chunks of glass that had fallen into the enclosure. Coming back from emptying the dustpan in the bin, Ava heard a creak and looking up saw the great jagged-edged piece of broken glass still attached to the bar at the top begin to move. She tried to cry out a warning, but the sound seemed to stick in her throat. From somewhere a shout did come. Joel's voice loud and horrified. 'Oh shit, look out!'

And the massive splinter slipped from the metal strip still holding it, hung for a moment, then broke away, glinting as it sliced through the air towards Lally.

Chapter Forty-Two

Somehow, whether it was her own instincts or Joel's warning, Ava found she had dragged Lally away just as the glass rained down to the floor. They held each other close, Lally gasping and sobbing on her shoulder.

Then Brad and Joel were there leading them both to the sofa in the sitting room. In her thin dressing gown Lally was shuddering violently and Ava couldn't stop shivering either. From somewhere Mel brought a tartan blanket to put over them and they huddled together. Ava felt Mel touch her hair, then saw her lean over to do the same to Lally. She was picking little chunks of glass from Lally's curls. Lally was no longer sobbing, but her breath came in hoarse gasps and the drumming in Ava's chest was so violent she pressed her hand to her breastbone under the blanket.

Mel brought a tray of coffees and sat across from them in one of the armchairs. 'Fucking hell that was intense.' She looked up at Joel as he came in, helping Paddy to limp behind him. He pushed Paddy into the chair next to Mel and sat on the arm of the sofa beside Ava.

Brad handing coffees round shook his head, 'How the hell did that happen?'

Paddy, his bare foot resting on the coffee table, the plaster visible on his heel said, 'Those glass enclosures look good, but they're not as safe as shower curtains. Apparently, it's not uncommon for them to shatter.'

Lally lurched up, pushing away the blanket and still gasping as she spoke. 'I don't believe this. Even after three of us could have been seriously hurt, you're still dismissing things as accidents or coincidence.'

Brad raised his hand. 'Now hang on, Lally.'

Paddy picked up a little piece of glass that must have fallen onto the coffee table from Lally or Ava's hair. 'The broken bits are quite thick and the edges are hardly sharp at all. I only cut myself because I stood on it hard. And the chunk that came down on you broke up before it hit you. Which is what it's designed to do.'

Joel leaned forward. 'It does happen, you know. Happened when I lived at home. They'd only put the screen over the bath the year before. The company said it was caused when it was moved too roughly, which gradually loosened the attachment at the top. One final careless slam and it gave way. My granddad blamed me for being so heavy-handed. I still am so it could have been my fault this time too.'

Ava could tell Lally was trying to speak calmly, 'So what exactly happened this morning, then?'

'All I did was pull the door open. Thought I heard a crack, looked up, and the whole thing collapsed in little pieces. Lucky I did hear that warning crack, because I was able to jump back as it shattered. Thing is, I'm always so dozy in the morning I wouldn't have noticed if there was damage to the glass already.'

Paddy nodded. 'I never look at it closely either. It was obviously just a simple accident. One of those things.'

When Lally pulled the blanket up over her shoulders again, Ava reached for her hand, squeezing her fingers. She was clearly very upset, but Paddy and Joel were convincing.

No one spoke again. Like her, they were probably too tired to keep going over it. One by one they began to move away and Ava drained her coffee mug. When she asked Lally if she was OK, she got back a smile and a nod, so she pulled down the blanket, tucked it around Lally again and went upstairs to dress and call Will.

He didn't answer and had left no message so she told him she was all right and he could try her anytime during the day, but they had a show this evening.

This would be a perfect time to call her mum. It wasn't one of the days when she went to work so she was likely to be home. It would be good to hear Daisy's voice, although she would have to be careful not to give away anything about what had just happened – or the conversation with her dad. Taking a deep breath, she reminded herself that Paddy and Joel were probably right. The broken shower screen, shocking though it was, especially on top of all the other horrible incidents, was very likely to have been an accident.

Her mum answered right away. 'Hello, sweetheart. How is everything?'

Just hearing that voice was enough to make Ava feel better. There was absolutely no need to worry her. 'Good, the plays are going well and we're hoping a big critic from the *Guardian* will be coming soon either tonight or in the next two days. After that I'll be finished here, at least for a while, so I thought I'd come and stay for a bit, if that's all right.'

'Oh, that's wonderful, Ava, of course we always want to see you.' A pause. 'And bring Will too.'

'No, Mum. I told you, we're having a break. I want to concentrate on my career, just like you always say I should.'

It must have come out wrong because she heard a little gasp from the other end. 'Oh, darling, I'm so sorry about the way I've been about him. I know he's a decent young man and he really cares for you. It isn't that at all.'

'I didn't mean it as a dig. You were right. I know that now. I was too young to commit myself and so was he. In fact we've both come to realise that. We haven't said it's all over, so who knows, we may get back together eventually, but a break will be good for us.'

'That's a relief, then. I don't really know why I worry about you because you've always been so much wiser than I was as a girl. In future I'll keep out of it.'

Ava couldn't hold back a chuckle. 'I'll believe that when I see it.'

Her mum was laughing too. 'I have got something to nag you about though. You never sent me the photos you promised.'

'Sorry, I forgot. I'll take some right away. And there's one of the cast together after our last show as well, so I'll send that too.' She had been about to say that Will had taken the picture, but it was best not to mention his visit. No need to talk about him more than necessary. Avoiding any chance of things going wrong again. Instead she said, 'You're always so busy worrying about me, but I hope you're taking care of yourself too.'

It might have been a mistake because the pause this time was too long. 'Has Dad been saying something?'

There was no point in denying it completely. 'Only that you're missing me.'

A faint hardness came into that sweet voice. 'Please don't come home just because you feel sorry for me, Ava.'

It was going wrong again. A pang of longing for the days when they had found it so easy to talk. 'I'm not. I want to come home. Want to see you and Dad. I always do.'

Daisy must have heard the little choke she'd tried to hide. 'Now I've upset you again. I'm hopeless these days, can't seem to do anything right.'

'Don't be silly, Mum. We're fine.'

'Are you sure?'

'Of course.'

She thought that might be the end, but heard a sighing breath down the line. 'It's things from the past, you know. Regrets. They're so difficult to cope with when it's too late to do anything about them.'

'You can tell me if it would help.'

'It's nothing. Honestly, Ava, I'm fine really. Don't worry about me.' A little laugh that did nothing to convince Ava. 'Just send me those photos and I'll be happy.'

As she came down from the attic, she thought how wonderful it would be if a few pictures could really make her mum happy. But at least getting them sent off right away with a nice message would show Ava was thinking of her.

Mel wasn't in her room, so Ava took a quick picture of the view from the window that she loved so much. She noticed

Mel had her own mum's picture next to her bed. In the bright light here, she looked even more like her daughter than when Ava had first seen it in the attic.

Then she went into the garden and snapped a few pictures of the cottage from different angles and the little town and river down the hill. When she looked up she saw Brad and Rose beckoning her from the sitting room window. Inside, a big holdall was sitting beside the front door and Brad said, 'Rose is off to her mum's now.'

Rose, who had been on the sofa, came and grabbed Ava's hands. 'I feel bad for leaving everyone like this, particularly you. Will you be OK?'

'Of course. You need to look after yourself, not start worrying about me.'

'Well, I'll be coming to the final show. So I'll see you soon.' She pulled Ava into a hug speaking very softly. 'You know we really like you, don't you? Brad and I would love it if you'd stay on after this tour is finished. Help with the music for the next plays and be in them of course.' When Ava said nothing, she stood back and looked at her intently. 'Don't say anything yet, just think about it.'

'What's going on? Conspiring again, are we?' Mel appeared. She must have come out of the annex.

Rose turned to her with a laugh. 'No, I was just asking Ava to make sure the place doesn't go to shit when I'm gone.' She kissed Ava's cheek. 'And look after Brad for me too. He'll be lost without my nagging.'

A hearty guffaw from Brad covered whatever Mel had been going to say as he swung Rose's bag up again, opened the front door and said, 'Back soon. Don't suppose I'll be asked to lunch.' As they walked to the van Ava heard Rose telling him that of course he would be asked to stay and he wasn't to refuse. Their laughter echoed back until the van engine came to life and they heard it pull away down the lane.

Mel slumped into a chair at the table, saying in a low voice that Ava was still sure she was meant to hear, 'Fucking bitch.'

Chapter Forty-Three

Anxious about the performance that evening, which everyone seemed convinced would see the critic in the audience, and wanting to get away from the atmosphere at the cottage, Ava spent the afternoon in the town. As she walked down, a message came from Will: *Sorry I haven't been in touch, but things are going crazy here. The awards are tonight and I seem to be doing endless interviews on top of work. Hope you're all right and that stupid incident didn't upset you too much. XXX*

She hadn't even registered the date of the awards and quickly sent back a good luck message, feeling guilty that she hadn't done it before or sent a proper card. But along with the guilt there was a pang. Of course he knew she was working and wouldn't be free to come with him. So he wouldn't even have thought to invite her. He was doing what she wanted him to do: keeping his distance and focusing on his career. Still, she couldn't help feeling abandoned and sad. At least she was alone. She couldn't face the thought of speaking to anyone from Chimera for a while.

It was no good thinking about Will or the awards. She'd have to check later to see if he'd won and to face the fact that he might be pictured with another woman smiling at his side. Instead, she tried to keep her mind occupied by taking a series of pictures for her parents. Probably too many, but it was the kind of place she knew they would love, even though it wasn't looking its best with dark clouds beginning to fill the sky.

She ate in the little coffee shop near the market again and as she sat there she sent off all the photos, including the one Will had taken after the show.

With the photos, Ava sent a message saying how much she was looking forward to being home soon. She wanted to add more, but couldn't think of anything that might not be misinterpreted. Once she was back, she'd work at sorting out her relationship with both her parents.

Although she longed to know what Daisy had meant by her *regrets*. The *things from the past* that were haunting her; she knew there was no way she could ask, but it was worrying. Especially as her taciturn dad had mentioned *things that happened not so long ago that brought it all back*. If her mum's ex had stalked her once, could he be doing it again? The thought was truly frightening. And it somehow felt more sinister in the light of what was going on with Chimera. The two things could hardly be connected, but knowing that didn't help. The world suddenly felt threatening.

When she got back to the cottage, she had a shower then lay on her bed. She put a chair in front of the door, determined to pretend she was asleep if anyone knocked. And she was almost dozing when she heard voices close by: so close they had to be coming from Mel's room. Mel's voice rose, clearly angry, 'Shut up, just shut up.' Then Ava heard the soft rumble of a man obviously trying to speak quietly. It was followed by another shout from Mel, 'Not when I've done telling her you won't.' Again the man's voice. Mel's reply was quieter, sounding breathless. 'You wouldn't, you know you wouldn't. Not to me.'

This time, the male voice was louder. 'Just try me then, Mel. Just you try me.' Although the voice was distorted with anger, Ava was almost sure it was Brad.

Quieter words from both of them, then Mel, 'Well just fuck off then,' and what sounded like a door slamming.

Ava lay for a while listening hard and only when the silence had gone on for ten minutes or so did she dare to go down the narrow staircase. The room below was empty and when she glanced from the window she could see Mel in the garden, standing staring over the valley, her arms crossed tight on her chest.

Ava had been certain the man's voice she'd heard had been Brad's, but when Joel came into the garden Mel rounded on him, her face contorted. Perhaps it had been him after all.

But Mel seemed to crumple and put her head on his shoulder. For some reason Ava found herself bracing as she waited for the kiss that she expected to come. Instead, Joel rubbed Mel's back and after a few moments they pulled apart and Mel wiped her eyes with the back of her hand. Although she couldn't see his face, Ava knew from the gentle shake of his head that Joel was trying to reason with her. But then she pushed him away, both hands on his chest, and stormed back into the house. He was still shaking his head when he followed her, but walking slowly so as not to catch up with her.

Chapter Forty-Four

Once they were all in the van, with Lally on one side and Joel on the other, Ava was relieved that they seemed to be trying to keep things light. They talked and laughed about all kinds of silly stuff. Joel telling bad jokes and Lally relating anecdotes from Chimera's early days. It sounded as if they'd had a lot of fun then and a mention of Dominic didn't cause any tension. Paddy joined in with one story, correcting Lally's version, and even Mel laughed, but Ava could tell it was forced.

Only Brad was quiet. He was driving and his hands looked tight on the wheel. Ava wondered if it was because of the argument with Mel, but it was more likely because the rain had begun to come down more and more steadily and the heavy clouds turned the afternoon to a misty twilight.

He was also obviously very anxious about the coming show. Apparently the village would be about the worst place for the critic to come, because it was so remote and they'd never been there before, so had no guaranteed audience.

Looking out at the rain, Ava shivered. She still hadn't got round to having her warm jacket cleaned after the accident and was only wearing a thin hoodie over her T-shirt. Beside her Lally huddled in a parka, but Joel on the other side took off his coat and draped it over her knee. 'Here you are. It's too warm for me.' She smiled a thank-you and pulled it up to her chest. It was dark wool, a bit threadbare, but it had a clean, outdoorsy smell and was very comforting.

The village they were heading for was in the centre of the Forest of Dean and as they got closer, Lally spoke more seriously. 'It's a weird place. A few huge houses and an enormous vicarage on one side of the village hall, then a run-down housing estate on the other. The vicar was keen for us to come, said he'd push to get us an audience, but I wonder how big a congregation he has. He's taken some flyers and I've posted more through doors, on the bus shelter and the village notice board, but I doubt they'll bring in much of a crowd. So once we're set up I'll go out and try to drum up more custom. Shame about the weather because the hall is a bit of a way from all the houses so that might put people off too.'

The rain was coming down fast, the sky thick with dark clouds that promised plenty more. Brad pulled into the empty car park. Lally had the keys so he let her out at the front to go through the hall and open the fire door at the back. He pulled up the van right behind it, but they all got wet as they moved the heavy lights and sound equipment inside. The door led into a big storeroom that would serve as their dressing room, so they had to carry everything through there and into the main hall.

When they'd got it all inside and were beginning to set up, Mel walked through the hall into the small foyer and looked out through the big front door. She let out a hooting laugh. 'Can you believe it? The rain's easing and the sun's coming out.'

Lally, taking off her waterproof jacket and shaking out the drops of rain, said, 'OK, I'm going to try and scare up some custom before it starts again. Come with me, Ava?'

There were no houses in sight as they left the hall – it certainly was isolated. Lally headed across the road and down a lane surrounded by trees, very like the one where they had crashed on that first day. The sunshine hadn't lasted and in her damp fleece Ava felt chilled. 'I think the hall is a converted outbuilding that used to belong to a farm, which is why it's so far from all the houses,' Lally told her as they walked. 'The vicarage and the posh houses are all over there.' She pointed back into the trees behind the hall. 'Down here is where the real villagers live, I guess.'

There were no picturesque cottages, but a huddle of box-shaped structures probably built in the 1950s and '60s. They were grouped around a series of worn grass areas, some of them with cars parked on top. On one, a group of kids kicked a ball about in the mud, until they saw Ava and Lally and stopped to stare at them.

Lally took one side of each grassed space and told Ava to visit the houses on the other side. 'Offer them two tickets for the price of one if they turn up. We want to get as many as possible. Won't make much money, but it'll look better if the critic comes.'

Ava found it acutely embarrassing and most of the people who answered her knock looked at her as if she was insane. Lally was obviously better at sales because Ava heard several bursts of laughter and a couple of times she called out, 'See you about 7.15 then, don't be late.'

After close to an hour and feeling seriously humiliated, Ava had extracted just two half promises, but as they made their way back to the hall, Lally said, 'You might be surprised. Sometimes it's the ones who seem less keen who actually turn up. And you did help me with one lot who thought they recognised you from *Factory Family*. Must have seen you in photos with Will. I didn't correct them.'

The hall was chilly and Ava noticed the others had only put out a few seats. It was better to add some if they ended up with a bigger turn-out than having rows of empty chairs. As she changed into her goddess costume, she was so cold she had to clench her jaw. Before the punters arrived – if any of them ever did – she ran around the hall to warm up, then retreated to the back room to do some stretches. It was raining again and when Lally came in she shook her head. 'No one yet.'

'What's the betting she comes tonight?' Brad muttered.

No need to ask who he meant. Ava said, 'What if we don't get many takers?' They'd had small audiences before, but never fewer than about thirty.

Lally answered, 'Less than ten and we try to persuade them to come to another show. In this case it'll have to be one of the last two. Otherwise it's a refund. At least tonight we can blame it on the weather.' But as she stepped outside again, she leaned back in and gave them a thumbs up, whispering, 'Yay, a little group in the foyer now. I'll go and capture them before they change their minds.'

Everyone was very quiet, Mel stretching and breathing heavily, stopping every so often to gulp some water, Brad pacing the room and giving the occasional sigh. Paddy sitting silently, staring into his hands just as always before a show.

Joel was hunched next to him and when Ava caught his eye, he winked at her, but she could see he was nervous. More nervous than she had ever seen him, but then she felt like that too. It was always more difficult to perform to a scanty audience. And if the critic was here as well? She gave herself a mental shake – mustn't think like that.

When Lally came back she was smiling, although it looked forced. 'At least twenty and I've bunched them in little groups spread all round.'

Brad asked, 'Anyone on her own?'

A headshake. 'No, but she might have brought someone with her. Anyway, if she's not here tonight that means she's most likely to come to the last one and we should get a good crowd there. Always do.' Their final performance was in the back room of a café in Gloucester where they'd proved popular in the past. Ava was looking forward to it. A lovely way to end.

Brad was clearly very much on edge and when Mel looked around and said, 'Damn it, I've left the mask I wear for the early scenes in the van,' he gave her a fierce look and threw the keys over, hitting her hand so that she let out an exaggerated, 'Ow! Chill, will you, I won't be a sec.'

When Ava's phone rang from amongst the pile of clothes she'd just taken off, he grunted, 'You should have switched that off already and locked it in the box.' It was her mum again. She didn't answer, but before she could put it in the metal box Brad was holding out, it buzzed with a voicemail. Ava clicked to listen to it, giving Brad a quick glance of apology, although they had at least five minutes to go. Time for more audience to arrive as well, so he had no real reason to complain.

Please, Ava, ring me when you can. It's probably nothing, but I'm really worried. It's those pictures you sent – one of those pictures you sent. I mean it's probably nothing, but – sorry, I said that before. You see, I think I recognised someone. Oh, I can't explain like this. Ring me please. Oh dear. She seemed to give up rather than finish.

Chapter Forty-Five

Staring around at everyone, wondering what her mum could mean; which of the photos she was talking about, Ava registered that Brad was looking hard at her, still holding open the metal box with the other mobiles inside, but she had to send a quick text: *Sorry, Mum, about to go on stage. I'll call you as soon as the show is over.*

She wished she hadn't listened. It was so peculiar and her mum sounded so disturbed. What the hell did she mean? How could she recognise anyone?

If only she could ring back right now, but the text would have to do and she switched off and dropped the phone into the box. Brad slammed it shut and locked it just as Lally came in. 'Right, a few more out here now, so a lot better than we expected. They look keen too.' Her upbeat tone was more, Ava guessed, to cheer them up than because of how she was actually feeling. Brad handed Lally the key to the box of phones and she pocketed it as usual.

Ava took a moment to close her eyes and try to clear her

mind as she heard Lally make her announcement about silencing mobiles, and their introductory music came on. She was almost sure the call from her mum had been nothing to worry about, but obviously Daisy was under some serious stress if even a couple of photos could upset her so much. They needed to talk so Ava could reassure her. It was hardly a good way to start a show, but – a deep breath – she'd speak to her as soon as they finished.

It wasn't their best performance. The audience was restless, sometimes whispering or laughing at inappropriate places. There seemed to be a little group of teenagers who'd probably just come in for something to do. The rain could be heard beating on the roof during some of the quieter scenes. A couple of times their lighting stuttered and threatened to fail, and the applause at the end was muted. She wasn't surprised when she peeped out from the dressing room a few minutes later to see that the place was empty. Behind her, Brad said, 'Well at least it looks as if the critic didn't come.'

Ava changed and took off her makeup as quickly as she could, then headed for the door to the main hall because she really needed to reassure herself by speaking to her mum as soon as possible. Looking over at her, as she laced her own boots, Mel, who was usually first to be ready said, 'Got a bus to catch or something?'

Ignoring her, Ava went out to Lally piling up the chairs. 'I need to make a call. Can I have the key to the phone box?' Without looking at her Lally reached into her pocket and handed it over and Ava headed back towards the dressing room.

Before she got there the hall plunged into blackness. A gasp from Lally echoed her own intake of breath. Disorientated, she moved towards where the dressing room should be, but stumbled over a chair, tripped and fell to her knees.

It was then she heard a burst of static that must be coming from their sound system. It was so loud, and the crackling so sharp, it was painful and Ava, still on her knees, pressed her hands to her ears. When the static stopped, she breathed again and began to stand.

But then, louder, much louder than the static had been, a torrent of music filled the air. At first it hurt her ears so much she couldn't identify what it was. But as it eased back to almost bearable, she realised it was something from the play. The sound of Mel's eerie singing.

Chapter Forty-Six

It was impossible to think with her ears battered by that piercing voice and it was a huge relief when the most wonderful silence filled the place again.

The silence lasted only a stunned second or two before everyone started shouting. The others were crowding from the dressing room and after a moment one voice rose above the others. 'For fuck sake, Joel, sort out that sound system. I'll try and get the lights on again.' It was Brad.

Ava struggled to her feet, pushing the chair she'd fallen over out of the way, but before she could move towards the others, there was another burst of sound. It took a moment to register that the metallic wailing must be the fire alarm. She heard Lally shout, 'Come on. We need to get outside,' and looking up Ava saw that the two Exit signs, one above the foyer door and the other over their dressing room, were still illuminated. The foyer was closer so she headed blindly towards it. As her eyes adjusted, the blackness turned to a fuzzy grey.

Out of the grey a figure loomed.

She shrank back.

Something clutched her arm.

And the grey shape became Lally, warm, solid and familiar. It was just Lally. She grabbed the hand that had clutched her arm and pulled Lally close. Then she and Lally staggered through the double doors into the little foyer.

Aware of the others crowding behind them, Ava pulled at the handles of the outside doors. They didn't move. When she gave up, Lally did the same thing. Her voice rose high. 'Jesus, what's going on? I didn't lock these doors. And who the fuck set off that alarm?'

From behind them, Paddy said, 'Never mind that now. Just get them open.'

Ava could feel Lally patting her own pockets and when she spoke there was panic in her voice. 'I haven't got the keys. I always put them in my pocket, but they're gone. My phone too.' A little gasp. 'Someone must have grabbed them when the lights went out.'

Chapter Forty-Seven

Realising that she was still holding the key to the phone box and mustn't lose it, Ava remembered her trousers had no pockets so she pulled down the neck of her T-shirt and pushed it into her bra. Then she felt all around the door handles and even dropped to her knees to pat her palms over the tiled floor. Nothing but dust.

Someone else was shaking the handles now, but over the piercing wails of the alarm Ava heard Joel say, 'It's no good, we'll have to go through the dressing room.'

It was darker back in the main hall, but Ava's eyes were beginning to adjust and she could just make out Joel's silhouette in front of the dressing room door. He shouted, 'I don't believe it. This one's locked too now. How did that happen?'

Brad called out, 'That's just great. So we're stuck in here. How on earth did someone get the keys and your phone without you noticing, Lally?'

Lally sounded close to tears. 'I don't know. There was a real crush at the end of the show. I think they were all keen to beat the next lot of rain. I felt people brushing against me in the foyer, but honestly I didn't feel anyone going through my pockets.'

Paddy said, 'There's no point getting at Lally.'

Lally sniffed. 'But what are we going to do?'

Paddy, a tall grey shadow in the gloom, said, 'Someone's obviously taken them. And locked us in too. Another of those bloody pranks. I tried the light switches, but they must have been turned off at the fuse box. It's all deliberate. But at least there's no sign of fire.'

Brad was breathing heavily. 'The bastards. I promised to call Rose right after the show. She'll probably be trying my phone already.'

Ava said, 'Well I've got the key to the safe box so if we can get into the dressing room we can call for help and you can speak to Rose.'

Paddy moved in front of the dressing room door, tapping it with his knuckles. 'The main doors are really solid, but I'm sure we could break in here.'

Lally again, her voice cracking, 'And get that bloody alarm turned off.'

Joel said, 'How the hell did someone manage to lock this door after we all came out?'

'Unless it was one of us…' Paddy paused and Ava saw a movement that could have been him holding up his hand against the burst of voices. 'Why would one of us do that?' 'Don't be stupid, Paddy.' 'That's total shit.'

'Well if we discount that,' Paddy sounded as calm as ever, 'someone else must have stayed in here after the show and locked it while we were trying to get out the front door. The same arsehole who did the alarm and the lights, I guess.'

Lally said, 'But I saw everyone out and I didn't lock the front door.'

Ava's mind was whirling. 'Is there anywhere in the foyer they could have hidden? Then they'd have been able to lock the front door while we were all in the dressing room and you were packing up the chairs.'

Brad said, 'Of course there's that cupboard in the foyer. The fuse box is in there too. So they obviously did the lights, then the alarm, which is just inside the main door, and once it was dark they could have slipped past us and into the dressing room.' Ava could almost hear him thinking. 'If they locked the dressing room door from the other side they could have got out the back door. The little bastards had it all worked out. They're probably outside now having a laugh at us.'

'I'll go and fix the lights.' This was from Joel. But then he stopped, his voice rising even louder above the wail of the alarm. 'Wait a minute, where's Mel?'

A pause as they all looked uneasily into the gloom. Lally said, 'If she was still in the dressing room when the alarm went, she would have gone out the back.'

Brad rapped on the dressing room door, his voice tense. 'Mel, Mel, are you in there?' There was no answer and when Paddy said, 'Ah,' as if he'd worked something out, Brad turned to him. 'Are you saying this is all down to Mel? But why?'

Paddy's, 'You tell me, Brad,' was said with a studied calm that made Brad grab his shoulder.

'Now come on, guys,' Lally said. 'It's no good getting at

each other. Let's just break this door down. That fucking noise is driving me mad.'

As if on cue the alarm stuttered to a halt and the lights flickered on. Joel came back from the foyer. 'That's better. At least we can see and hear ourselves think now. And I bet Mel's been trying to shout to us from outside, but we couldn't hear her over that racket.'

Lally nodded. 'If she couldn't raise us, she's most likely gone to the vicarage for the spare keys. She came here with me when I collected the other set, so she knows where it is.'

Joel said, 'That's right. So maybe hold off breaking down doors until we're sure we need to.'

Brad's hands were clenched in front of him as if he wanted to punch someone but couldn't decide who. 'But we can't just wait and hope. Rose will be going mad.'

Running her hands through her curls, Lally looked around at them all. 'I don't mind trying to climb out a window. Then go round the back to see if I can get in there for the safe box. If I can't do that I could go to the vicarage.'

The windows in the main hall were so high they were unreachable, but Lally was heading towards the foyer. 'The one out here is lower and might just be big enough for me to get through.'

As soon as she looked at the window, Ava could see it was too small for any of the men and probably for Lally too. It was quite high with only the narrowest ledge at the bottom. Paddy reached up and managed to shove the latch open and push the window back. 'Not sure anyone but Mel could get through here.'

Ava saw Lally and Joel glancing at her and said, 'It'll be a squeeze, but I'll give it a try. Except I've no idea where the vicarage is.'

'The posh bit of the village is behind the hall. There's only one road through the trees so you can't miss it. Are you sure?' Lally asked.

Ava didn't like the idea at all. Obviously none of this was accidental. Someone was orchestrating it. And she thought about what Brad had said: *They're probably outside now.* But she was desperate to find out what was wrong with her mum and Brad needed to call Rose. She didn't have a choice.

Brad said, 'But go round the back first. Check on Mel and see if you can get that box. Then we can just call the vicar. Get him to bring the keys.'

Joel touched her shoulder and leaned close, whispering, 'Are you sure? Don't feel you have to.'

The warmth of his hand felt good and she turned with a smile. 'I'm fine, but let's get on with it. It's late and I don't want to get the vicar out of bed. Come on, lift me up.'

Almost without knowing she had done it, she'd put her foot onto his clasped hands. He hoisted her with a grunted, 'Go on.' She felt Paddy supporting her back and was able to put one foot onto the ledge, grabbing the metal window frame with both hands. When her two feet were balanced on the ledge, she scrambled through the opening – it was just big enough for her. She jabbed her knee on the metal frame, but with Paddy's hands still supporting her she managed to twist her legs in front and sit on the outside windowsill.

After the lighted foyer it was very dark outside, only the gleam of one faint street lamp across the road. Joel's voice sounded suddenly far away. 'Let yourself down gently on the other side. Don't twist your ankle.'

Hands behind her, clinging onto the frame, she lowered her feet as far down the outside wall as they would go. It was so dark that she couldn't see anything, including the ground, but she took a deep breath and let herself go, her back scraping on the brick wall as she came down. Landing with a jolt made her bite her tongue and she fell forward onto her knees. The concrete surface was hard and she stood quickly. Then waited for her eyes to adjust after the bright foyer. She wasn't going to move until she could see better.

A shiver went through her. Not just because it was cold, but because Brad's words had come back to her again: *They're probably outside now, having a laugh at us.*

Chapter Forty-Eight

The earlier downpours had stopped, but an insistent drizzle was coming down. The gravel of the car park sounded loud under her shoes and once she trod on something that cracked beneath her sole. A piece of glass or a snail shell. But she went as fast as she could with the lights from the hall to guide her.

She stopped when she reached the corner, her breath catching in her throat. If Brad was right and there were some thugs hanging about enjoying the mischief they'd caused, there was no guarantee they wouldn't turn nasty if they saw her.

But there was no one to be seen when she peered round the corner. No one and nothing. Nothing at all.

The Chimera van was gone.

A deep breath. That could explain it. Maybe this whole thing was just a distraction while someone stole the van. Those kids from the audience perhaps. That would make sense.

She ran to the back door. It was a fire door so there was no handle to try, but there was a small window to one side, even smaller than the one in the foyer and she knew she was too big to squeeze through. But if Mel was inside she could pass the safe box out.

Her taps on the window sounded horribly loud in the silent darkness, but she leaned so close she could feel the cold glass on her lips and called Mel's name, once, then twice more. No answer.

She made her way back to the front of the hall, scanned the rest of the car park and the road outside, then called up to the window she'd climbed down from. 'The back door's shut and the van's gone.'

There was silence for a moment. Then Lally shouted, 'What about Mel?'

'I couldn't raise her so she may have got out.' Without a bunk up she couldn't get back in the way she had come out and anyway she wanted to be doing something. She could hear the others talking together, but couldn't make out the words, so she called, 'I might as well go to the vicarage. If Mel's gone there, I'll probably meet her on her way back.'

Joel shouted, 'Are you sure?'

She shook her head, although there was no one to see her. 'It won't take me long, will it?'

Lally's voice, 'No, it's only ten or fifteen minutes if you hurry. But don't go if you don't want to.'

'I'd rather be moving than standing all alone out here in the drizzle.' And before anyone else could speak, she was heading for the car park gates.

What she hadn't allowed herself to think was that she had been terrified of the dark as a kid. So scared that she had to have a night light until she was a teenager. And she had never been out alone in such a remote place. Tonight, there were no stars and she got only occasional glimpses of a pale sliver of moon when the clouds parted for a moment.

The street lamp close to the hall was feeble, but better than nothing. There was another on the road at the back that must lead to the village. But where the road disappeared into the woods, she couldn't see any lights at all. Her hoodie was still in the dressing room and she was only wearing a thin T-shirt; as she approached the trees she began to shiver so hard she had to clench her teeth to stop them from chattering. She told herself it was just the cold.

Fully into the trees now, she looked up at the steel-coloured sky. The forest, tall and black, pressed in on her from both sides and she began to half-walk, half-run, unable to go faster because her breath seemed trapped in her chest. It felt heavy as if she'd suddenly developed asthma. In her mind she repeated Lally's words, *only ten or fifteen minutes, ten or fifteen minutes.*

It was ridiculous. She slowed her steps until she was pacing steadily onwards, keeping her eyes on the road ahead, and trying to make her breathing match her steps. What a wimp she was. Scared of water and scared of the dark. It was people you needed to be scared of and no one else was likely to be out around here this late. The only thing to worry about was the vicar's reaction when she turned up at his door.

At first the woods seemed silent, as if the bulk of the trees had smothered every sound, but as she walked on she gradually became aware of rustlings and cracklings and noticed occasional flickers of movement. Small night-time animals and birds, she told herself. She quickened her pace, still trying to keep her breathing steady.

But she couldn't hold back a gasp that was almost a cry as a flare of brilliant light flashed down the narrow road towards her.

Chapter Forty-Nine

The light flashed on and off, on and off, as Ava stood unmoving.

It was a signal. She was sure of that. But whether meant for her or not she didn't know and she wasn't going into that light until she was sure who was flashing it. So she remained frozen, until the light went off. Then she moved into the trees.

The light flashed once more and stayed on. And as she waited, she heard someone moving on the road. Then a voice. 'Ava, you nerd, it's me. Come on, I've got the van and the hall keys.' Mel. Of course.

Ava stepped into the light. 'You scared the wits out of me.' Mel laughed, gave her a little shove and they began to walk together up the road. The light she'd seen was the headlights of the van and she could just make it out parked on the narrow verge at the side of the lane. It was facing towards the hall, which made sense if Mel was on her way back from the vicarage. She said, 'I didn't hear an engine. Is there something wrong with the van?'

'No, it's fine. I just spotted you coming along.'

Ava wondered why she hadn't driven right up to her, but asked, 'Did you get out of the back door? It was shut when I went round.'

A pause and now they were in the beam of light she could see Mel's eyes narrow as they looked over at her. 'It slammed closed after me and it's a fire door so I couldn't open it again. But I thought you lot would come out the front. I tried to get in there when you didn't appear, but it seemed to be locked.'

'It was. Someone stole Lally's keys so I had to climb through a window. But it's all right. There wasn't really a fire.' Again, she wondered why Mel hadn't asked about that. But instead, 'How did you get the van started?'

Mel grinned. 'That was the best bit of luck. Before the show I had to go out for the mask I wear in the first scenes and as I came back, I put the van keys in my jeans pocket. I forgot to give them to Brad and he was in such a state, fussing about your phone, that he forgot too. And I'd already put my jeans back on when those jokers started up.'

They climbed into the van. Ava had suspicions about Mel, but if this latest prank was down to her, it seemed to be over now. Best to say nothing. Let the rest of them work it out between them. She'd be gone soon and Chimera wasn't her problem.

She was really cold and remembering the coat Joel had lent her on the drive here, she reached behind her and groped over the back seat for it, but as she did so a phone began ringing. And she realised that the safe box was on the floor back there. Mel had brought it with her. 'That might be Brad's phone. It's probably Rose.'

When Mel turned to her Ava could tell, despite the gloom, that she was nodding very slowly. 'I know who it is. She's been ringing non-stop.' Her voice was icy. 'Typical Brad. Nags the rest of us to switch our phones off and leaves his on. If I could have got the box open I'd have flung that one out of the window.'

'For god's sake, Mel. Rose is pregnant.' Ava twisted in her seat and stretched her arm out, managing to move the box a fraction closer.

'And don't we all know it?' Ava had heard her sound bitter before, but never with this despairing note in her voice. 'Yeah, darling Rose will be shitting herself. Good.'

It was so harsh Ava felt herself flinch. 'You don't mean that, Mel. I know you don't.'

'Oh yeah? Since when did you become a mind reader?'

There was no point in arguing and she had managed to get her hand under the box, where the ringing had stopped. As she pulled the box onto her lap, she kept her voice neutral, 'OK, let's just get back, shall we? They were thinking about breaking down a door.'

She groped down the neck of her T-shirt for the key. She had to send a message to her mum. Fitting the key into the lock, she took out her own phone and pressed to start it up. Mel had turned the engine on, but when she saw what Ava was doing she switched off again and put on the inside light, blinking as she looked at the box. 'How did you get that open? I thought someone took all the keys.'

'They must have missed this one because it's so small.' Her phone came on and beeped with a voicemail, then another and another. The first two messages were from her mum, but the final one was from her dad. They were obviously desperate to reach her.

She turned to look at Mel. 'It's my parents. There must be an emergency.' Hand shaking, she pressed to listen to the final message: *Ava, love. It's your dad. I don't know if you've heard the voicemails from your mum, but try not to worry about them too much and please don't ring her back until the morning.* A pause and a cough before he croaked on. *I've managed to get her pills down her and she's finally asleep. I'm sure she's working herself into a state about nothing, but text me as soon as you can.* A long pause. *Well bye, love.*

Ava looked through the windscreen, trying to keep calm; telling herself to wait until she'd heard the previous messages before she started panicking. The most recent one from her mum said:

I don't know why you haven't called me, but I really am worried. Dad says I'm being silly and I expect I am. He's probably just a lad who looks like… But – oh, Ava – after what's happened I'll just feel better if I can speak to you.

Mel turned off the inside light and switched the engine on again, driving slowly down the lane. Ava clicked on the message that had been sent first.

Ava, darling, the show must be over by now, but you haven't called back so you must be too busy, but I need to tell you this. One of those pictures you sent has really worried me. There's a young man I'm sure I recognise. Oh dear, I don't exactly recognise him. It's just he looks so like my ex-husband, I think it must be him. Ava realised she was screwing up her eyes, trying to understand what her mum was saying. It didn't make sense.

It must be my son, you see. The son I had to leave behind. Ava, I never told you or even Dad, but he contacted me when he was eighteen, but… a sob and she stopped. When she carried on she was choking on her words. *I know it was wrong, but I couldn't bear to see him. I was scared he'd be like his dad or he'd tell his dad where I was. I was afraid, Ava, and not just for me. That man was so malicious. Please, Ava, I need to speak to you.*

Chapter Fifty

Her mind reeling, Ava sent a text to her dad:

I'm so sorry I didn't call Mum earlier, I couldn't get to my phone. Tell her I'm fine and I'll call in the morning. I don't know who she thinks she recognises in those photos, but do let her know that all the men in the group here are lovely. In any case I'll be home in a few days so we can talk it all through then. Love to you both. XXX

She hoped that was enough to reassure them.

When there was no answer to the text after a few seconds, she dropped her phone back in the box and placed it on the floor by her feet. Her dad was probably in bed by now too. If only she'd been able to call earlier.

Shaking her head, she became aware that Mel was driving far too slowly. 'Come on, Mel, we need to get back.' They came to a gap in the trees that seemed to lead to a bridle path and she gasped when Mel turned the wheel fast to the left, bumping onto the path and along for a few yards before stopping and switching off the lights again. Ava said, 'What are you playing at?'

'I just need a minute.' Off the road like this they wouldn't be seen by anyone coming along, which Ava guessed was what Mel wanted to avoid. She put her hand on her door, ready to jump out and run back to the lane if she heard voices or traffic.

Mel leaned back, her hands in her hair. 'What have they been saying back there?'

'Nothing. I don't know what you mean.'

'Don't even bother, Ava, you're a useless liar.'

'Look, Mel, let's just go. Then you can talk to them yourself.'

Mel sat up and turned to stare at her. 'I bet they're blaming me for it all, aren't they?'

Ava was suddenly tired of the whole thing and found herself blurting out, 'And did you have something to do with tonight?'

Mel's laugh was so loud there was a rustle in the trees nearby as if she'd startled some wild thing out there. 'What do you think?'

Ava shook her head. She needed this to be over. 'I don't know and I'm leaving soon, Mel. It's really nothing to do with me anymore.'

Leaning back again and closing her eyes with a huge sigh, Mel said, 'I've always liked talking to you, you know. So would you like to hear it all now? I think you deserve it.'

'There's no need, honestly, Mel. Let's just go.'

It was as if she hadn't spoken. 'I was going to end it tonight anyway. A grand finale.'

She was obviously determined to explain before they went back so Ava said, 'What did you do?'

'Tonight I had a couple of kids helping me. Gave them tickets to the show and a tenner each. They picked Lally's pockets, did the lights, the alarm and locked the front door, then ran round to bring me the keys.' She laughed. 'Never thought it would work and even if they managed all that, I was sure you'd spoil it because you always take so long getting ready, but you dashed out of the dressing room first tonight, which was perfect.'

'But why? I mean why do it? And the rest of it too.'

A huge sigh. 'It started out as just a couple of pranks. Having a laugh, you know. Winding them up. But I couldn't stop. Not until I showed them what they'd done to me. And made them sorry.' As she spoke, Mel's voice stumbled and weakened. Ava could tell she was fighting tears.

So it was all down to her. Ava forced herself to keep her voice gentle. 'Oh, Mel.'

Mel went on, ignoring her. 'Rose, dear sweet Rose, was supposed to be my best friend back in the day. Would you believe it? But she decided she had to have Brad. Probably just to spite me. She knows he still loves me and that's why she wants rid of me, the jealous bitch.'

There was nothing she could say and when she reached out to touch Mel's knee, Mel jerked it away, her voice becoming hard again. 'Brad thinks he's such a stud. Bet he's tried it on with you, hasn't he?' She didn't wait for an answer. 'The fling he had with Lally really hurt her but I doubt he even remembers it.' A laugh that was a bit too loud. 'Probably helped put her off men completely and who can blame her?' Her tone softened. 'But he was different with me. We had something special until Rose got in the way. And now she's going to chase me out of the group.'

It was sad and Ava guessed there was some truth in it. It must be uncomfortable for Brad and Rose having a resentful ex around. She felt sorry for Mel, but she needed to move on. 'It must be hard on you, but you're so talented. Why not make a clean break?'

Mel rounded on her. 'That would suit you, wouldn't it? It's what they want, of course. To replace me with you. I mean Brad has a bit of a thing for you and Rose thinks you'll be easier to handle than I am.'

That was ridiculous. 'Brad's not interested in me and I've got no interest in him, so don't let that worry you.'

A sly laugh. 'How do you think you got the job?' She didn't wait for an answer. 'Brad saw you in a photo with darling Will, basically cyber stalked you, and sent Joel to suss you out. Making it look like chance. He's hoping Will's contacts can be useful. A lot more ambitious than he makes out, is our Brad. Rose too. Both desperate to show their awful mothers they can cut it in the legit theatre. Make some money too.'

It was probably just malicious lies, but it hurt. It hurt because it was so close to what Ava had feared. She swallowed down the sour taste of it. Couldn't give Mel the satisfaction of knowing the barb had hit home. When she could speak coolly enough, she said, 'Well, you needn't worry about me trying to replace you. I've already decided to leave after the last show.'

Mel went on, 'Who knows, this might be the end of bloody Chimera anyway. Once I tell them everything and they realise what fools we've made of them, they'll start tearing each other apart.'

'We? Who else is in on it?' It made sense that there was someone else involved. Mel could hardly have done all those things herself. Even with the help of kids.

It was too dark to see the mottled stone of Mel's eyes, but Ava caught a glimmer from them.

'Oh, Ava, wouldn't you like to know?' A little chuckle. 'But don't worry, it'll all be out it the open soon. I've got no reason to keep quiet now.'

The same phone rang again – poor Rose – but seeing Mel's warning look, she didn't try to get to it. It would be worse if Mel grabbed it from her. She spoke over the tune. 'Did you really damage your own instruments?'

'Of course not. I guess that might have been frustrated burglars like the police said. But my money's on Rose.' Mel's head jerked back towards the phone as it stopped ringing. 'It's the kind of sneaky thing she'd do, taking advantage of a situation to get back at someone she hated.' She tapped her chest. 'Yours truly.'

Ava gazed out at the dark woods all around them and saw a low shadow slinking across a gap in the trees. A badger or a fox. Time was getting on. They needed to go back. She looked at Mel. Her arms were crossed tight over her slender chest and Ava wondered if she might be able to grab the van keys. 'What about the car crash Lally and I had and the shower screen? Someone could have been badly hurt.'

A little laugh. 'Nah, the shower screen was dramatic, but no one was in real danger. And the car accident was just that – an accident.' A glint from her eyes in the dimness and Ava could tell she was smiling. 'As far as I know, that is.'

'What's that supposed to mean?'

She turned to look into the trees, then shook her head. 'Ah, well, I'd love to tell you everything now, but you'll know soon enough.'

It looked as if she was prepared to sit here forever and Ava was fed up; wasn't going to humour her any longer. She didn't bother to keep her annoyance from her voice when she said, 'Look, if you want to stay here all night, that's up to you. But I'm cold and tired, so I'll take the phones and walk back.'

Her hand was on her door when Mel turned on the engine. 'OK, I give up. Might as well go back now.' And they reversed so fast that Ava was afraid they'd hit a tree. But on the road again Mel slowed down. After a few yards she gave a shaky laugh and said, 'Perfect.' Then twisted the wheel sharply to the right.

This time the gap in the trees was even smaller and when they plunged into it, branches slapped against the windscreen as they jolted over the rough ground. 'What the hell are you doing, Mel?'

The only answer was another, harsher, laugh.

Chapter Fifty-One

Ava clung onto the dashboard, her jaw juddering so hard she felt as if her teeth might crack. Overhanging branches scraped on the roof of the van and Ava expected them to crash into a tree at any moment.

It seemed like hours, but eventually they came to a stop in a small clearing. Breathing heavily, Mel switched off the engine and put on the inside light, turning to Ava with a smile. But it was an odd smile, half weary, half angry. 'I think we'll just sit here a bit longer.'

Ava had to swallow before she could speak. It was hours since she'd had anything to drink. 'Come on, Mel. This is getting stupid.' She tried to say it jokingly, but her voice was so hoarse it came out as aggressive.

Mel reached for something at her side and Ava felt a thrill of fear. Mel was being so weird. She tried to disguise her flinch, to make it look like she was just shifting in her seat. But Mel was only holding out a bottle of water. Ava shook her head and Mel let out one of her hoots of laughter. 'It's not drugged if that's what's scaring you.'

'I'm not scared. Just fed up. This is pointless, Mel. The others might be out by now. So why not just go back and tell them it was a joke that misfired? I won't contradict you.'

Mel looked hard at her. Her eyes flashed. 'But it isn't a joke. None of it has been a joke. It's serious. It's about me and Dominic and all the other people that lot back there have shat on or are planning to shit on. We wanted to shock them out of their complacency. To show Brad, Rose and the rest that if they treat people like dogs, they're eventually going to get bitten.' Her voice shook and she rested her head against the window beside her, reaching up to turn off the light again.

'So are you in this with Dominic?' In the darkness Ava thought Mel was shaking her head, but whether that was an answer or not she couldn't tell. Although Mel was turned away from her, her face pressed against her window, Ava sensed she was crying. She reached out to touch her, but Mel's hand brushed hers away.

She felt suddenly very angry. 'And all the horrible things that have happened to me? Were they just to scare me away?'

Another big sigh, as if the question was just an annoyance. Ava gritted her teeth. 'All right. Let's just get back, please.'

Mel rubbed her sleeve across her face then sat up very straight, switched the engine and headlights on and began to move the van forward, then back, trying to turn it around in the small space. When she bumped lightly into a tree she said, 'It's no good, you'll have to get out and guide me.'

There was nothing else for it. Ava lowered her window so she could shout instructions to Mel and jumped down from the van so fast she almost twisted her ankle, still feeling angry. It was tricky, but eventually the van was facing the right direction.

But as she ran to get in again it shot forward and moved fast away from her. At first she followed thinking Mel had put her foot down too hard. But it was soon clear this was intentional. Even when she could no longer hear the engine, she waited, hoping Mel would come back. That it was another not-very-funny joke.

But she didn't and as Ava stood gazing helplessly into the dark, she wanted to beat her head against one of the trees surrounding her. What an idiot she was. She'd known all along that Mel wasn't to be trusted. At least she should have grabbed her phone before she got out.

She wondered if Mel regretted what she'd told Ava and wanted to get to the others first and give her side of the story. Maybe she was going to disappear completely. Or perhaps she'd decided to do something else crazy like crash the van. Just now she had seemed bitter and twisted enough for anything. None of that mattered to Ava anyway. All she wanted was to get out of these wretched woods and get warm.

A bird squawked nearby and she heard a fox yelp in the distance. That was all. Apart from that there was silence.

And the sense of being completely alone.

She peered into the black shadows between the trees. Nothing and no one. Although it wasn't actually raining, big drops from the earlier storm fell onto her face from the overhanging leaves and she brushed away a hank of wet hair that clung across her eyes. She had never been so cold. Another surge of anger went through her as she cursed Mel again. But she had no time for that. She had to work out how to get back to the road. The others would hardly come looking for her this deep into the woods and this far from the vicarage.

A sudden thought stopped her. What if they were all in on this? But, no, that was surely ridiculous. Although Mel must be unhinged, the others were far more grounded. Unless this was some bizarre initiation ritual. Or a kind of performance. She looked quickly round imagining a camera somewhere nearby. Filming her. A real-life *Blair Witch Project*. She could almost see Mel back at the hall laughing with the rest of them about how they'd made a fool of the newcomer.

The anger flared again, but then began to give way to misery. When she thought about her fragile mum waiting for her to call, and getting so desperate she'd had to go back on her medication, she wanted to cry. Fucking Mel and whoever else was involved. This was no joke.

Trudging on through the clinging mud, she prayed for a hint of light from a house or even a street lamp, although this far in the country and this late at night – or early in the morning – that was probably too much to hope for. All she could see was the grey sky and the black sentinels of trees all around her.

She had no idea where she was going or how to get back to some kind of pathway. It was too dark to make out the tracks of the van or she could have followed them. The adrenaline drained away replaced by a huge weight of exhaustion and she wanted nothing more than to find a soft patch of grass and to sleep. But she couldn't stop shivering.

Another yelp from that fox. And then something else, something longer and more like a scream: a human scream. She pressed her fingers to her mouth, holding back her own cries, telling herself it was still just the fox or some other animal. Nothing to hurt her. All the same she had to clench her jaw and force her breath to slow down, telling herself over and over to keep calm. But she was soon shuddering as the mud alternately sucked at her feet or had her sliding and fighting to keep upright.

Pretty sure that Mel had at least one accomplice, she thought about who that might be. Mel had mentioned Dominic. He was obviously very angry with the rest of the group and he'd always worked closely with Mel. She remembered those low whistles in the night and the time she'd gone down to the toilet and Mel hadn't been in her bed. The whistles could have been a signal from Dominic telling her to come down and meet him. And Joel thought he might have been the man she'd seen walking back to the station around the time their rehearsal space above the pub was vandalised.

If it wasn't him though it could be any of the others. Most of the things Mel had said just now had been about how badly Rose and Brad had treated her, so it was unlikely to be them. If Joel was Mel's mystery lover, and Ava still thought he might be, he would be the obvious one to help her. But Ava couldn't think of any other reason he might have to get involved.

And what about Lally? Mel had mentioned her as well as Dominic just now, saying Brad had hurt her badly when he broke off their relationship. So Lally must have issues with him too. And she was very close to Dominic. Had told Ava she really loved him. It made sense that she might want to get revenge on Brad for herself, but also for Dominic.

Then there was Paddy. What about him?

She slumped against a tree. It could be any of them. She couldn't think straight. Clutching her arms around her body did nothing to warm her and the chill inside was worse than the cold outside. She couldn't ignore the fact that the tricks that had been played on Ava herself had seemed targeted. But why? Was it just because Mel feared she planned to supplant her or was there someone else in the group who wanted to hurt her?

Chapter Fifty-Two

She just didn't understand any of this. And walking, or stumbling, through the trees was taking up too much energy for her to think clearly. She seemed to be getting nowhere. Could have been walking in circles for all she knew. If only she had her phone.

It was no use thinking like that. The others were bound to be out by now and would be searching for her.

A different sound. And she was running towards it before she'd even registered what she was hearing. It was a car or van that must be travelling along the road. She stumbled through the trees, but even as she chased the sound it was getting further away and she still couldn't see any sign of the road.

She stopped and listened hard. And, yes, surely that was another engine. A different one. This time it sounded like a motorbike. She ran towards it, but yet again the sound faded and died until she knew there was no point in trying to chase it any longer. When she stopped she felt the tears of frustration fill her eyes. If she had been lost before, she was now completely disorientated.

Too shattered to go on, she crumpled down onto the damp ground, leaning back against the slimy trunk of a tree. A few minutes' rest was what she needed to clear her mind and give her the energy to find a way out.

Despite the chill air, she found herself slipping in and out of sleep, jolting back to awareness every time her head slumped forward, but never able to come fully awake. Half dreaming, she kept worrying, not about herself, but about her mother. In those last calls she'd sounded desperate. Surely she was fantasising about seeing her son in one of the Chimera photos. That would be the wildest of all coincidences.

Still she couldn't help puzzling over which of the men her mum might have meant. Had a momentary fantasy of Joel or Brad as her stepbrother. But of course, it could be Paddy. Then she shook herself… This was ridiculous. It wasn't any of them. Just her mum's paranoia.

Paranoia brought on, Ava guessed, by whatever had been going on that had upset her. That phrase she'd used: *after what's happened*? Ava recalled her father saying something similar earlier on: *a few things have happened recently that have brought it all back.* She should have paid more attention. Asked more questions; forced them to tell her everything. When she was home again they would have to talk properly.

It seemed as if only a few minutes had passed, but when she next opened her eyes, it was to pale light and bursts of birdsong. She scrambled to her feet. How much time had gone by she couldn't tell, but this close to midsummer dawn came very early.

She shook her head hard to try to wake properly, holding

onto the tree to steady herself because she was dizzy and all her joints felt weak. Everything was sore, as if she'd been partying hard. Harder than she'd ever partied. Her whole body felt stiff and she was shivering uncontrollably. Still groggy, she pressed against the tree, glad of its solidity and the hint of warmth from its rough bark. She felt a hundred years old. But most of all she was thirsty. She had never been so thirsty. And pain was pounding through her head.

At least she could see now, although the early light was still weak. There was nothing for it, but to make a choice and to go that way. She couldn't be too far from some kind of road. The woods glinted in the hazy dawn: all the greenery silvered with drops of rain or dew. It might have looked pretty if she hadn't felt so horrible.

She ran her hands through her hair, picking out bits of leaf and twig and wondering how bad she looked. Could imagine frightening a dog walker as she staggered from the trees: like some kind of forest monster. When she spotted a narrow pathway leading through the trees, she guessed it must be a route people took when walking here. It was too early for anyone to be out, but chances were it would lead her to some kind of road back to civilisation.

And, ahead, she saw what could be a bridle path, maybe even be the one Mel had driven into. She began to half-run half-stumble towards it, her legs heavy, almost numb.

The path wound through the trees. There was nothing to tell her if she was going the best way, but after a few yards she thought she saw tyre marks in the distance. They were wide ones from a big vehicle. Like the Chimera van.

Nothing around her looked familiar, but she followed the tracks, expecting them eventually to lead her back to the road.

But she was disappointed when they swerved into a gap in the trees. If they were from the Chimera van that probably meant that Mel had parked up for the rest of night, once she'd off-loaded Ava. Hoping to make them all suffer a bit longer, maybe, or dreading what she'd have to face when she saw everyone again. Whatever it was, Ava certainly didn't want to see her any time soon. So she threaded her way through the trees, trying to keep hidden.

She stopped moving.

Someone was nearby. She could hear their feet crunching through the bracken. It would be a local, someone who could help her, lead her to a path. Perhaps take her to the vicarage or the nearest house. But she quashed the urge to call out when she heard the unmistakable sound of a van door sliding open or closed.

She crept forward and as she came closer, she could see that it *was* the Chimera van, obviously parked here to keep it out of sight. Staying shielded by trees, she peered at it. It was positioned so that only the driver's side was visible and in the early light she could just make out what looked like someone in the driver's seat. Not moving, probably asleep. For a second she was tempted to run up, fling back the door and try to grab the keys. But she was too tired. Couldn't outrun anyone the way she was feeling.

That sound again: a door sliding back and a figure coming round from the passenger side.

It was a man.

Paddy.

Ava couldn't hold back a small gasp and he looked towards where she was hiding. He was wearing his padded jacket again so he must have been back into the dressing room. His face was very pale and the way he held onto the van as he walked around it suggested he was as tired as she was. He listened for a moment, 'Ava? Is that you?' When he moved his head, listening again, she didn't stir or breathe. He'd been in the van. Mel must be in there too. Still in the driver's seat. They'd been in this together. Whether they'd decided it was over or not she wasn't about to trust either of them.

When he seemed to stop listening, probably thinking he'd imagined her gasp, she let herself take in a tiny sip of air. He was leaning against the van, his hand on the end of the chimera design where the tail of the snake curled across the driver's door. And he just stood there, staring ahead, breathing deep and heavy, although she knew he couldn't see her. Long minutes passed as he stayed there totally still. Ava didn't let herself move either.

Then, as if making a decision, Paddy pulled back the driver's door, jumping away as it slid open.

And Ava's heart, a huge heavy stone, plummeted down through her.

Mel must have been slumped against the door and as it opened the top half of her body fell out, her arms flopping free. She hung there totally still. And in the clear morning light Ava could see that the pale sleeves of her shirt were blotched, no soaked, in red. The red that had come from the gash in her outstretched neck and dripped down her pale face.

Chapter Fifty-Three

Ava stood, clutching the tree she was standing behind. It seemed as if the world stopped and then started moving again. But moving in a weird and jerky way. Even the light seemed different. No longer a gentle morning light filtered through fluttering leaves. Instead, the scene had the floodlit brilliance of a film set. Yet those floodlights flashed on and off as she tried to take in what she was seeing and somehow avoid the sight of the thing, that was, but couldn't be, Mel. It – she – was hanging as if about to topple onto the ground. In a ghastly frozen tableau.

Of course – and she almost laughed, although it would have been a bitter laugh – this was another of their ridiculous tricks. Mel was good at makeup. She did a wonderful job with Ava's face for her goddess part. Although the pose looked incredibly awkward, she was a dancer and Ava had often marvelled at how flexible she was. It was something she envied. Had seen Mel contort herself into some really difficult positions during the shows.

But Mel didn't move.

Didn't rear up and give one of her hoots of laughter as Ava expected. Just hung there. Obviously and absolutely dead.

And Paddy stood as if frozen, just staring. Staring not at poor dead Mel, but at his own bloody hands stretched out in front of him.

Ava stepped back and something cracked under her foot. Paddy looked up. 'Ava? Ava, is that you?' And she began to run.

She could hear him following, crashing through the trees and bushes, and calling her, 'Ava, stop. It's all right. It's Paddy. We got out. I came to find you.' There was no way she was going to stop. She was hardly aware of the brambles tearing at her arms and legs, only pausing for a second when something sharp whipped across her neck. Pulling it away with a wince she ran on, hoping, praying, she'd meet a dog walker.

Knowing Paddy must be close behind she chanced a look back. It was a mistake. She didn't see the ditch, just in front of her, and crashed down into it. As she tried to scramble out of the water and up the other side, her feet slid on the mud and she fell back again, scrabbling on her hands and knees to try to gain some purchase on the wet soil. It was no good and she gave up and began to run through the water at the bottom of the ditch. It was getting deeper. Becoming almost a stream. And the sticky mud beneath the water made running impossible. It didn't matter because Paddy with his long legs was almost upon her: running along the side of the ditch.

Lurching to a halt she bent and picked up a big stone and turned to face him. He loomed above her, looking down and shaking his head as if confused.

They were both panting. She was in shadow, but he stood in full sunlight: tall, handsome, his face flushed and his rich-brown eyes bright. 'What the hell, Ava? Why are you running away?' He held out his hand for her to take so he could pull her up to him. Gripping the stone so hard it hurt, she raised it to her shoulder where he could see it clearly. He dropped his own hand, the flush fading from his cheeks. 'You don't think I hurt Mel, do you? Why the fuck would I?'

When she spoke, she couldn't stop her voice from choking with sobs. She was so tired and now she had stopped running the image of poor Mel, her tiny body so pitiful and undignified, flashed into her mind again. 'You were there in the van with her. The two of you must have cooked up all these mad schemes together.'

He took a step back, staring at her. Then ran his blood-coated hand over his head. His hair was still in its neat pony-tail and although the bottoms of his jeans were muddy and there was a bramble clinging across the front of his dark jacket, he still managed to look neat. But his face was contorted with something she couldn't identify. Grief or anger, she couldn't be sure. Maybe it was a mixture of both. Or he could of course be acting.

Keeping him talking was the thing to do. She had no idea if she would have the nerve to hit him with that stone if he came down to grab her. No idea if he had the knife that had killed Mel with him, but the longer she could keep him talking, the greater the chance of someone coming along. 'Mel told me everything. Admitted she'd done it to get back at Rose and Brad and admitted someone else was in it with her.'

He made a move, to come down or just a gesture of denial,

she didn't know. She raised the stone higher. *Keep talking.* 'Mel didn't seem to care anymore. Otherwise she wouldn't have told me. Knew she was going to have to leave the group and I think she was planning to admit that you were involved too. Then you would have to go as well.'

When he made another move, she stepped back, but the other side of the ditch was so close to her heels she couldn't go far. He didn't come down to the bottom, just sat on the bank, his long legs sliding forward until they were almost touching her feet. The sunlight picked out every crease and line on his face and he looked more like forty or fifty than under thirty.

He swallowed, the lines around his eyes deepening, then spoke in the same calm, reasonable tone he used when he was directing. 'Ava, this is ridiculous. I could just as well say you killed Mel.' His voice wobbled on the name, but he carried on. 'You were there too, after all.' As he talked he rubbed his hands, first the palms then the backs, in the damp grass at his side. Then wiped them on his jeans. She watched, mesmerised by the careful way he checked for dried blood under his nails and between his fingers. Without meaning to she tried to step back again and almost lost her footing.

Paddy wasn't looking at her now. Staring down at his hands as he rubbed and rubbed them; his thoughts obviously far away. 'She must have done it herself. I knew she was unhappy and just like you said, she realised she'd have no place in the group after this. She really loved Brad, you know. It must have been agony for her seeing him so settled with Rose.'

Neither of them spoke. Ava's mind was whirling. What he said did make sense. For all her bravado, Mel had obviously been very unhappy and maybe it was only planning this whole shitshow that had kept her from seeing how pointless her schemes were. Rose and Brad were together and once their baby was born, they would be more of a couple than Mel and Brad had ever been. Perhaps last night was the first time she'd let herself see that.

And she could never be part of the group again. The group that had been her family for years. So it was possible that she'd killed herself. Of course it was. And she thought of Mel's words: *I was going to end it tonight anyway.*

Paddy shook his head and she could feel his eyes resting on her. His voice was slow and soft. 'I didn't have anything to do with those pranks, you know. And even if I had I'd have no reason to worry about what Mel might say because I'm leaving Chimera. It's just been no good for me without Dominic.'

When she met his eyes, she let herself sit on the other side of the ditch. He looked as if he was telling the truth. And she was so tired and so horrified about Mel that she wanted to believe him. Couldn't bear the thought that he might have done that to her. 'But what were you doing in the van?'

'I came looking for the two of you. Couldn't find you anywhere in the village, so I thought I'd try around here. I saw the tyre tracks, followed them and spotted the van. I climbed in the passenger side thinking Mel was asleep.' He swallowed and closed his eyes, his hand, clean now, smoothing his hair again.

She spoke slowly, trying to keep him talking. Hoping someone would come along. 'What happened after I got out of the hall?'

He leaned back with a sigh. Thinking he was persuading

her. 'When we'd given you plenty of time to get to the vicarage and back, we managed to prise open the dressing room door and get out the fire door. By then I think we'd all guessed Mel must be behind it.'

'So how did you know where to find me?'

'We didn't. We've searched everywhere. Thought you'd be at the vicarage or down in the housing estate.'

'Where are all the others then?'

'Brad called Rose from the vicarage and then came back here to look for you. Lally called a taxi to go back and get the Harley to do a wider search.' Those motorbike sounds must have been Lally.

'Joel went to the housing estate and I tried the posh houses. We were all meant to meet back at the hall, but I thought I'd give Brad a hand searching the woods. Didn't find him and was about to give up when I spotted those tyre tracks.'

He glanced back the way they had come – to the van and to Mel – and his voice wavered. 'We'll have to phone the police now of course, but I haven't got a phone. The vicar lent one to Brad so we need to go back to the hall to meet him.' He gave her a small smile that she thought was meant to be encouraging and reached his hand out to her again.

This time she took it. She wasn't convinced, but if he thought she was he would have no reason to hurt her. And she couldn't get away from him by running – unless she got him to drop his guard.

His hand was cool and damp from the grass. He pulled her up as if she weighed nothing. He was very strong. 'Come on, let's get to a phone.' He looked down at her, beginning to unzip his jacket. 'You're shivering, put this on.' She couldn't refuse; it would make him suspicious and the jacket felt wonderfully warm.

When he took her elbow, saying, 'Lean on me,' her breath caught in her throat. She was so tired and she wanted to believe him. She wanted this nightmare to be over, but she was still holding the stone and slipped it into the jacket pocket as she pulled it around her.

Chapter Fifty-Four

After a few yards the trees seemed to be thinning and she squinted through them praying for a movement that might mean someone else was nearby. She stopped and pulled away from Paddy, bending down to fiddle with her shoe. He waited, still too close, and she started fussing with the other one.

A loud burst of music made them both jump, but Ava was ready to go and she started running towards it before Paddy could move. The music was 'Amazing Grace'. Must be coming from a mobile phone. Although it stopped very quickly, she carried on running as fast as she could. Paddy called after her, 'Wait for me. You're going to hurt yourself.'

But she didn't look back, just stumbled on through the trees and bramble. She had begun to cry, praying to the unknown walker: *Please, please wait for me. Don't go away.*

Paddy was close behind her, but she burst through the trees and slammed into another man coming along fast. He grabbed her to stop her falling.

It was Joel.

The impact had knocked the breath out of her and her legs seemed to have stopped working. She found herself sliding to her knees, her cheek rubbing against the rough wool of Joel's coat. It felt damp, smelling of sour rain.

She struggled to her feet, stepping away from him. After all the tricks, she knew there was no one she dared trust. He was saying, 'Ava, Jesus, where have you been all night? Are you all right?' his words coming on heavy breaths.

Then he looked over her head, talking to Paddy. 'Well done, mate. I met Brad at the hall and he's so worried about Rose he called a taxi and has gone back. So he gave me the phone. He'd looked here already, but that was in the dark and I thought it was worth another try, but you beat me to it.'

She could see Joel properly now. See those familiar gold-brown eyes crinkled with concern as he reached out as if to caress her cheek or to push back her hair. When she flinched away, he raised his hand, telling her it was all right. He wouldn't touch her.

What he said seemed to confirm Paddy's story and vice versa. But an image, a horrible image, of poor Mel hanging from the van, flashed sharply into her mind. And if it wasn't suicide; if someone had killed Mel, it had to be someone from Chimera. She needed to stay vigilant.

She tried to speak, but nothing came out at first. A painful swallow and she managed to choke the words from her dry throat. 'It's Mel, Joel, she's dead.'

He stared, as if trying to register her words. 'What did you say? What are you talking about?' His eyes flashed to Paddy.

Paddy knelt heavily on the grass. 'It's true.' Like Joel, he seemed to be gasping for breath. 'I found her. In the Chimera van. She's killed herself, Joel.' Joel looked from Paddy to Ava. She could only nod and give a kind of shrug. Paddy gasped again. 'She told Ava she was behind it all.'

Joel looked up to the sky and she followed his gaze. After yesterday's rain it was going to be a lovely day. The sun was shining properly and it was beginning to get warm. He had already pulled one sleeve of his coat from his shoulder. Now he took off the rest and let it fall over his arm.

Ava forced herself to speak. 'She had the keys to the van all the time. So she got out of the dressing room and drove over here to wait. She and the bastard who was in it with her had it all worked out. When I came along she drove me deep into the woods and left me there.' Her head felt so heavy she could hardly hold it upright.

Paddy pushed himself to his feet, seeming as tired as Ava felt. 'Was that the vicar's phone we heard just now? We need to call the police.'

Of course, the 'Amazing Grace' tune had come from the vicar's mobile. Joel stared back into the woods. Then grabbed Paddy's arm. When he spoke, his voice sounded almost angry. 'Show me her first.'

Ava expected Paddy to argue; to ask if Joel didn't believe them, but he nodded and turned back to the trees. Joel looked down at her. There were dark half-moons under his eyes, but his gaze was the same clear gold as always. 'You should wait here. Take it easy. We won't be long.'

She sat down and watched them both disappear, longing for it to be over. But when she lay back and closed her eyes she had a sudden memory of singing and laughing with Mel after that first rehearsal, as Mel imitated Paddy's deep voice.

Although she had never liked her, she realised she had to go back to the van. To be with Mel.

She still suspected Paddy and how could she be sure of Joel? Even if neither of them had killed Mel, they could have been involved with all the pranks. And they shouldn't get away with it. Whoever had helped Mel was at least partly responsible for her death. She couldn't leave her alone with them.

Chapter Fifty-Five

She was on her feet and heading after them before she knew what she was doing.

They were both standing close to the van, just looking. In the warming air there was a horrible smell. With a thrill of disgust, she saw an insect settle on Mel's neck. On the red slash across it.

Paddy moved away, reaching with one hand for a tree and bending over double as if about to vomit – she felt the same. Swallowing hard and glad she hadn't eaten for hours she forced herself to move a little closer; peering into the van. On the floor, right beside the long seat where Mel lay, she saw a knife. It looked like a Stanley knife.

And she thought again of Mel's words: *I was going to end it tonight anyway.* If only Ava had listened more carefully. Had asked her what she meant, maybe she could have persuaded her out of it. Instead she'd got angry with her. A huge sob burst from her throat. So loud, so unexpected, it startled her.

It must have startled Joel too because he turned to her. Face so white she thought he was about to collapse and eyes stretched wide. Even the gold in them seemed to have dulled and the odd thought came to her that they looked like the old pennies her dad collected.

His head shook as if he was an old man. 'She must have been desperate,' he said. A groan as he rubbed his hand across his face, leaving a dark streak on his stubbly cheek. 'My god, I can't believe this.' Then he closed his eyes and she saw his chest rise and fall.

Paddy's words were so breathy she could hardly hear them. 'We need to get the police.' Ava moved back, leaning against a tree. Paddy again, 'Call the police, Joel. Now.'

Joel didn't react. As if he couldn't hear. Or as if he was in so much shock he couldn't understand. Then he seemed to shake himself and very gently placed the coat he had been carrying over the dreadful thing she could hardly think of as Mel anymore.

Walking back, he looked, like Paddy, as if he'd aged years, his feet dragging. His hands and his shirt had blood on them and when she looked down at her own hands, she realised they were bloodstained too. She rubbed them over her trousers. They were so dark that the stains didn't show. As if that mattered. And what a terrible thing to think at a time like this.

Joel had placed the coat wool side down so that the lining was showing. Its vivid red colour was like a huge patch of blood. Following her glance, he jerked his head back towards it. 'I covered her up.' Ava looked away again.

Paddy said, louder this time, 'Joel, the police.'

For a moment Joel seemed to be listening to his own thoughts. 'Shouldn't have touched anything, but I couldn't leave her there like that.' Stumbling over the words, he put his hand to his chest, leaving a red mark on his T-shirt. When he looked down at it, he shuddered. She wondered how close he and Mel had really been.

As if coming back to himself, Joel wiped his hand on his T-shirt again and pulled a mobile from his pocket. He shook his head. After a moment she heard him say, 'Yes, I need to report a death. It looks as if she cut her throat.' He was pacing back and forth as he spoke and she couldn't hear any more but when he finished he gave a huge sigh. 'It was difficult to tell them exactly where we are so they want someone to wait here and one of us to go up to the road to show them the way.'

Paddy said, 'OK, I'll go. Come with me, Ava?'

'I don't think I could make it.' It was true, she had never felt so tired. And Paddy had been in the van. But it was nearly over and the police would soon be here. She slid down to sit on the wet earth underneath the tree.

After he had gone, she half expected Joel to come and sit beside her. When he didn't, but began to pace up and down in the clearing, she allowed herself to close her eyes. Glad not to have to see poor Mel and to be able to rest for a moment.

Joel's voice, so croaky it was more like a growl, jolted her alert. Unbelievably she had been almost asleep. 'You say Mel told you someone else was involved? Did you believe her?'

She shook her head, trying to sort out her thoughts. 'I don't see how she could have done all those things on her own.' She didn't want to talk about this. Not only because she was too tired but because, even though she really liked Joel, she couldn't dismiss him as Mel's possible accomplice.

'Back in the hall Brad said he thought Dominic might be

involved. Paddy didn't like it, but Mel and Dom were close and he was certainly mad at the whole group.'

'I don't know what to think. I just want it all to be over.'

'Well, the police will be here soon.' He looked down at her and went to sit against a nearby tree. She was glad he was giving her space.

Sitting there together, they waited. Not speaking: both dazed. The only sounds were their breaths and the buzz of another insect hovering nearby but, thank god, staying away from the van – for now. Ava just wished the police would get there. So she could tell them what had happened and begin to process it properly.

Her time in the van with Mel kept running on an endless loop through her head. The way, after the bravado, she had seemed to despair. Had pressed her head against the window to hide her tears. And Ava had just been impatient with her.

When she forced herself to stop thinking of that she saw herself standing by that tree, watching Paddy pull back the door to let the sad little body fall out. And Paddy staring and staring at his own hands.

Unable to sit still, she pulled herself to her feet, made dizzy by the sudden movement. The words were out of her mouth before she realised she was going to speak. 'Do you really think Mel killed herself?'

Joel twisted right round, looking hard at her. 'Of course, what else?'

She swallowed. 'Paddy was in the van when I got to it. He said he'd only been there a few minutes. Had climbed in to see what was up with Mel, but at first I thought…'

On his knees now, Joel stared into her eyes. 'You thought he'd killed her?'

Ava nodded. The way he said it made it sound ridiculous. 'I thought he might have been helping her with all the pranks and realised she was going to tell everyone.' She walked a few steps away. 'That was my first thought and I ran, but Paddy followed me. He denied having anything to do with it.'

When she turned back to him again he was also on his feet, running his fingers through his hair so that it stood up in spikes. It was a gesture that reminded her, agonisingly, of Mel. 'Did you believe him?'

'I don't know. I honestly don't know.'

'My god, Ava.' She could almost see him thinking, staring into space, his breath rasping.

Her heart was beating hard. She could see he was taking it seriously now. They stood staring at each other as that horrible buzzing noise filled the air.

When her legs would no longer support her, Ava sat down again. Joel knelt in front of her. 'Look, the police will be here soon. None of this might mean anything. We're both in shock after all. I don't know about you, but I can hardly think straight. We'll have to talk to them, but let's keep it as simple as we can for now. It's up to you what you say, but I won't mention what you've said about Paddy or about Mel saying she had an accomplice. I'll just stick to the plain facts of what happened.'

Ava nodded. Above all she wanted time to think. Paddy's story that he'd just got into the van to check on Mel was perfectly possible. And the police could surely tell if it was suicide or not. Joel was right. She'd keep it simple and let them do their job.

Chapter Fifty-Six

The sound of a motorbike, and she saw a police car and an ambulance coming slowly into the clearing, with Lally following on the Harley. Paddy got out of the car, but stayed beside it as if he couldn't bear to come any closer.

Just the sight of Lally, taking off her helmet and shaking out her curls, looking so ordinary and familiar, made tears surge into Ava's eyes. She was so, so, tired.

A gentle touch on her shoulder and a woman was kneeling in front of her. Joel was gone, standing with Paddy and Lally. The woman said, 'I'm DC Yvette Madison. Do you need to go to hospital?' When Ava shook her head, muttering that she was just tired, the woman went on, 'If you feel able, we could take you to the station right away to give us your statement?' Ava nodded, wanting so much to get that out of the way.

'Is there anything you can tell me now?'

Ava looked up at the others and saw Paddy glance back. The police officer seemed to notice. 'Your friend told us you went to look for Mel, but she left you in the woods and that he found the – her – body. Is that right?'

She nodded. 'I saw Paddy pull back the door and Mel…' That image flashed again and she gasped and swayed. When the dizziness receded, she looked at the officer and rubbed her eyes to clear them. 'I'm sorry. I can't think straight.'

The woman patted her shoulder. 'That's OK.' She helped Ava to stand and pointed to another police car that had just pulled up. As they walked towards it she heard Lally say, 'Shall I go with her? Joel and Paddy can come on the bike.' Without waiting for an answer, Ava clutched Lally's hand and almost pulled her with her. The policewoman got in the passenger seat.

As they drove, Ava wondered if Lally was thinking, like her, of how horribly different it was from their journey out yesterday. A yesterday that seemed impossibly remote. Even Mel had seemed cheerful, although she must have known what she was going to do. Did she also know how it would end? Ava couldn't believe it and forced that final image from her mind.

Lally leaned close to her, her voice shaking. 'I can't believe any of this. Still can't believe Mel hated us so much. I mean she did stuff to me and even to you that was evil.'

When Ava tried to speak, she began to cough. She waved her hand in front of her mouth and Lally handed her a bottle of water. She took great gulps, almost choking on it. Finally, she managed, 'Do you think she, or whoever was helping her, caused our car accident on my first day?'

Lally gasped. 'Oh my god, no. However bitter she was, she wouldn't have done that. And she hadn't even met you then.'

'She didn't exactly deny it and she thought I'd been brought in to replace her.'

Ava guessed she'd hit a nerve when Lally flushed and took the water bottle, checking the lid was tight before putting it into her bag. When she spoke, it was as if the words were dragged out of her. 'I wasn't meant to be driving that day. It should have been Mel, but I'd been out in the car all morning and was delayed so I rang to say I'd go on and pick you up.'

Turning away, Lally stared from the window. They were on a main road now and the morning sun was bright, flashes of light flaring off the other cars as they sped along. But Ava pulled Paddy's jacket around her, still feeling cold. Eventually Lally said, 'If Mel had been driving, and knew exactly where the branch was, it would have been easy to avoid it. She didn't mean to hurt you, just give you a scare. And to make herself look like a brilliant driver, your saviour, at the same time.'

When Ava stayed silent, Lally turned to her. 'I bet she roped in a few local kids to help her.'

Ava hoped she was right.

Chapter Fifty-Seven

DC Madison leaned back in her chair. 'So what happened after you ran away from Paddy?'

Ava took a gulp of tea. 'He followed and told me they'd been looking for me.' Another gulp, very aware of the eyes of the two police officers on her. 'We headed towards the road and heard a phone ringing and it was Joel. Then we all went back to the van.' She gasped, suddenly short of breath.

After being so cold all night she was hot now. She'd taken off Paddy's jacket, but her face was throbbing and sweat prickled under her arms. The day had warmed and the bare room they were in was airless.

DC Madison was tall and dark with lovely cheekbones. She seemed kind: unthreatening, but all Ava wanted was to get out of there, afraid she might say something to incriminate Paddy. She was almost certain now that he couldn't have done anything to hurt Mel. 'I only ran away because I was so upset when I saw Mel.'

'So why did you go back to the van with Paddy and Joel?'

'I don't know. Scared to be on my own, I guess.' She knew she sounded pathetic, but it was better than admitting that she had suspected Paddy and even Joel. And the one thing she hadn't mentioned about her time with Mel was the hint that she had an accomplice in the group. Like Joel said, it was best not to complicate things. After all, Mel hadn't named anyone and Lally was right that she could have got local kids to help her. Different ones each time in all likelihood. Even if Dominic had been involved, he would surely have no reason to hurt Mel.

When it was over, DC Madison handed her a card. 'We may need to speak to you again, but in the meantime if anything else comes to mind do phone me.'

Lally's interview had obviously been shorter than hers, but she was waiting for Ava so they could travel back in the police car together. As soon as she got in Ava fell asleep and the next thing she registered was Lally nudging her. 'Come on, we're there.' And it was so like Ava's very first day, when she arrived battered and bruised at the cottage, with Lally by her side, that she felt disorientated.

But there was no Rose to greet them. No welcoming fire as they stepped through the door. Just a pile of cold ash in the grate and the dark dregs of coffee in a couple of mugs on the low table. She hurried to the kitchen, desperate for a drink. Lally stood behind her as she glugged down a glass of water and then refilled it. 'You must be exhausted. I'm tired enough, but I didn't spend hours lost in the woods. Do you want to go straight to bed?'

Ava leaned on the sink as the floor seemed to shift under her feet. 'I need to clean up first.'

Gulping down another glass of water, she heard Lally

moving away. 'I'll run the bath for you.' She climbed the stairs feeling as if each step was getting higher. At the top she had to stop and rest against the wall. Lally gestured to the bathroom. 'I've put a couple of towels in there. No need to go up to your room yet.'

They looked at each other and Ava knew their thoughts were the same. *No need to go through Mel's room until you can face it.*

In the bathroom mirror her face was filthy, eyes sunk in shadowed hollows. And when she noticed the streak of red across her throat the floor shimmered again and she had to clutch the edge of the bath to keep from falling. It was just a scratch where a long bramble had caught her as she ran from Paddy, but it made that image surge back.

There was another blotch of red on her cheek, looking like a more serious cut, but when she rubbed it away with a wetted pad of toilet paper there was no mark underneath. Another sway and another surge of nausea. It must have been Mel's blood, although she couldn't recall touching her. She washed her hands under the hot tap and scrubbed at her cheek again.

In the bath she didn't dare to lie back in case she dozed off, but it was good to get clean again. She washed her hair, wrapping it in a towel. A tap on the door. Lally. 'I brought you some peppermint tea. Didn't think you'd want coffee in case it kept you awake. Although, looking at you, I don't think anything would.'

She handed Ava the mug and sat on the toilet. It was so like what Mel had done on that first day that Ava stared into the mug and swallowed a gulp of scented liquid so hot it burned her tongue and hurt as it went down. Lally said, 'Brad and Rose have borrowed her mum's car and are driving over to see Mel's parents. They know them quite well.'

Ava put down her mug and grabbed a towel. How could she have forgotten her mum? Hadn't even thought to ask the police if they'd found the phones in the van. 'I've got to send a message to my parents. They were trying to ring me last night. They'll be worried.'

In Lally's room, still wrapped in one towel, her hair piled under another, she sent an email to both her parents' addresses, telling them that she'd lost her phone and would call when she got a replacement. *But I'm fine and there's nothing to worry about.* It wasn't true of course and she would have smiled if she hadn't felt so awful. Here she was, keeping the truth from them again. The same thing she'd always been angry with them about. But she promised herself she would tell them everything when she saw them.

Then she remembered Will's award show and quickly Googled to check it out. Will hadn't won. He must be wondering why she hadn't messaged him, so she did. She said she was sorry, but was sure he wasn't too disappointed. There was no need to tell him anything else.

She couldn't resist scrolling through some of the pictures of the event. The only ones of Will as he arrived showed him alone and at the end he appeared hugging Mariella, who had won something. A surge of guilt went through her. How could she even be thinking of things like this when Mel was dead? Another flash of that image.

She hurried through Mel's room, trying not to look at it. Didn't want to see the bed with the covers pulled back, the dent in the pillow, or the clutter Mel always left everywhere. But she was too hyped to sleep so she dressed, came down again, and made herself take a deep breath. Mel's parents might come to collect her things and someone needed to clear up first. She tidied the bed and picked up some striped socks, an open book and a sheaf of papers from the floor, placing them neatly on the windowsill along with a penny whistle and a couple of CDs. She made sure the photo of Mel's mum was in a prominent position.

Lally was downstairs eating toast. She told Ava to sit and handed her a couple of slices. Although she should have been hungry Ava had no appetite, but she was glad of an excuse to do something other than talk.

Then she saw Lally's smile, an odd and sad little smile, but still a smile. She said, 'There was something I was about to tell you before you rushed out of the bathroom. About an email I just got.' Looking as if she might be about to cry, she went on, 'It was from that critic we were expecting last night. Apparently, she'd already been. To the show above the pub when Will came. She waited in the bar to talk to us afterwards, but we all went back to the cottage right away, with Will.'

Ava felt her throat close up. It didn't matter anymore. Lally reached over and grabbed her hand. 'She sent a copy of the review. It's a rave. She adored the play and thinks you could be a star.' A long pause, eyes fixed on Ava. 'I know we'll have to cancel the last two shows, but I'm sure all the horrible times are over. So please, Ava, will you think about staying with us? We need you.'

Chapter Fifty-Eight

To Ava's relief, Lally didn't wait for an answer. Just yawned and said she had to get some sleep. 'You should go up too.'

In the attic room, however, Ava looked at the bed and knew it was hopeless, she would just lie awake thinking about Mel. She needed to wait until she was so exhausted she would sleep right away and without dreams. So she scrabbled through her bag and found some cream, smoothing it over her sore cheek and the bramble scratch on her throat.

Then she went down and took some coffee into the garden, sitting in her usual spot on the low wall. She could hardly believe it was the same day she'd woken to in the woods. It was hot. The sun beat down on her and the view she'd loved since her first day here was too bright: the green of the grass so vivid it hurt her eyes. Flashes of brilliance reflected from the windows of cars driving along the road through the little town. The heat amplified the smell of the herbs in the overgrown patch by the French windows and the lavender was so heady it made her feel sick.

She was about to go inside where it was cool when the Harley roared into the lane and she sat where she was, not wanting to talk to anyone. But Joel and Paddy came out with mugs of coffee. Joel sitting beside her and Paddy standing, staring down the valley. After a while, he said, 'Are you OK? Did you manage to sleep?'

'I haven't even tried. I know I'd just lie there thinking.'

Joel scrubbed at his hair. 'I might be too hyped up to sleep as well.'

Paddy said, 'Were the cops all right with you?'

She turned to him. 'Yeah, and I'm glad I got it over with.' There was something pleading in his look and she felt sorry for him. Surely he hadn't had anything to do with Mel's death. 'You'd told them a lot already. When you showed them the way to us,' she said, wishing she'd made her voice softer.

Joel's shoulder was touching hers and he moved it gently as if to comfort her. Paddy gave a rasp of laughter. 'That's right, I admitted you ran away from me.'

'I'm sorry. I was just so frightened.'

Another tiny pressure from Joel's shoulder against her own. 'Of course you were,' he said. 'And I got the impression that they've definitely pegged it as suicide.' His hand came to his hair again and his voice broke on the words, 'Poor little Mel.'

Paddy's voice sounded shaky too. 'It took a while, but they didn't grill us or anything. One thing they did say was that they hadn't found our phones in the van. Apparently, the safe box was there, but it was empty.'

Ava twisted round so she could see them both. 'The phones

were definitely there when I was with her. I used mine and I heard Brad's ringing.'

A pause, then Joel, 'Mel must have got rid of them.'

Ava said, 'To hide evidence, maybe.'

Paddy's voice had a hard note. 'Of her accomplice, you mean?' When neither of them answered, he drained his mug. 'I need to get some sleep.'

Chapter Fifty-Nine

A breeze had sprung up and it felt more comfortable sitting in the garden. Joel didn't speak, seeming to know Ava couldn't face talking. But she became restless and went back into the cottage, pouring some water and drinking it down fast, although she was no longer thirsty.

Joel came into the kitchen saying, 'Do you fancy a walk? I don't know what to do with myself.'

She nodded. 'Nor me.' A walk might help tire her enough to sleep for a bit. Get this day over with. But she still wasn't sure of anyone from Chimera. Joel closed and locked the French windows. 'Best not to leave them open with Lally and Paddy sleeping.'

He was assuming she would come with him and she wanted to, but she couldn't take chances – even with Joel. So she grabbed a notepad from the drawer and scribbled: *Joel and I are out for a walk. Back soon. Ava X*

She left it in the middle of the table where it couldn't be missed. Making sure he saw it too.

But it was a relief to get away from the cottage and she was glad when he led her up the hill in a different direction from the way she'd walked with Lally. She wanted to go somewhere with no memories.

Joel pointed to a stile and they climbed over into a field with grazing sheep, a footpath snaking across it. She was very aware of the emptiness all around them.

They walked slowly and she stayed silent; almost holding her breath, sensing there was something he wanted to say. Eventually, 'I feel so bad that I got you involved in all this. I bet you wish we'd never met at that party.'

It wasn't what she'd expected, although she couldn't have said what that was. 'Of course I don't.' She looked round at him. 'Did Lally tell you the critic came to the show above the pub and has written a rave review?'

He turned to her, smiling. 'No, but that makes me feel better. I'd hate to think it's all been bad. Will you stay, do you think? I'm sure they want you to.'

'Lally asked me that today, but I don't think so.'

'I'm not sure if I want to go on either.'

'Mel said this would destroy Chimera.'

Joel ran his hand through his hair. 'And I wouldn't be surprised if it did. Poor Lally will be devastated.'

'Do you think so?'

'Oh, yes. Have you forgotten that day when we walked back from town and she called Chimera her family?'

She had forgotten, but she recalled it now. She'd been startled, almost frightened, by the ferocity in Lally's voice as she said: *Chimera is my family now. And screw anyone who tries to damage it.* But surely those were just words, they didn't mean anything.

They'd reached a gate and Joel pushed it open to let her go first. 'These are called kissing gates because only one person can get through at a time and you're meant to kiss over them.' She stepped away, pushing the gate towards him so he could follow.

He looked up, squinting against the sun and Ava could see there was something else on his mind. Something about Mel she guessed, wondering, yet again, how close they had been and what that might mean. 'What is it?'

Empty of sheep, this field was scattered with tiny violets and buttercups. It was flat going, yet Ava could hear Joel breathing rapidly beside her. He blurted out, 'It was my fault Mel killed herself.'

It was so unexpected she could only gasp. 'What do you mean?'

He stopped moving, turning to stare down at her, his eyes glinting in the sunshine. 'I'd begun to suspect it was her. Doing all those stupid things. And that day, that last afternoon, she had a fight with Brad and I guessed she was going to do something else.'

Ava remembered the argument she'd almost overheard between Brad and Mel in Mel's bedroom, when Mel had told him to fuck off, and later had pushed Joel away. 'I saw her getting angry with you in the garden.'

He nodded. 'That was when I warned her. Told her I knew what she'd been up to and it couldn't go on any longer.' He rubbed his hand over his mouth. 'I said I was going to tell Brad. And, Ava, oh god, she said…'

'What did she say?'

The words were choked out as they walked slowly on. 'She said if I did she'd have to leave the group. And if she couldn't be in Chimera, if she couldn't be with Brad, she'd kill herself. And it would be my fault.'

Ava looked down at the rough grass, staring at a patch of daisies by her feet. If what he said was true it explained everything. 'Did you tell the police all this?'

He sounded close to tears 'Yes, and I feel horrible about it. It means her family will know she wanted to die.'

She put her hand out to stop him and grabbed both his forearms, squeezing to emphasise her words. 'It wasn't your fault, or Brad's. He couldn't help loving Rose and you couldn't have kept quiet once you guessed what Mel was doing.'

'Thank you for saying that.' He hugged her and she rubbed his back, feeling his heart beating against hers. When she moved away he reached out and stroked her hair whispering, 'Oh, Ava.' Then he pulled her close again.

And he kissed her.

It was soft and sweet, but she didn't respond and drew back again. She couldn't let herself relax, still couldn't trust anyone. And there was something else. Something she didn't understand.

He gave a trembling sigh. 'No good?'

She shook her head. 'It's just with, you know, with everything that's going on.' Her own sigh echoed his. 'I'm so tired.'

'And there's still Will, isn't there?'

'I don't know, honestly I don't know, and I can't think about it now.' She met his eyes again and smiled. *Perhaps one day.*

She took his hand, holding on as they turned to walk back. Because there *was* something that drew her to him, but it was so different from what she felt with Will, she didn't know how to interpret it. It was as if she had always known him. And perhaps that was the problem. He seemed like an old friend – almost a brother.

Her hand came to her mouth where she could still feel the linger of his lips. Her heart jolting in her chest, so hard she put her hand to her breastbone to calm it.

Because she knew.

'Oh my god, it's you, isn't it?'

Chapter Sixty

He gasped and looked around at the wide fields as if afraid someone had crept up on them. 'What do you mean?'

'You must know. Must have known who I was all this time.' She pulled her hand away, the anger surging through her. 'My mum, Daisy, phoned me after she saw the pictures I sent her. Said she recognised the son she'd lost in one of them. It was you, wasn't it?' She walked on fast, before twisting back to face him. 'And I bet you knew who I was from the start.'

His slow head shake was no denial. If anything, he looked relieved. 'Ah, that.'

The fields around them seemed to waver as if she was hallucinating. It was so difficult to reconcile the image she'd had of her mum's lost child with this man. The Joel she found so attractive. 'I don't understand.'

Joel raised his hands, whether in apology or to tell her she was safe and he wouldn't come any closer, she couldn't tell. He said, 'I contacted her when I was eighteen and she blew me off.

Said it was too late and she was still scared of my dad. I told her I didn't even speak to him anymore, but it was no good. I hoped she'd change her mind, but she didn't. Then I spotted you in the papers with Will.'

'And it's just coincidence that we met and I joined Chimera?' Her laugh must have told him there was no use lying.

'I got drunk with Brad one night and we started talking about our crappy families. I told him I had a stepsister I'd never met. Will had been in the news that week and I showed Brad a photo of the two of you at some flashy do. He got all excited and checked you out. Managed to find out about the party and I blagged my way in. I just wanted to meet you. It was Brad who was desperate to get you into Chimera.'

It was almost what Mel had suggested and it still hurt. 'But you went along with it, Joel, why?'

The sun brightened the gold in his eyes. 'I hoped we could be friends and you'd help me get to know my mum. Help me show her I'm nothing like my father.' A little choke. 'That's all it was at first, but I got to like you so much, I began to hope for more.'

'And if I hadn't sent her your picture, would you have let me introduce you without telling me the truth?' She didn't know if she felt more anger or pity for him. 'She's so fragile, Joel. The photo upset her so much I can't imagine what seeing you would do to her.'

'But that's just it. I want the chance to show her I'm nothing like him. To help make her happy. And I would never have tried to meet her under false pretences. I still won't.'

A sudden thought. Her mum and dad had both talked about things that had *happened recently*. 'Have you been trying to contact my mum?' She hesitated. 'To contact Daisy again recently?'

A shrug and a slow, sad headshake. 'No, and I promise I never will. I just hope she might change her mind when you tell her what I'm really like.'

'Well, something has happened to worry her and I'm sure it's connected with your father.'

'He died a few months ago and my grandma might have got in touch to tell her. Can you believe I never even knew Daisy's name until I was eighteen? Then I found out that my gran had always known. Knew where she lived and about her new family. Always one for empty gestures, my gran. I mean, I haven't seen my father for years, but she expected me to go to his funeral. Even though she couldn't stand the guy either. So it would make sense that she'd contact his ex.'

That could explain it. Ava seemed to remember her dad saying her mum was upset because something had brought back painful memories.

They had reached the kissing gate again and Ava hurried ahead to get through it before him. But he had slowed his steps and instead of coming through he leaned on it, talking so softly she had to come closer to hear. 'You know, my grandma always said how like my dad I was, and never in a good way. And the only time I've ever felt any sympathy for him is when I realised how awful it must have been to grow up with a mother who couldn't stand the sight of you. I hate the thought that I look like him.'

She had no idea what to think.

But he was smiling at her, a sweet pleading smile that held so much pain she couldn't help saying, 'Your eyes are just like hers.' A breath while she made herself process what she'd said.

'I knew there was something about you. Your eyes always made me feel safe and happy because they're so like my… like your mum's.' How come she'd never registered that until now?

Very tentatively, he reached out for her and she let him lay a hand on her arm, the gate still between them. 'Thank you for that. It means a lot. And I'm so sorry for all of it. The whole thing just galloped away from me. I planned to tell you who I was at the party and when I couldn't get up the nerve, I was going to do it as soon as they offered you a place in the group. But then you had that accident on the way and everything else started up. After that we never got a moment alone. I did try a couple of times. In my room that day. And before, when I asked you to come down to the pub.'

'So do any of the others know about this?'

He shook he said, 'Just Brad, and I swore him to secrecy.'

Ava was so confused and disturbed, she had no idea what to say or even to think.

Joel said, 'It's a lot, I know, and with all the rest of it.' He took a breath, 'With poor Mel and everything, neither of us is thinking clearly.' He ran his hand through his hair. 'I'm so sorry. The whole thing was a mistake.'

All she could do was to shake her head. 'I need to get back. Be alone for a bit.' And she hurried away from him across the field. He didn't follow.

Chapter Sixty-One

There was a car she didn't recognise parked by the cottage and she heard a burst of laughter from inside. As she came through the door, Rose called to her from the kitchen. All she wanted was to go to her room, but she found everyone sitting at the table and when Brad held up a bottle of red wine she let him pour her a glass.

Rose, looking larger than ever, moved awkwardly over to let Ava sit beside her on the bench. 'How are you feeling? Did you sleep?'

'No, I'm going up to try in a minute.' She took a sip of wine. 'This might help.'

The sun had disappeared behind a bank of dark cloud and Brad got up to turn on the light above the table. It was too bright, bleaching all their faces, and she blinked, feeling that same sense of unreality she'd had with Joel.

Brad said, 'We were just talking about Mel. Her mum was very keen that we do something to celebrate her.'

If they were discussing Mel, she wondered why they had

been laughing and Rose must have seen that in her expression because she said, 'We were remembering the good times. The funny things that happened before it all went wrong. We want it to be as positive as it can be.'

Lally topped up her own glass. 'But let's wait and work out something rather than rushing it.'

Paddy smoothed his hand over his hair. Ava noticed he had no wine, just a bottle of water in front of him. 'This isn't the way I wanted to tell everyone, but I've been asked to direct a show in Manchester, starting more or less right away, so it might be difficult if we don't do something soon.'

'Nice of you to let us know.' Lally was clearly annoyed. This was news to her and, from their expressions, Brad and Rose too.

Ava took a breath. 'Of course I'd like to come to anything you do for Mel, but I hadn't known her for long so I won't expect to be involved.'

Rose took her hand. 'But you have to be. You are staying with us, aren't you?'

Before she could speak, Lally said, 'Brad's got some news. Important news.'

Brad coughed. His face had flushed. 'We've had an email and Rose has had a phone call. A big producer has been in touch, after that great review. Wants to take the play on tour in major theatres and then to the West End.'

Ava swallowed a long gulp of wine. It was already making her feel more relaxed. 'That's wonderful news. Congratulations, everyone.' She raised her glass and drank again.

Rose took her hand, holding it tightly. 'And to you too. It

wouldn't have happened without your wonderful performance.'

She laughed. 'You'll be even better, Rose. After all it's your part.'

'No, you've made it yours, Ava. The whole play becomes a different beast with you in it.' This was Brad and Ava's eyes went to Rose, surprised to see her smiling and nodding. 'It's true,' she said. 'I'm not half the actor you are. And I don't plan to come back to work for a while after this.' She rubbed her hand over her bump.

It was so flattering that Ava closed her eyes and leaned back, a vision of West End stardom flashing into her mind.

Joel clattering in brought her back to reality. He said, 'It looks like rain again,' stopping as he saw them all looking at him. 'Did I interrupt a meeting?' He met Ava's eyes and she gave a tiny headshake. She wasn't about to tell the others who he was. That was between the two of them.

Lally said, 'We've been talking about doing something for Mel and trying to persuade Ava to help us take *Dark Matter* on tour in theatres. Brad's had a wonderful offer.'

Paddy gave a small chuckle and held up the wine bottle. As he poured a glass for Joel, he said, 'I'm not going to be involved. They can easily recast me and I've done the directing already.'

Joel raised his glass, leaning against the sink. 'Same applies to me, I guess.'

Lally reached over and gave his thigh a little punch, laughing as she almost overbalanced. 'I'm sure we can find something for you to do.' Ava wondered how much she'd had to drink.

The relaxed feeling had gone, replaced by that dreamlike

sensation again and a churning in her stomach. She put down her glass. 'Look, this is all a bit much after everything. I can't take it in.' She stood. 'I need a lie down.'

Someone had tidied Mel's room properly now. So that, apart from her mum's photo on the windowsill and the jazzy duvet cover, it looked nothing like a place Mel might live in. That made it easier to pass through, but as she climbed the attic stairs a huge lump rose in Ava's throat. How quickly that lively presence had been erased.

Taking off her shoes and lying on her bed, she tried to calm her mind. It was all too much to take in. Not only Mel, but the reality of who Joel was, and now the idea that she could be starring on the West End stage.

A noise on the attic stairs and she went to look. It was Lally, who must have stumbled as she came up because she was sitting halfway up, rubbing her arm and laughing. Ava pulled her in and she plonked heavily onto the bed. 'Those stairs aren't easy when you've had a few drinks.' She laughed again, but there was a flicker of pain in her eyes.

Ava reached for her hand. 'Are you all right?'

'Yeah, just letting it all get to me, I guess.' She fumbled in her back pocket and brought out a phone. 'There were a couple of replies to your emails. I've forwarded them to Rose's mobile for you.'

Ava took the phone. 'Thanks, I'll bring it down when I'm finished.'

But Lally didn't go. She leaned crookedly forward, looking into Ava's eyes. Her voice wavered. 'You're going to stay, aren't you? This could be your big break.'

'I'm sure Rose will change her mind. Or they could find someone else for the part. Someone much better.' When Lally shook her head, she laughed. 'Well, someone with a higher profile anyway.'

'I don't think so. That reviewer loved you and the producer is really keen to get you. If you don't agree he might even back out.'

Ava looked down at her own clenched hands. 'I'm going to need time to think it through.'

Lally rubbed her knee. 'It's been a nightmare for you, I know, but Mel's gone now.'

'She said all this might finish Chimera.'

'Did she?' Lally's tone was icy and she crossed her arms tight over her chest, suddenly seeming completely sober.

Ava felt bad. Wished she hadn't said it.

Then Lally smiled, her voice softening. 'But you surely don't want that to happen. We're not so bad, are we?'

Ava met her smile. 'Of course not.'

'And if the play's a success it will be so good for Mel's parents to know that her music is getting heard. Whatever Mel said, she'd be thrilled about that. Dominic's songs too. And we might even tempt him back. You'd love working with him.'

Ava could see she was convincing herself it was going to happen. 'Look, I can't think straight. Let me check my messages and have a rest.'

On her feet, her eyes looking bleary with drink again, Lally went to the door and Ava stood and watched her go down the stairs, afraid she would fall. But she seemed completely steady this time and at the bottom she turned and looked back. 'Do stay, please. The play really wouldn't be the same without you. Nor Chimera. You're part of us now.'

Chapter Sixty-Two

Ava was so confused she felt like screaming. When she'd imagined getting her big break she'd always thought it would be a thrilling moment. The only thing that would matter. But this was nothing like that and she couldn't even begin to think about it until she'd made sure her mum was all right. The same reply had come from both her parents: *Glad you're all right, but please ring as soon as you can. We're still worried.*

She called her mum. 'Oh, thank goodness. I've been frantic. Last night when you didn't answer I was sure something had happened to you.'

'I'm fine. Just lost my phone.' Ava had decided she couldn't tell her about Joel on the phone, so she spoke fast. Didn't want to give her mum the chance to ask any awkward questions. 'Look, Mum, I'm borrowing this mobile and someone else is waiting to use it. I'm going to be home in the next couple of days and we can talk about everything then.'

'But the photo?' It came out fast on gasping breaths. 'That boy looks so like him, you see, but Dad says it couldn't be.'

'I'm sorry, Mum, I have to go. Just don't worry about me, please. Everyone here is lovely.' It wasn't enough and she felt cruel, cutting her off like that, but it would have been worse trying to explain it all when they couldn't see each other. When she couldn't hug her mum and let her know Joel was no threat to them.

Will had also emailed her: *Hope you managed to get through to your parents and calm them down. They rang me last night obviously really worried. But OMG, Ava, I saw that review in the* Guardian. *I'm so happy for you. Didn't I say you were brilliant! I've been boasting about you all day!*

She didn't expect him to be available, but he answered right away, raving about the review before she could say anything, but when she simply said, 'Thank you,' he came straight in with, 'What's wrong? What's happened?'

And it all poured out. Everything that had happened with Mel. Will just listened. Now and then she heard a sharp intake of breath, but he let her talk it through. When she finished she was crying.

'Oh my god, Ava, I wish I was there with you. I knew something was going on. Your hair being cut and those horrible phone calls, but I can't believe it was all down to that funny little Mel. And she's killed herself? What a nightmare.'

'I haven't told Mum and Dad yet. Want to wait until I see them. The last two performances are off, of course, and I've talked to the police so I can go home as soon as I like.'

'Just let me know when and I'll come and get you. And, before you start objecting, I won't take no for an answer, but

I'll drive you to your parents. Won't be expecting you to come back to the flat with me.'

Although she was tempted to tell him about Joel, she held off. She hadn't had time to digest that yet and as for the others asking her to go on with Chimera, she wouldn't even let herself think about that until she'd had a sleep and her mind was clearer.

After they said goodbye she lay on her bed, looking up at the dark clouds. The rain was coming down fast, beating on the skylight, and she was glad. It hadn't seemed right for the weather to be so lovely, when all Mel's sparkle and mischief had turned to horror.

Joel called from the bottom of the attic stairs. 'If you're done with the phone, I'd better call my grandparents. The news is likely to be in the local papers and they're bound to mention the name of the group.'

It was going to be impossible to sleep and Ava suddenly wanted to see him again. To see if that would help make sense of the turmoil she was in about him. So she carried the phone down.

In Mel's little room the rain streamed down the windows. It turned the view Ava loved into a watercolour wash of green. Joel was sitting on the bed holding the photo of Mel's mother. His voice was almost a whisper. 'Her poor mum.'

Ava nodded and sat beside him. They looked at the photo together for a few silent minutes. Then she said, 'So you still keep in touch with your grandparents?'

'On and off. I mean they brought me up.'

'What about your dad?

'Basically dumped me on them when I was about three. I hardly ever saw him.' He put down the photograph and turned to her. 'I'm so sorry about everything. I just wish I'd come right out and told you who I was at that party.'

When she didn't speak, he gave a little smile. 'Of course, if I had, I don't suppose you would have joined Chimera.' He was right and she wasn't sure how she felt about the idea that the past few weeks might never have happened. She'd have missed the nightmare with Mel, but wouldn't have been able to do the play. Or to get to know Joel.

He took a deep breath. 'Did you tell your mum about me?'

She shook her head. 'Couldn't do something like that on the phone.'

'What will you say?'

'That I've met you and I like you.' She turned to look into his eyes. 'But, Joel, I won't try to persuade her to see you. That has to be up to her.'

'I know and you're right. I can't ask you to work on her for me. I should never have got you involved. But once I told Brad about you, he was so keen he practically begged me to meet you.'

'What did he say when you told him you hadn't explained who you were?'

'He wasn't bothered. I think he was glad. Thought it might have put you off. Told me to wait till you got here. And I don't think he told any of the others.' When she nodded, not really surprised, he said, 'Will you stay? Do the theatre tour with them?'

She shrugged.

He picked up the photo frame again and Ava said what had been on her mind. 'You were close to Mel, weren't you?'

'At the beginning, when I first met the group, when I started helping Dominic, Mel was always there too. She was so friendly and we got close.' A deep heaving breath and Ava put her hand on his forearm. 'But it all went to shit.'

'Why?'

He looked at her, his eyes clouded, like dull old pennies again. She could see a muscle clenching in his jaw and she waited. Another deep breath. 'I want to be honest with you from now on, but I'm scared you'll hate me.' She didn't dare speak, just gently squeezed his arm. 'You see there's a reason why I suspected Mel.' A long pause as he picked at a thread on his sweater. 'She tried to get me involved when she first started all that stuff.'

Ava could only gasp and decades seemed to pass before he spoke again: the words tumbling out. 'She told me she wanted to play a practical joke. Knew I grew up in the Forest of Dean so asked me to get hold of some kids to help. There was a guy I was at school with who was always up for anything and he had a kid brother just like him. So I asked the kid to recruit a couple of mates. She gave them a few quid to do it.'

'To put Coke in the van engine?'

'Yes, although she claimed she just asked them to siphon off the petrol, so we'd be stranded for a while. She seemed so upset when the van was shot to pieces that I believed her.' Ava heard him breathe in hard. 'If I'm honest I wanted to believe her because she persuaded the group to give me a chance when Dominic left, even though I wasn't that well qualified.'

When she didn't speak, Joel put his hand on her knee. She tensed, but didn't pull away. 'But then there was the graffiti on the van. I had nothing to do with that, but I realised it was the same kids. So I got hold of them and made it clear they'd be in deep shit if they did anything for her again. And I told myself that was it.'

'But it wasn't.'

'She swore none of the rest had anything to do with her and I wanted to believe her. I mean when her own instruments were damaged I knew she would never do that. So I persuaded myself she was telling the truth. Until the last day.'

Ava stared out at the rain-washed fields. She was so tired. When she turned back to Joel she could see the desperation in his eyes. 'I'm so sorry, Ava. I was stupid.'

She nodded. Knew Mel was manipulative. A wave of weariness flooded her and she found herself leaning into him, knowing he wouldn't try to kiss her again. It was good feeling close to him and, with her head resting on his shoulder, she let herself relax. Just for now she wanted to stop thinking. To allow her mind to stop churning. She could work out what to do when she was away from here.

But Joel's sweater was wool and her cheek still felt sore. She seemed to have developed a patch of eczema since she'd scrubbed the dried blood away with the wad of toilet paper. The blood that had come from Mel.

Even as she thought it, that image flashed into her mind again. Mel hanging from the van door, the bright blood that had gushed from her throat already congealing and darkening in the sun. She sat up and a huge shudder went through her.

Joel put the photo frame on the wide window ledge. 'I'm sorry. I've made you think about it again.' He pushed a strand of hair away from her eyes. 'I'll go and make my phone call.'

When he'd gone, she sat for a while gazing at the rain rippling down the window and rubbing her cheek. She'd put on some cream, but it didn't seem to be doing any good.

Lally or Rose might have something better. Rose and Brad's door was open. They must still be downstairs. She knocked on

Lally's and when there was no answer she opened it a crack. Lally was lying fully clothed on the bed, one leg and one arm hanging over the side and Ava caught her breath. It was so like Mel. But Lally grunted and turned awkwardly. It was obvious she was drunk. If she hadn't felt so sick about it all Ava might have smiled. That was one way to deal with this whole nightmare. Maybe she should try it.

As she closed the door, Brad ran up and into his own room, grabbing a weekend bag. He said, 'Rose thinks the baby's coming. Paddy's driving us. I've had too much to drink.'

Ava ran down after him, to see Paddy helping Rose up the path, holding a big umbrella over her. At the open door she called out, 'Good luck,' as Brad hurried after them.

Rubbing her cheek again she remembered the first-aid box Rose had used when the shower glass shattered. Joel was making coffee and she pulled open a couple of drawers, but couldn't find it. 'Any idea where they keep the first-aid box?'

Joel found it in a corner cupboard. 'Did you hurt yourself?'

'It's just a bit of eczema.'

He went to the door of the annex. 'I might have some cream for that.'

'My own fault, I scrubbed it too hard.' Resisting the urge to scratch, Ava touched her cheek. Every time she did so she imagined the patch of dried blood was still there and could feel again the horror of realising, as she rubbed it away, that it wasn't her blood, but Mel's.

But then another scene from that horrible morning flashed in front of her. The time when she sat waiting for the police. And it seemed even more vivid now. The blood-red lining of Joel's coat covering Mel's body. The sound of the fly buzzing too close, and that dreadful smell.

Her breath stopped.

The world juddered to a halt, just as it had when Mel's body flopped from the van.

Her cheek seemed to be burning. The dried blood she'd rubbed from it had been Mel's and yet she hadn't touched Mel's body. And there had been blood on her hands too. Her mind spun back. She hadn't touched poor Mel. Hadn't gone close enough to get blood on her hands or her face. Hadn't touched Paddy's hands until after he'd rubbed them clean on the grass.

But when she met Joel. When she collapsed, she had touched *him*. Her cheek had rubbed against his coat as she slid down. And his coat had felt damp and smelled sour – like the smell lingering around the van. Around poor dead Mel.

Chapter Sixty-Three

Reaching for the table to steady herself, she knocked the first-aid box to the floor. The clatter sounded very loud in the silence. Joel must have heard it and he called, 'Everything all right?'

Somehow she got the words out. 'I'm fine, just dropped something.' She needed to think this through calmly before she faced him. 'Don't worry about that cream. I've remembered Lally said she had something. I know where she keeps it.'

She ran up to the attic, putting a chair against the door, thinking frantically. The coat – Joel's coat – something about it had been niggling at the back of her mind all this time. And the blood on her own cheek where it should never have been.

On the journey to the hall Ava was cold and Joel had given her his coat. When she got out, she had left it on the back seat of the van. And it had still been there when she was with Mel later that night. She was sure of that. Could almost feel the fabric under her fingers as she reached for it. But it had been scrunched up in the corner. Too far for her to catch hold and pull it towards her.

Which meant it was in the van when Mel died. And Joel must have been there too. Before Paddy got to it.

She jumped at his voice. 'Coffee down here. Or shall I bring some up for you?' He sounded just the same and yet so, so, different.

'I'll be down in a minute.' Although her heart was pounding so violently she could feel it in her throat and even her temples, she had to act normally. It might not be true. After all she'd been sure Paddy had done it and now she was equally sure he hadn't. And what reason could Joel have for killing Mel?

She knew one answer already: the same reason she'd thought of for Paddy. That he'd been her accomplice and he wanted to stop her telling everyone. Joel had admitted just now that he'd helped Mel at the start, but what if he'd been involved all the time?

He had arrived at the van so soon after she saw Paddy that he could easily have been hiding somewhere nearby. And she couldn't ignore the coat.

She swayed and sat heavily on the bed as she imagined how it might have been. Him climbing into the van and putting on the coat to protect his other clothes. Then grabbing Mel's head, pulling it back and cutting her throat. Afterwards, when he went back with Ava and Paddy, he'd put his coat over Mel's body, not just because he couldn't bear to look at her, but to make sure there was a good reason for it to have Mel's blood on it.

He had been keen to tell Ava that Mel had threatened suicide and had made sure the police knew as well. But that wasn't what Mel had said to her. Although she'd said she was going to end it all, Ava had never really believed that meant she planned to kill herself. What she seemed to mean was that she was going to admit everything, which would surely include revealing who'd helped her. But was that a good enough reason for Joel to kill her? Surely not. And knowing who he was now – that he was her mum's lost son – she couldn't bear to believe it. She clutched both hands to her head, pressing hard against her temples. She had to know for sure.

When Joel called up again, she went down and took the mug of coffee he held out to her. When she thanked him she avoided his eyes and stood looking out of the French windows. The rain had stopped and a mist was rising from the valley.

As he moved about behind her, she shook her head; amazed at her own thoughts. This was Joel she was thinking about and she was turning him into a killer. She must be wrong. She wanted to be wrong. If she told the police what she suspected they would have to follow up. And that would be awful for Joel if he was innocent, which surely he was. And so terrible for her mum too. Ava couldn't put them through that unless she was absolutely sure.

Running through her memories of that night and the following morning, she tried to persuade herself that she was wrong, that Joel's coat hadn't been in the van when Mel drove away with it. She had a sudden impulse to ask him about it right now. To give him the chance to supply a simple, obvious explanation.

But she couldn't do that, at least not yet. She put down her untouched coffee. 'I think I'll go for a walk. Need to clear my head.'

'Do you want company?'

'No.' She knew it was too shrill and tried to soften the next words. 'I just need to think things through.'

He said, 'Those clouds still look threatening and Paddy's taken the umbrella.'

She looked around and saw Paddy's jacket still on the chair where she'd hung it and pulled it on. She had to get away right now.

Walking down the hill she had no idea where she was heading or what she was intending to do. The pub was closed from three to six each afternoon and it was only 5.30. So there was no way she could go in and borrow a phone to call DC Madison. But she didn't want to do that anyway. Not yet, not until she'd got it clear in her own head.

She carried on walking past the pub, heading for the town. She'd feel better around people.

Even as she thought that, she was shocked at herself. Was she scared of Joel? Not just bothered by the idea of confronting him with her suspicions, but actually scared?

The day was brightening, thin shafts of sunlight piercing through the trees, and the mist rising from the valley made the town below seem to float in a billow of cloud. She wanted to be down there, in the little café, sipping a cup of coffee and watching the market stall-holders packing up for the night.

By the time she heard his footsteps he was already close behind her. Had been coming along quietly for some time.

Chapter Sixty-Four

Joel took her arm, bringing her towards him. His eyes sparked with the golden glints she loved. 'You should come back. It's going to pour again soon.'

'I'm all right. Just going to walk down to town. Lots of thinking to do.'

He must have seen something in her expression or heard the tiny shake in her voice because he took her arm again, scanning her face. 'What is it, Ava? What's wrong?'

She shook her head, 'Nothing.'

His voice was low and soft. 'It's to do with Mel, isn't it?

And this time she didn't resist the impulse. 'I've remembered that your coat was still in the van when I was with Mel last night.'

He looked sad, very sad, and she realised he must have guessed what she was thinking before she even left the cottage. 'I wondered if you'd noticed that. I was going to tell you when we were walking earlier on. Should have taken the fucking coat off right away, before you collapsed on me.' The tiniest of laughs. 'But I wasn't thinking straight.'

A spike of fear shot through her and all she could say was, 'What happened?' She began moving faster, aiming for the little bridge. Once there she'd be nearly in town.

Although he sounded shaken, he continued walking next to her as if they were out for a stroll. 'What I told you was true. I did warn off those kids and tell Mel to stop all the tricks, but when I confronted her, she said she wasn't done yet and if I didn't help her she'd blame me for all of it. Even said she'd make out I'd told Dominic a load of lies to convince him to leave.'

Ava turned away from him. Wishing she didn't have to know. When she didn't speak, Joel slid his arm around her and she tensed as they came to a standstill, but didn't pull away. Told herself it was all right. She forced her voice not to quiver too much. 'But all those things, all those dangerous things?'

Hands on her waist, he swung her round. 'I kept trying to stop her. That branch across the road with you and Lally, was the last straw. She swore she'd be driving.' Ava swayed, feeling as if she was back in the car with Lally as it swerved across the road. Remembering him coming back late on the Harley. Remembering that strange expression on his face when he saw her sitting unhurt at the table. It must have been relief. He must have put the branch there.

But he was still talking. 'I told her it couldn't go on. Hoped she'd stop, but she didn't. All the rest of it was down to her and she focused her tricks on you because she wanted to get rid of you. You were a threat to her position in the group and it didn't help when she realised I'd fallen for you.'

Her hair, the phone calls to Will's studio and about his so-called accident – the fake police officer on the phone had been a woman. He carried on, 'And each time she promised that would be the last one.'

'She surely didn't smash her own instruments?'

He still held her tight. Looking hard at her, as if trying to gauge her reactions. 'I was desperate. Had to show her what it was like.'

A deep breath and she made herself say it. 'So what happened? Last night?'

'She knew you were probably leaving and had some mad idea that she was getting Brad back; that he'd sent Rose away so he could be with Mel. Told me she wouldn't be doing anything else. But that fight you overheard must have been him blowing her off, because when she came into the garden I could see she was furious. I guessed she was going to do something. Begged her not to, just like I told you, but of course she wouldn't listen.'

'So you helped her?'

'No, no way. And I didn't know when she'd do anything else. Certainly didn't expect it so soon. But I made sure I didn't put my phone in the safe box and when I got out of the hall I called her. She'd kept hers too of course. She told me where she was and instead of going to the housing estate, I went to meet her.'

That explained why all their phones were gone. He couldn't have the police checking his and Mel's. Getting rid of the lot of them meant there would be no focus on those two. He'd been thinking clearly enough to do that.

His eyes were too bright: feverish. She could still hardly believe any of this. And yet she did believe it. He said, 'She wanted me to think she had hurt you: run you over. I was so frightened. Felt so bad that I didn't stop you from climbing through that window. But she talked about it as if it was a big joke.'

Ava couldn't breathe. 'So that's why you had to…?'

His hands fell from her waist and he stepped away from her, staring. His hand came to his chest as if to calm his heart. 'Had to what, Ava?' When she just looked and shook her head, his hand clenched and he brought the fist up to press against his mouth. 'Jesus, you don't think I killed her, do you? My god, Ava. What do you take me for?'

As if of its own accord her hand was at her cheek. There had been blood there. She hadn't imagined it. And there was only one way it could have got on her face or even her hands. From his coat. He had to have been there when Mel's throat was cut. 'Well what happened then?' All she really wanted now was to get away from him; to pretend none of this was true.

He grabbed a hank of his brown hair. Her mum's hair was the same colour, but threaded through with grey. 'She killed herself of course. Saw how impossible it would be to get away with it. Otherwise she wouldn't have told you the truth.'

She thought but didn't say: *Or did you realise she was going to tell about you too, so you had to shut her up?* At the same time a part of her – a big part of her – wanted to believe him. 'Tell me then.'

He rubbed his face. The stubble rasping under his hand. 'I'd put on my coat because I was cold, that was all.' A noise between a gasp and a huge sob burst out of him. 'Then I saw she had that knife in her hand and she started waving it about. Slashed it towards me, then held it to her own throat.'

She stepped back – waiting. Wanting to run, but needing to

know. Glad she was wearing Paddy's jacket and that the stone she'd picked up that day was still in the pocket. It was difficult to breathe.

'I tried to get the knife from her. She said she thought she might have killed you, but had made sure everyone would think it was me. I grabbed her hand, the hand with the knife. Just to stop her. Then – I don't know what happened, but, oh god...' His hands were over his eyes, but she knew what he was seeing.

She didn't want to hear any more. He had told so many lies, she didn't know what to believe. But she knew she couldn't keep it to herself. Amazed that her voice sounded so calm, she said, 'This is no good, Joel. You have to explain the rest to the police. Not to me.'

He reached for her, grasping her shoulders. 'I can't, Ava. I just can't. They won't believe me. Please tell me you won't say anything.'

The desperation in his voice frightened her more than any show of anger would have done. He must know they could find damning evidence if they had reason to look. She pulled away, managing to say, 'OK, OK, but just let me go now.'

Instead, he dragged her towards him again, hard this time.

Chapter Sixty-Five

When he trod on her toe, she let out a yelp and he said, 'Sorry, sorry. I just want to talk to you for a minute more.'

Reaching into her pocket to clutch the stone, she forced her voice to sound strong. Like the water goddess in the play. 'This is no good, Joel.'

Her words seemed to bring him to himself and his hands dropped. She was running before she knew she had moved. Could hear him coming behind. His words a panted chorus, 'Wait, Ava, please wait.'

He caught her just before the bridge.

Clutching her arm and staring into her eyes he said, 'I'm sorry if I frightened you, or hurt you. But you need to listen. I was stupid to help Mel with all those tricks, but you don't really think I could kill her, do you?'

The lie came out surprisingly easily. 'No, no, I don't. It was just shock, that's all.'

'But you have to promise. They think it was suicide so you just have to stay quiet. You don't need to say anything else to them.' She could almost see his mind working. 'Just think about how much it would hurt her if you did.'

Calm, talk calmly. 'Her, Joel? Who do you mean?'

A beam of sunlight shone through the clouds and his eyes were gold again. 'My mum. I'm talking about my mum. I'm still her son. So just think what it would do to her if she thought her own child might be a killer.'

She swallowed. He couldn't have said anything more certain to make her doubt what she should do. Because it was true. Her mum already blamed herself for leaving him. If she thought it might have contributed to making him a murderer Ava couldn't bear to think how she would feel.

It was as if he could see her thoughts and the tiniest flicker of relief crossed his face. 'Come on, let's go back.'

Looking at the ground because she was afraid of what her expression would show, Ava stepped onto the bridge. She had to get away. To think it through properly. 'I still need to go into town.'

His fingers gripping her arm this time were steel pincers. 'No, you don't. Everything will be closed.' His voice was steel too.

Ava remembered what her nan had said about his father: *One of those good-looking charmers. All sweetness and light, but turns nasty when you cross him.* It was difficult to breathe. 'I just want to walk around for a bit. Check out the train times for when I go home.' She knew she was gasping because what she saw in his eyes now terrified her. How could she have been fooled all this time?

He pushed her against the rails of the bridge. 'I said, come back. It's going to rain.' A hard little laugh. 'Don't want you to get wet.'

Pressed against him she could feel his heart drumming. Or it could have been her own. It was horribly like earlier on when they had hugged and he had kissed her. He wasn't going to kiss her now, although his face was almost touching hers and his breath fluttered her hair. His eyes glittered, the fire in them turned to a harsh blaze.

A twisted little smile that made her flinch. 'You realise they could just as well be made to believe you killed Mel? After all, you were with her before Paddy or I even got there. I bet the police spotted the blood on your hands and face. And you had good reason to hate her. Everyone knows she tried to make your life a misery.'

When she shook her head, he brought his face even closer, whispering now, 'Just think what that would do to your dear mum. Or I should say my dear mum. Because she is really my mother – not yours at all.'

Such a wave of anger swept through her that she pushed back hard against him, kicking his shin and shoving her elbow into his stomach. Then she slipped past and off the bridge towards the town.

But she hadn't hit him hard enough and this time when he caught her he dragged her back to the river bank. As they jolted along she could only gasp, 'Joel, don't do this. It's no good.'

The bank was slippery from the rain, the water green with weed and the reflection of the darkening sky overhead.

And she knew.

Knew he was going to push her in; hold her down until she drowned. Like her mother.

'I'm sorry.' This time there was no fake regret in his voice. 'But I can't trust you. So this is the only way.'

Her voice was hardly there. 'We can work something out. I know we can.'

'I'll have to tell the police everything. Everything you confessed to me back at the house. That you killed Mel.' He was talking fast. 'And that you went for a walk and didn't come back. I'll tell them how bad I feel because I didn't guess that the guilt would make you kill yourself. Even though I knew about your mother's death. And that you sometimes thought of jumping into the river. Lally will remember that too.'

Ava could see how pleased he was to have worked out such a neat little story. Made all the pieces fit. But in his satisfaction he let himself relax for a split second as he moved his hands to her shoulders.

And she managed to reach into her pocket and pull out the stone.

A crunching sound – stone against bone – as it struck his temple.

One hand rose to touch his head. He looked confused. Then his eyes misted over.

And he fell.

She jumped away as he crashed face down into the river. Breath catching at her throat, heart pummelling in her chest, she dragged him away from the water and forced him over onto his back.

His eyes were closed. Blood and water dripping from his face.

She stumbled away. Had to get help. Had to get to town. As she ran she prayed: *Please, please, oh please.*

Not praying, this time, that he wouldn't catch her. She knew he wouldn't be getting up.

But praying – praying so hard – that she hadn't killed him.

Chapter Sixty-Six

Something thumped hard against her legs. A dog. It ran past her as she crumpled to her knees, fighting to get up again. To keep going.

But a hand reached for her, pulling her to her feet. 'All right, love, it's all right. We've got you.' Ava blinked to clear her sight. It was an elderly man. An elderly couple because coming behind him was a tiny woman.

Ava gasped, 'Please, we have to get help. An ambulance.' But the woman already had a phone in her hand. As she spoke, giving crisp instructions, the man called for their dog. 'Come on, Georgie, you silly creature.'

The woman came close to Ava. 'OK, now just you wait quietly here with us. They won't be long. And don't worry. We saw what happened.'

All she could get out was, 'He… I hit him with a stone.'

The woman who only reached her shoulder put her arm around her. It was comforting, too comforting because it made the tears come. Great gulping sobs. And the woman said, 'Quite right too. The evil swine was trying to drown you.'

It was morning before Ava got back to the cottage. In a police car yet again, but Paddy and Lally, who were in the kitchen, didn't see it. Lally was at the table looking hungover and Paddy standing talking on a phone. He put it down as she came through the door. 'Hey, Rose is fine and the baby's great. A big bouncing girl.'

Lally laughed and stretched. 'That's wonderful. I'll be happy for them once my head stops thumping.'

When Ava collapsed onto a chair, Lally leaned forward and Paddy came close. Lally said, 'What's wrong? You look worse than I feel. We thought you were out for an early morning walk. Where's Joel?'

She told them everything, pausing only once to drink from the glass of water Paddy placed beside her. Had to get it all out in one go. Although she heard a few gasps and an *Oh my god* from Lally, there was a long silence when she finished.

As she'd talked Lally had grabbed her hands across the table and Paddy pulled up a chair to sit beside her, rubbing her shoulder when she choked on a sob. Finally, he said, 'It's unbelievable.' He shook his head. 'Yet I believe it all.' It was so like what she had thought that she almost smiled.

Squeezing her hands, Lally said, 'You really think he was trying to kill you?'

She nodded. 'And I thought I'd killed him. But they say I couldn't have hit him as hard as I thought. It was only enough to knock him out for a few minutes.'

Paddy spoke thoughtfully. 'That thing with his coat? When he put it over Mel? I thought it was odd. Wrong somehow, although it seemed to make sense at the time. And I remember wondering how you got blood on your face because it wasn't there when you ran away from me.'

'If he put the coat on deliberately to shield his clothes, that was very calculating.' Lally sat back, staring into space. 'It makes you shiver.'

Ava sighed. 'I don't suppose we'll ever know the exact truth. He's too good a liar. At least they should get him for attempting to murder me. Those witnesses were pretty sure of what they saw.'

She borrowed Paddy's temporary phone to call Will saying, 'I can't tell you anything now. Please don't ask me. Just come.' He had a meeting that afternoon and when she refused to let him cancel he said he'd get there as early as he could next morning.

She, Lally and Paddy sat talking for hours. When Paddy said, 'Looks like Mel got her wish. This really is the end of Chimera, I guess,' Ava looked at Lally.

But Lally just ran her hands through her curls. 'Yeah, I was so upset about that yesterday. Couldn't accept it, but, you know I think it's time. Time for us to grow up and move on. Believe it or not, I have got friends outside the group. And Brad and Rose will want the cottage to themselves now. They should have time alone with the baby.'

Paddy turned to Ava. 'But you should do the play. It's going to take a while to set up and Brad doesn't think the producer wants him in the cast. Just hasn't told him yet. You're the one he's interested in. But the play's Brad's which is what matters to him.' His cheekbones flushed and he looked down at his phone. 'I spoke to Dominic and he's really pleased about his music being used. And Mel's, of course.'

Lally smiled and nodded at him. 'That's good.' Then she turned to Ava. 'So will you do the part? If the play really does get off the ground? You'd be a fool to turn it down. And you won't have any of us around to remind you of all this.'

Paddy laughed. 'We'll come to your first night of course, but even playwrights are not encouraged to hang around once rehearsals start.'

They were right. It would be a fresh start. Not a continuation of Chimera. So maybe.

Mostly, though, they talked about what had happened. Trying to make sense of it all. The one thing Ava hadn't told them was that Joel was her mum's biological son. Brad knew, so they would find out, but she couldn't bear to talk about it anymore.

She had explained it to DC Madison who, thank god, was on duty again to take her statement. In fact, that was the first thing that seemed to surprise her. She'd looked so unfazed by everything else that Ava wondered if they already suspected Joel.

At the end of the interview Madison said, 'You'll need to tell your mum all this.' And when Ava nodded she added, 'That's going to be one very difficult conversation for you.'

Chapter Sixty-Seven

Unbelievably, when she finally went to bed she slept the deepest sleep, as if her mind didn't have the energy to manufacture dreams. Maybe because the reality was as twisted as any nightmare.

And Will arrived so early that she was only just up and ready. Lally and Paddy were still asleep and she was glad to avoid any goodbyes.

Will drove more carefully than usual and didn't speak until they were well on their way. 'Would it help to tell me?'

A deep breath and she realised she had been sitting forward, her own foot pressing down on a phantom accelerator, wanting him to go faster. To put many miles between herself and Chimera. Although she'd talked so much about it already it was different telling him. And she needed to do it. To prepare for what she would have to say to her mum later on.

When she'd finished he took a huge breath. 'So he's not that badly hurt? Thank god for that. But they surely couldn't have blamed you anyway. It was self-defence.' He rubbed her knee. 'Don't worry.'

'I'm not, not about that. I mean there were the witnesses and DC Madison was kind. And as she showed me out to the car she said that Joel was talking to them and she thought it wouldn't take too long to sort it all out. Think she was trying to reassure me.'

They were silent for a while, then he said, 'So what will you tell your mum?'

'Everything. I have to tell her everything. There have been too many half-truths and evasions.'

When she woke, the car was pulling up outside her parents' little house. Will squeezed her hand and whispered, 'I won't stay and I won't phone until you call me. But remember I'll always be there.'

He left her at the front door. Said hello to her dad and refused the offer of tea. Then, with another squeeze of her hand, he was gone. He knew she needed to get this conversation done.

'Nice lad,' her dad said, putting her bags on the floor beside the stairs. 'Good of him to do this, I wouldn't have wanted to leave Mum.' Even in her shaky state Ava found herself smiling. They were the warmest words he'd ever said about Will.

Inside, her mum came hurrying downstairs, holding her cardigan tight around her. She looked calm, but when she pulled Ava into a hug, her voice wobbled. 'Thank god, oh thank god. I've been so worried about you. I knew something was very wrong. Needed to see you.'

Although so many questions hovered around them they waited, keeping to the normal home-coming ritual. Savouring the precious moments when everything was the same as always.

Her dad boiled the kettle and made them mugs of tea and her mum got out the biscuit tin. It wasn't until they were all sitting at the little kitchen table that her mum took a huge shaky breath and said, 'Tell me now, sweetheart. I knew as soon as I looked at you that it was bad, but I can bear it. So long as you're all right.'

She reached over and squeezed the soft hand that had soothed her through all the years whenever she was ill or sad and said, 'Of course I'm all right. I've got you and Dad, haven't I?'

Then she looked into the golden brown of her mum's eyes and, very gently, she began to tell her everything.

Halfway through the story Daisy looked away and pulled her hand back from Ava's, clenching it on the kitchen table in front of her. When Ava stopped talking, the three of them sat silently as long minutes passed. Ava could hear Daisy breathing and the occasional squeak as her dad shifted on his chair. When she could stand it no longer she asked, 'Are you all right, Mum?'

Daisy pushed herself to her feet, resting her hand on her husband's shoulder as she passed him before standing in front of the sink and staring into the garden. 'It's my fault.' Her voice was so quiet Ava had to strain to hear.

Her dad seemed about to stand, but lowered himself back onto his seat when Ava said, 'Don't be silly. None of it is your fault.'

When her mum turned back to them, Ava could see tears

glittering in her eyes. 'I should have met him when he asked to see me. Explained why I couldn't come for him when he was little. Told him I loved him. I've made so many terrible mistakes.'

Her husband said, 'Ava's right, love. You did nothing wrong. Never have done,' and stood as if going to reach for her, but she held up a hand to stop him.

Looking away from them both. Looking towards the kitchen door she answered, 'Oh, but I have done wrong, my darling. Very wrong.'

Following her gaze, Ava saw she was staring, not at the door, but at the little gallery of family photos they had hanging in the space beside it. She wondered if her mum was thinking that there should have been a picture of Joel amongst them.

Then Daisy turned those gleaming eyes, so like his, back to Ava and shook her head. 'I'm so, so, sorry.' And she headed for the door.

But as she passed the little photo gallery, her fingers trailed across the glass of one of the pictures, lingering on a face for a moment.

Ava heard an intake of breath from her dad and Daisy must have heard it too because she twisted round to say to him, 'I'm so sorry, my darling. So very sorry.'

The picture was of Ava as a baby. And with her, smiling down at her, was her mother. Her real mother, just before she drowned. Daisy's finger stroked Jane's face and Ava was suddenly afraid. She didn't want to speak, but couldn't stop herself. 'Mum, what is it?'

Daisy turned her golden gaze to her, her finger still soothing Jane's face. And those images came to Ava once more.

The images of Jane disappearing under the water as the green weeds pulled her down too fast for her to scream for help.

But this time they came with such sharp clarity it was as if she was seeing the real scene. Seeing it through Daisy's eyes.

She saw Jane struggling to free herself from the dark coils, before disappearing under the swirling water. Not far away, on the bank, her husband, unaware, played with little Ava and smiled across at Daisy. And after one long look, Daisy's eyes slid away from the churning water to smile back at him.

Then the water began to still, as Jane stopped struggling. Knowing no one was coming to help her.

Daisy's, 'Sorry, so sorry,' was only a whisper this time as she closed her eyes and turned away.

And Ava and her dad stood staring as she walked slowly up the stairs. Alone.

Acknowledgments

First and foremost, I'd like to thank you, dear reader, and especially if you've read, or are planning to read, any of my other titles. Without you there'd be no point!

Thank you also to all the reviewers who take the time to share the book love – reviews really matter to authors. And all you wonderful book bloggers who give so much support to authors with no thought of reward, please know that you are deeply appreciated.

Huge thanks of course must go to the amazing people at One More Chapter. It really does take a village to produce a book. Above all to Charlotte Ledger, editor extraordinaire – what would OMC be without you? To my eagle-eyed and perceptive copyeditor, Nicky Lovick, and proofreader, Simon Fox. And to Lucy Bennett for the gorgeous cover design.

I want to thank too, all supporters of books, especially everyone working in libraries and bookshops. And special thanks to the UK Crime Book Club. Check it out on FB if you want to chat with fellow crime book lovers and authors and see interviews with your favourite writers. You won't regret joining.

Much love and big hugs to the whole Curran/Farmer crew, including my perfect first readers: Sue Curran and Jack Curran. Not forgetting my writing friends who keep me going when the going gets tough – love you all.

Last but not least, my thanks and apologies go to all the actors I've worked with – you are all stars. Chimera couldn't have been born without you, but it shares only your qualities. The bad bits are (nearly) all invented.

YOUR NUMBER ONE STOP

ONE MORE CHAPTER

FOR PAGETURNING BOOKS

The author and One More Chapter would like to thank everyone who contributed to the publication of this story...

Analytics
Emma Harvey
Connor Hayes
Maria Osa

Audio
Charlotte Brown

Contracts
Florence Shepherd

Design
Lucy Bennett
Fiona Greenway
Holly Macdonald
Liane Payne
Dean Russell
Caroline Young

Digital Sales
Michael Davies
Fliss Porter
Georgina Ugen
Kelly Webster

Editorial
Simon Fox
Charlotte Ledger
Nicky Lovick
Bethan Morgan
Jennie Rothwell
Kimberley Young

Harper360
Emily Gerbner
Jean Marie Kelly
Juliette Pasquini
emma sullivan
Sophia Wilhelm

HarperCollins Canada
Peter Borcsok

International Sales
Hannah Avery
Alice Gomer
Phillipa Walker

Marketing & Publicity
Emma Petfield
Sara Roberts

Operations
Melissa Okusanya
Hannah Stamp

Production
Emily Chan
Denis Manson
Francesca Tuzzeo

Rights
Lana Beckwith
Samuel Birkett
Agnes Rigou
Zoe Shine
Aisling Smyth

The HarperCollins Distribution Team

The HarperCollins Finance & Royalties Team

The HarperCollins Legal Team

The HarperCollins Technology Team

Trade Marketing
Ben Hurd

UK Sales
Yazmeen Akhtar
Laura Carpenter
Isabel Coburn
Jay Cochrane
Sarah Munro
Gemma Rayner
Erin White
Leah Woods

And every other essential link in the chain from delivery drivers to booksellers to librarians and beyond!

YOUR NUMBER ONE STOP

ONE MORE CHAPTER

FOR PAGETURNING BOOKS

One More Chapter is an
award-winning global
division of HarperCollins.

Subscribe to our newsletter to get our latest eBook deals and stay up to date with all our new releases!

signup.harpercollins.co.uk/
join/signup-omc

Meet the team at
www.onemorechapter.com

Follow us!

@OneMoreChapter_

@OneMoreChapter

@onemorechapterhc

Do you write unputdownable fiction?
We love to hear from new voices.
Find out how to submit your novel at
www.onemorechapter.com/submissions